SỌMADỊNA

ALSO BY AKWAEKE EMEZI

For young adults:

Pet

Bitter

For adults:

Freshwater

The Death of Vivek Oji

Dear Senthuran

Content Warning: Everything

You Made a Fool of Death with Your Beauty

Little Rot

ṢỌMADỊNA

AKWAEKE EMEZI

faber

First published in the US by Alfred A. Knopf
An imprint of Random House Children's Books
A division of Penguin Random House LLC, New York in 2025
First published in the UK in 2025 by Faber and Faber Limited,
The Bindery, 51 Hatton Garden, London, EC1N 8HN
faber.co.uk

Typeset in Garamond Premier
Printed and bound by CPI Group (UK) Ltd, Croydon, CR0 4YY

A CIP record for this book
is available from the British Library

ISBN 978-0-571-38303-0

Printed and bound in the UK on FSC® certified paper in line with our continuing commitment to ethical business practices, sustainability and the environment.
For further information see faber.co.uk/environmental-policy

Our authorised representative in the EU for product safety is
Easy Access System Europe, Mustamäe tee 50, 10621 Tallinn, Estonia
gpsr.requests@easproject.com

2 4 6 8 10 9 7 5 3 1

For Bun, Shadow, Smalljoy,
and Smoke.
Small gods, you are safe in
God's hands.

PROLOGUE

MAMA ALWAYS SAID THAT EVERYTHING STARTED THE DAY THEY came for Nkadi, her firstborn, the golden leopard of our family. My twin, Jayaike, would disagree – he says it started before we were even born, that it started with the Split, the great breaking of the earth – that it started with the war. This was the kind of thing he said quietly, when we were lying in our bed with our legs thrown over each other, whispering under the heaviness of night. In our town, talking about the Split is not something you do when the sun has woken up, or in places where ears can hear you. In fact, left to me, I wouldn't be talking about the Split at all. It's so far away from us in time, what can it matter now? The past has happened; leave it alone.

Jayaike says I sound like Mama when I say things like that, as if I'm afraid of looking over my shoulder. Maybe he's always been the brave twin – after all, he's the one who used to catch our grandmother Ahụdi on the moonlit nights when he knew she wouldn't refuse us stories. That's when he'd ask her about the Split, and the Starvation War, and her husband, Kesandụ, our dead grandfather. Since Jayaike is one ear and I am the other, I always listened to the stories, even when some of them turned into streams from her eyes, even when they hurt her. Jayaike would press his mouth to Ahụdi's hand when this happened, but I could have told him he didn't have to worry. Our grandmother never stopped a story just because it was breaking her heart.

Ahụdi told us things they refused to teach us in school, things that Papa pretends not to hear when you ask him, things that Mama will slap you for even bringing up. I'm not the only one who doesn't like to talk about the past – I learned it from somewhere, but my twin challenges the silence I want. Jayaike and I can't tell other people the things Ahụdi tells us, that's how heavy they are. I tried it once with one of our teachers, when I thought I could be brave like my brother. I told the teacher that she was wrong, that war was never necessary and it was certainly not noble, not when so many people died. The teacher didn't even allow me to finish class. She sent me home immediately with a warning, and Mama shouted at me, told me I shouldn't be contradicting my elders. This was part of how I learned to be quiet.

When I told Ahụdi, she just shook her head. 'Some people

don't want to hear true things, Sọmadịna. You have to be careful which air you speak it into.'

In school, they tell us things as if they're true. They tell us that nothing happens beyond the Split, the yawning chasm that breaks our islands away from any other part of the world. And even if it did, they add, it is impossible to cross the Split, so why disturb yourself with this nonsense? All we need to know, the teachers say, is that the Split ended the Starvation War, that we lost hundreds of dịbịas, and that we are now free because of it.

It was Ahụdi who told us about the decision the dịbịas made to create the Split, when too many children had swelled and died of hunger, when the war was a mad thing rampaging through our land. The dịbịas had always been our masters of medicine and spirit, our guides to the primordial mother, the deity Ala. She was the earth, the underworld, the sacred crocodile crawling up the banks of the river, and we were her children, two-legged and fumbling on land. The dịbịas were responsible for us; they could not fail. Our grandfather Kesandụ had been one of them.

'We tried to keep magic out of the war,' my grandmother explained. 'It is always too dangerous. One person brings their magic and another brings a more powerful one, and the next thing you know, there is no land left to even fight over and who is going to explain that to the deity?' Ahụdi folded her legs on her mat, and in the hushed evening, our little fire threw sheets of light across her face. Jayaike and I were roasting cashews in the coals, our eyes wide as we ate our grandmother's story.

'Magic can remove everything,' she told us. 'It can remove everything you have ever loved or wanted or seen. Like that!' She snapped her fingers sharply, and we jumped in alarm. The night felt wide and dark at my back. I tried to imagine our compound being removed, Mama and Papa gone like a snap, let alone the whole of our town, the thick forests that encircle us, the water past the forest. It was beyond the stretch of my mind, but I believed our grandmother. Jayaike and I always believed our grandmother. She told us that the war started because when we were all one land, our neighbors got greedy and tried to take our land from us. We fought back, but our enemies poisoned the waters of our rivers and destroyed our crops and livestock until our people were dying of hunger. That's why it's called the Starvation War, for the bodies of children floating black in our dead rivers. The crocodiles ate the corpses and blasphemy lived everywhere. The dịbịas decided that in order to save us, they would have to break the earth and invite in the sea to separate us from those who were killing.

'What if we had all drowned?' I once asked Ahụdi. 'When the water came in.'

She had held my hands and smiled. 'Then we would still be free,' she replied. 'We would still be free.'

The Split changed everything in our history, but to understand what our world became, you have to understand what our world was before. I wish I could imagine it, but all I had were fragments of stories from Ahụdi, whispers of truth in what they told us at school, and it wasn't enough to put together a correct picture. What I know is that we were always a powerful people, some of us with gifts from the mother deity. That is what we called magic, when the deity touched you, when a piece of the spirit world found its way into your flesh and gave you an ability beyond what was normal, the tooth of the crocodile working its way under your skin. The Split changed all of that.

When the dịbịas broke the earth, one of the deity's bodies, it caused a ripple of power beyond anything that had been seen before or since. The land shattered into islands, and our enemies fell into the water, where if they didn't die in the crocodiles' jaws, they drowned. Magic tore through the air, far too much of it, and it clawed its way through our towns and villages like a god's rampaging anger. It was as if we had angered Ala by breaking the earth and in return she suffocated us with gifts, those abilities we used to pray for; she forced them down our throats. Not everyone can survive being touched by a god, and a person can only hold one gift at a time, except for the dịbịas, who can hold several. So, if you already had a gift before, either your body closed itself off to refuse the influx of magic, or you died.

If you didn't have a gift and lacked the capacity to hold one, you died. It didn't matter if you were young or old, sick or healthy, you died. Infants, elders, the strong and the weak – they were all reduced to one thing: if their spirit could handle the deity's hand.

Ahụdi said this is what war did, it killed people from start to finish; it killed people in consequences that don't pay attention to time. When the shock wave from the Split had passed, everyone on our island had gifts – at least, everyone who was still alive. I never knew if we used to be many more than we are now. I just knew that everyone in the world I was born into had a gift, a blessing bitten into us by the unforgiving jaw of a god, and it would never leave our lineage. It passed on through the blood, to the children, and their children, and in this way, we belonged wholly to the mother deity, the survivors scarred with her heavy favor. My grandmother was a healer, and she never forgot what that wave of magic did to our people, both those it killed and those who had the magic forced on them. She knew how a god's touch can ravage your flesh, and she told my twin and me how no one goes near the Split till today. It lies somewhere beyond our sight, abandoned and unknown.

I was one of the children born in the generation after the Split. My parents were very young when it happened, and Ahụdi told me not to ask them what it was like to have the magic enter. 'The crocodile may bless us,' she said, 'but its bite still hurts.' She knew how true that proverb was. She'd known it since her husband, Kesandụ, died at the Split and left her to raise my father.

As for the magic, I knew what to expect, for myself and my twin. At some point, my body would start to change, just like my older sister, Nkadi's, and then my gift would come in. When that happened, I'd go to our town elders so they could make a record of it. Our elders liked things to be in order, as if organization could erase the trauma of the war, as if that would keep us safe. They liked to know exactly what everyone in our town was capable of, but I never met anyone who turned their gift toward violence. Most people just used their gifts in their work, like messengers who traveled through time and space, or builders with extra strength. My parents didn't. Jayaike thought it was because they both had dịbịas as parents and didn't want to shape their whole lives around the magic. They both chose to become farmers, even though Mama could travel anywhere in a second, even though Papa could speak without words.

The only people who never had to report their gifts were the dịbịas, the ones who held our medicine, who had the deity's ear, who acted as the deity's mouth. They were blessed, or cursed, depending on who you asked. I had always been painfully curious about them because both my grandfathers were dịbịas, but a dịbịa was made up of secrets, and people sewed their mouths shut when I asked. Ahụdi told me a few stories about Kesandụ, but they were all gentle human things that made me wish I had met him, that Papa hadn't lost his father. There were no dịbịa secrets in those stories. Mama's father was the real enigma, mostly because he was still alive. We never saw him and Mama never spoke of him, didn't even allow Ahụdi to tell us his name.

We knew he lived in the Sacred Forest, because that's where all dịbịas lived, south of the river where we never fished because the crocodiles lived in those waters. Every dịbịa retreated into the Sacred Forest when their gifts appeared, to train for years before they started offering their services to the people. If a dịbịa ever turned their back on the deity to become a ritualist – a person who sacrificed humans to amplify their gifts for the sake of power – then the other dịbịas would kill them and abandon their body in the Sacred Forest. No one had seen this happen in a long time, not even Ahụdi, but I still wondered what kind of bones lay decaying on that consecrated land. I had never stepped foot in the Sacred Forest, but I heard stories that the birds inside there spoke with human voices and that the trees were so old and tall, clouds formed at their crowns. Our own forest – the People's Forest – seemed boring in comparison, just trees and leaves and bushes and streams, springs of clear water and birds that did nothing but sing. Back when I was too young for a gift, my whole life seemed boring. I wanted more than stories.

The dịbịas had always been strange, and after they broke the earth, they became even stranger. Some people thought they had too much power – how else could they have decided to wound a god by creating the Split? Rumors were whispered that in doing so, the dịbịas had stopped obeying the deity and taken matters into their own hands, and that was why we were culled by the gifts – because they had skirted too close to ritualist disobedience. Other people claimed that although the dịbịas could communicate with the deity, that wasn't the same as serving her, and that if the deity ceased to be useful, the dịbịas could destroy her. I never knew which one was true; how could you destroy a god? What I did know was the taste of fear every time a dịbịa came to our town, like bitter kola crushed between my back teeth.

Years later, I wondered if Mama was right, if my fear was a prophecy or an announcement, if our world did fall apart on the day the dịbịas came to collect my sister.

CHAPTER ONE

THE FIRST TIME I MET MY MOTHER'S FATHER, JAYAIKE AND I WERE thirteen. I remember that morning well. It was cold, and I was making pap in the big pot, stirring it with the long wooden spoon as it thickened. Jayaike was frying the akara on another fire next to me, lifting them out with a metal ladle and draining the oil before collecting them in a bowl and then dropping in the batter for the next batch. We were quiet because sometimes talking spoiled things. It was better to breathe in the cold morning air and enjoy the way Mama would stroke our cheek when she walked past with a basket of wrung clothes. She was stringing up the drying line when the first apprentices walked into the compound and hesitated at the gate, calling out a greeting. They were wearing red cloth and their faces were half masks, with white chalk covering the left side. The rest of their skin was fully coated in the chalk, and some of it had cracked into jagged lines running over their bodies. Their feet were dusty.

Mama turned her head at their greeting, then stood very still for a few seconds. She bent down to put the spool of thick thread next to the basket, and she looked so old when she straightened slowly.

'Where is he?' she asked, beckoning for them to enter and come closer to her. The two children came and knelt at her feet, touching their fingertips to her big toes and murmuring more greetings. She touched their shaved heads absentmindedly, her eyes blinking quickly as she looked toward the gate.

'Where is he?' she asked again, with more force this time.

I stopped stirring the pot and looked at Jayaike in confusion – who was she talking about? My twin stood up, unfolding with a small frown of concentration as he scanned the compound. He looked like he was expecting trouble. I had already heard trouble in Mama's mouth, so if that's what Jayaike was looking for, I could have easily told him where to find it. It was everywhere in how her voice broke when the tall man entered our gate without a pause, striding in as if he owned our land.

'No,' Mama whispered in a small, scared voice. 'Biko, no.'

I swear the air shifted in that moment. Our compound looked just the same as it always had – the goats eating a patch of grass in a corner, a chicken scratching in the sand, white flowers climbing over our fence – but something inhuman exhaled and inhaled, a cold breeze brushing past my cheek. The stranger who had walked in was bald and his face was shaved to show the folds of his skin. His cloth was a deeper red than the apprentices', and he threw it over his shoulder with a smooth ease. When he glanced in my direction, I felt my skin prickle. I immediately put down my spoon and turned to my brother.

'Quick, help me take the pot off the fire.' My twin didn't waste time asking me for reasons. He helped me lift the pot onto the ground; then we took the pan of oil off the fire, covered the pap and the akara, and reached for each other's hand in the same moment. The touch of Jayaike's hard fingers helped my feet feel better about the ground we were standing on.

'Go and get Papa,' I said, squeezing his hand and keeping my eyes on our mother. She was trembling, but I think I was the only one who could notice. Her shaking was so fine and delicate, like rain on a spider's web. Jayaike nodded and ran off to the back of the house, and I walked closer, trying to stay quiet. I wished I could disappear so that the stranger wouldn't see me, but Mama had never shaken like this before, so I had to come and make her stop. That kind of shaking is never good.

The man was speaking to her as I walked up. 'By the river, is this how you greet me, Ngọzị? I don't even get an embrace?'

Mama put her hand to her chest and pressed down. 'Do you know how long it has been since I heard your voice?' she asked.

Her voice was doing that shaking thing like her body. I didn't like it. The man's eyes did something soft and he put his hand on my mother's cheek. I had never seen a man who was not Papa touch my mother, and it alarmed me, so I ran forward and grabbed her other hand, the one that was not helping her chest. They both looked down at me and the man smiled. He was much older than I had thought; he was definitely an elder, yet I had never seen him at any of the gatherings. The faint stubble on his cheeks was white with age.

'Who is this one?' he asked, and Mama pushed me behind her.

'Whoever you are looking for is not here!' Her voice was harsh, unwelcoming. 'You have the wrong compound.'

The man dropped his hand and looked very sad. 'Well, it cannot be her; she is too small. I have the right compound, Ngọzị. I'm here for the Ada.'

Mama's hand tightened on my flesh, but I squirmed away, now curious.

'It's our Ada you want? It's not me. I'm not the first daughter.' I narrowed my eyes at this stranger. 'Who are you? Why do you want Nkadi?'

Mama made an annoyed sound and pushed me toward the house. 'Go inside!' she shouted. 'And tell your sister to stay inside as well!'

Her order left her mouth too late. Jayaike had already come

back with both Papa and Nkadi. Our senior sister was fifteen years old at the time. Her black hair was threaded neatly and her brown eyes were calm above her sharp cheekbones, her dark gold skin glistening with oil. She had just finished having her bath. Even though she was older than us, she was small and agile, our young leopard, our gleaming one. Papa had his hand on her shoulder but his eyes on Mama, and there was a sadness there that resembled that of the stranger's, who had leaned forward toward me, speaking softly.

'My name is Zerenjọ,' he said. 'I am your mother's father. What is your name?'

I frowned and looked for my mother in his face. He was a stranger, but if he was telling the truth, then he was also a dịbịa, and that thrilled me. 'Sọmadịna,' I said. 'Did you come from the Sacred Forest?'

Mama slapped me behind my head when I said that.

'Don't ask him questions,' she hissed, and I thought she would grab or push me again, but she didn't. She just stood there, looking at us like she was falling. Jayaike came and stood next to me. We had always been precisely the same height, and Mama let us wear our hair in the same way: fist-tight tiny curls stiffly reaching up. We weren't exactly identical, but the way we wore our faces and moved our skin made it clear to people that we were one person. Jayaike was the color of red soil, the kind that turns so smooth when you add water to it, while I was like dark loam, Papa said, the rich, almost-black earth that grows everything. It made me an especial child of our mother deity Ala, he said, very much a farmer's daughter. My hair was black like Nkadi's hair, and Jayaike's was the same dark gold as her skin. We loved to find ourselves in her, just like finding our long fingers on Papa's hands and our thick eyebrows on Mama's face. Apart from our different shades, it was like they used the same tools to build us – our features and bones were identical. Like I said, we were one person.

Our grandfather rocked back and looked at us intently. 'Your twins are growing well, Ngọzị,' he said slowly, scanning first my face, then Jayaike's.

We stared straight back, skin prickling, and our fingers found each other as they always did. We had a bond that Ahụdi first sensed when we were babies. Even if we were separated, we cried and laughed at the same time, as if we could feel each other's emotions. Ahụdi said it wasn't a gift, that it was just part of being twins. In my head, the bond was like a soft rope connecting us, bleached white like an old bone.

'Is it now you're seeing them?' Mama spat out. 'Did you even know you had a family? You have been gone for years!' She threw the words as if she hoped to hurt him more than she was hurting. Papa had his arm wrapped around her, but she still stood like a trembling and lonely tree. 'And now you want to come and collect my firstborn, just like that? Not even here to see your family, but to take mine from me?'

Zerenjọ stood up and dusted his red cloth, then let his hands fall so the palms opened out and faced Mama.

'I know how hard this is, Ngọzị. I watched my mother cry when they took me, and I prayed no one would come for my children. I do not have the words to tell you how sorry I am to be coming for yours. I wish I could apologize for the ways I have not been here, but it would be an old, old conversation. We do this every time. I have never loved you any less, never spent a morning without you on my mind, never stopped wondering if the things that happened had not happened, so that I could be with my family, here. But things happened the way that they did, and we are where we are.'

'What things?' I asked, annoyed. He was upsetting Mama and he was keeping dịbịa secrets, talking in circles instead of telling me things I was dying to hear. What was his mother like, our great-grandmother? Did being a dịbịa mean that Mama lost him completely? If he was here to take Nkadi, how much were we about to lose her?

Nkadi touched my mouth and shook her head at me. When I looked at her, her eyes were shining with water and the air around her was vibrating like it does when she's excited, a thing that only started a year or two ago. I reached up to trace the marks Mama had put in her skin from the last time she was born and died. She always belonged to Mama more than she belonged to any of us – she was our mother's most precious thing because she was alive, because she was a spirit child who passed through other bodies before this one, children that Mama bore, children that died until Nkadi decided to stay. Some people would say this means she's not really Mama's firstborn, but Mama would point out that the dead children were all Nkadi, and so the spirit is still her firstborn even if the flesh is not.

'Are you going to go with him?' I asked Nkadi. Did she have a choice? Would she choose us over the forest and this strange man?

'Stop asking questions,' whispered Jayaike. 'Of course she is going. That's why Mama is crying.'

Our mother hid her face in Papa's shoulder and sobbed without sound. Papa was silent as well, his face turned toward her and his hand making circles on her back. I knew his voice would be soft in her head, soothing her. He glanced over at Nkadi and smiled at her, nudging her to go to our grandfather. She looked at Mama, worried for a moment, but then she took cautious steps toward the dịbịa.

'Grandfather,' she said, and knelt at his feet, touching her fingertips to his toes. He held her shoulders and pulled her up into an embrace.

'My child.' His voice was thick and he cleared his throat. 'You know why I am here.'

'Yes.' She nodded. 'I'm becoming a dịbịa.' Her voice started out strong, but then it stumbled. 'I—I have to go and train with you in the Sacred Forest.' A spike of jealousy ran through my chest.

'What if it's all wrong?' Mama was desperate now, pleading. 'What if that's not what's happening to her?'

'You know better, Ngọzị.' Grandfather adjusted his cloth again, and I suddenly realized the color was that of dried blood. What did he need to hide? 'Her powers will be too strong to manage at home, too dangerous for your other children. I wish I could have left her with you for a few more years, but it has become very clear that she needs to start training now, no later.' His voice gentled as he looked at Mama. 'I saw how powerfully you fought to keep her in this world, Ngọzị. Trust me, I have no intention of letting her gifts take her out of it. The girl will be safe with me.'

Mama crumpled a little against my father, and her voice was so tired. 'It is too much. First her deaths, and now this? Will I ever sleep at night?'

Nkadi ran into her arms and pressed her head to our mother's chest. 'I am alive,' she reminded her. 'I will learn so much from Grandfather and then I will come back. I promise. I will come back to you.'

Mama gave her a small smile and held her tightly. 'Ah, my daughter. If there is one thing you know how to do well, it is to come back to me.'

Jayaike and I put our arms around them as we listened

to Papa's voice in our heads, whispering words of comfort. I wondered if any of this made Papa think of his own father, the dịbịa Kesandụ, Ahụdi's husband who had died in the Split.

Zerenjọ bowed his head slightly and gestured to his apprentices that it was time to go. 'I will leave you to say your goodbyes. Send her to the tallest palm tree after the sun reaches its peak. We will wait there for her. May we all see tomorrow.' He left quietly, the two boys walking side by side behind him.

When Mama said that it all started that day, she meant that some of her joy went out with Nkadi, and it left behind the suffering that gifts can bring, a suffering that grew and grew until it overflowed our compound and went wild. But we didn't think about all that in that moment. We didn't know what was about to happen. We just stood in the middle of our compound with our arms around each other, breakfast cold in the pot and clean cloths lying unhung in the basket, and we stood there for a long time.

CHAPTER TWO

OUR MOTHER WASN'T A COLD WOMAN. MAMA WAS MANY OTHER things – stern, disciplined, patient – not cold, but she didn't run hot either. If anything, she was cool like settled iron, steady and strong. Papa was the one who brought heat and warmth, and sometimes, like iron, she took on his heat and you could see it in her smile. She rarely held us, but she was always there, always constant. I think with all of Nkadi's past deaths, Mama became guarded with how she showed her love, just in case her children would be taken away again. When my grandfather took Nkadi, something in Mama shuttered closed. She didn't take on any of Papa's heat. She smelled like sorrow, and her silence felt like someone who had either just stopped screaming or was about to start. I missed Nkadi too, but at least I cried about it, my twin and I weeping and Papa wrapping us in his arms. Mama's eyes floated away when she saw us. We kept going, day after day, without our golden leopard, and that was how we settled into a new, slightly emptier way of living.

Mama said Jayaike could move into Nkadi's old room, which meant he and I would no longer share a room. She had tried separating us years ago because people said it was somehow for us to still be sleeping in the same bed. They said Nkadi and I should be sharing a room while Jayaike slept alone, but when Mama tried it, Jayaike and I simply stopped eating. No amount of threats or beatings could change our minds, and after three days, Papa stepped in and gave us back our room. Mama gave us separate beds, but we pushed them together and slept cuddled with each other as usual. Eventually, she just ignored it all: our disobedience and the neighbors' talk. After Nkadi left, Jayaike refused her room again, and this time, Mama didn't try to force it. She just turned it into a spare room, and I swear I saw the light in her eyes dim.

On the third full moon, Nkadi came home for a visit, surprising us when she walked into the compound, and Mama lit up like a wildfire. She clutched Nkadi to her chest and wept over her, then killed a chicken and made pepper soup. Jayaike and I ate out of the same bowl as our sister and stared at her. Her head had been shaved and traces of white chalk clung around her ears, like she had washed hurriedly before coming to see us. I wanted to ask her everything. I wanted to crawl into her head and explore everything she had seen.

'By the river, if your eyes fall into this soup the way you're looking at me, I will just eat them up,' she warned. We giggled in delight and exploded into questions, tired of holding them in.

'What did they use to shave your head? Did it hurt?'

'Have you seen the god? Have you spoken to Ala?'

'What is our grandfather like? Does he beat you?'

'Do they make you drink crocodile blood?' I asked this last one in a whisper. It was a rumor I'd heard at school and I was scared of what the answer might be, scared of who my sister might have become.

Nkadi just laughed and ate a piece of liver. 'I can't tell you anything about training. It's a secret.'

Jayaike frowned. 'But you can tell us about Grandfather, no? Is he like Mama?'

Nkadi thought for a moment. 'He's softer,' she said finally. 'And sadder.'

I almost scoffed. How could anyone be sadder than Mama had been since Nkadi left?

'Mama only lives for you,' Jayaike told her, as if he could read my mind. 'She's the most sad when you're gone.'

Nkadi cast a worried look in our parents' direction. Mama was leaning against Papa as he laughed and fed her bits of tender chicken like she was a queen.

'I'll come back every third moon,' she promised, but my twin pouted.

'It won't be enough,' he said. 'We're not enough for her.'

I looked at him, surprised he would say that out loud, and Nkadi frowned. 'You don't know how much she wanted you both,' she said. 'Don't talk like that, you hear?'

He fell silent, but I knew he wasn't convinced. When Nkadi left after two days and Mama lost all her spark again, I wasn't convinced either.

Nkadi kept her promise and came every third full moon, but each time she seemed less and less like our sister and more and more like a dịbịa, smelling of secret powers and with eyes that looked too far away. Jayaike and I got used to her absence, got used to the dimness of our mother's eyes, and pressed even closer to our father because Papa always saw us. In some ways, it felt like we were more his children than we were Mama's. He was the one we told about the little sagas that unfolded in school, where we learned how to make things, how to turn clay into vessels, how the crops cycled with the seasons, things we could go and apply at home.

There was this boy in our age group called Ụwafụlamiro. He was different, but not in the way Nkadi was different, where everyone knew she was a spirit that had come from somewhere else. Ụwafụlamiro was different in a way that made people want to throw stones at him. He was the color of chalk, from his hair to his eyelashes and skin, and they called him a ghost behind his back. Some people said he was cursed and that it would bring unhappy things to your house if you spoke to him or looked into his eyes. The other children at school didn't like Ụwafụlamiro, and sometimes they teased him or walked in wide circles to avoid him. Jayaike and I didn't pay much attention to him until the day of the fight.

It was a wet, rainy afternoon after classes and we were preparing to walk home when we heard noise and shouting from a tight knot of students in the far corner of the playground. When we pushed through everyone, we saw Ụwafụlamiro in the center, sitting on top of Chidị, one of the well-liked boys in our age group, smashing his swollen face with cracked knuckles. The other students were shouting for him to stop, but no one was actually stepping in to stop him, and there was blood soaking into the mud below them.

I was horrified. It was the first violent thing I had witnessed, and it made my stomach twist. Before I realized it, I was grabbing his pale arm and wrenching it away from Chidị's pulped face.

'Are you mad?!' I was shaking with anger. 'What kind of animal are you to start behaving like this?' I put both hands on his chest and shoved him off Chidị, wanting to watch him fall into the red soupy soil. Instead, Ụwafụlamiro rolled and was back on his feet, baring his teeth at me.

'Who do you think you are, small girl?' There was an ugly cut on one side of his face, and blood was crusted down his cheek and neck. He looked like a wild animal. 'Get out of here before I show you pepper!'

No one had ever dared to speak to me like that before, and I reacted sharply, aiming my hand at his wounded face, thinking to rake his cut open further. I never made the strike – Jayaike stepped in front of me and pinned my arm to my side, giving me a reproachful look.

'It's enough now,' he said to Ụwafụlamiro. 'The teachers are coming. Go home.'

The ghostly boy looked at Jayaike for a brief moment, his white eyelashes flickering; then he turned and walked away. The students cleared a path as he moved through them, murmuring like a swarm of flies, but no one would look at him. He treated them as if they were invisible too, his back straight as if he was walking in empty air.

Jayaike grabbed my arm and dragged me away, toward home. I went with him, silent and resentful. I could feel his irritation through our twin bond, but I just felt annoyed that he was annoyed with me. We walked for a few minutes in the light rain until I couldn't take it anymore.

'I didn't do anything wrong! He was beating Chidị!'

The self-righteousness in my voice was like fire to dry thatch, and Jayaike exploded.

'You don't *think,* Sọmadịna! And you don't see anything! You just march over everybody like a mad elephant!'

I stopped in my tracks. 'What did you just call me?!'

Jayaike threw his hands up in the air. 'Did you even see the knife?!'

That took me by surprise and I blinked a few times. 'What knife?' Jayaike actually looked at me with contempt, and I felt it sear me. *'What knife?'*

'By the river, you're a fool.' He shook his head. 'Chidị cut Ụwafụlamiro first.'

I scoffed at my twin, ignoring a prickle skimming over my skin. 'You're lying. How do you know?'

'There was a knife lying next to them, if you had used your eyes. It's Chidị's knife; he's brought it to school before to show off and you know he comes from a closed-minded family. He's always saying wicked things about Ụwafụlamiro and now he tried to cut up his face, so who's the one behaving like an animal?'

He shook his head at me and started walking away. I stood alone as the taste of guilt washed up my throat. Jayaike was right. Chidị's father was the local blacksmith and his family did hold some beliefs that were very old and very closed. I had heard rumors that they thought twins were evil and should have been left to die, thrown into the Sacred Forest. I ran after Jayaike and grabbed his hand.

'I will say sorry to him tomorrow, Jayaike.'

He just nodded tightly and we went home.

The next day, Ụwafụlamiro's face was sewn up and my mouth felt thick as I apologized to him. He was gentler when he was not angry, and he stammered as he accepted my apology. Jayaike invited him to come to our house, and from there, we became friends. When we told Papa this story, he looked at me gravely and cupped my chin in his hand as he spoke silently into my mind. *Be more like your brother, Sọmadịna. He takes his time.*

I knew Papa was right. When we turned fourteen, we thought our gifts would arrive soon. It would be dangerous to be someone who couldn't control themselves, who was rash and impatient like I was. It was already dangerous for us in ways that our parents wouldn't talk about, but I wasn't a fool and I wasn't born yesterday. Jayaike and I were the first twins born in a few generations and we weren't that far away from a time when twins would be killed for being blasphemous. The dịbịas had stopped the practice, but people take longer to forget. I heard the whispers at school, that Mama only gave birth to abnormal things, like twins, or like a spirit child who turned out to be a dịbịa. The whispers were only whispers for now, because Mama and Papa kept their heads down and worked hard, but I could spoil that for them if I wasn't careful. I shouldn't have been picking fights with people at school, not when Jayaike and I had so much at stake.

We didn't realize it then, but looking back, we didn't stand a chance.

There is a pattern to things with our people and the magic.

When your body started to change, the magic would enter you and the gift would be born – a bequest from Ala, a welcome into the threshold of adulthood, the crocodile crawling over your spirit and gifting you with its bite. I had spent my whole life wondering what my gift would be, especially after Nkadi's power took her to the Sacred Forest. It was inevitable that we would be strong, my twin and I. Didn't we come from a line of dịbịas on not one but both sides of our bloodline? I fantasized about my gift arriving in a blaze of glory, preferably while at school, so the rest of our age group would marvel at it. I looked forward to my body changing with less anticipation, but it was just as inevitable, or so we had been taught.

It didn't happen.

At fourteen, we could all pretend it was just delayed. We could ignore the glances our parents gave our bodies as Jayaike and I shot up like maize stalks, tall and thin and smooth. At fifteen, no one could ignore it anymore. All our age mates were morphing into new flesh. Ụwafụlamiro's shoulders grew even broader, and the bones of his face changed as his voice developed long fissures. Jayaike and I did not change. The whispers grew louder. Mama's eyes sharpened and her mouth thinned when she looked at us, but she said nothing. She gave me my waistbeads as was the ritual for every girl who turned fifteen, but they felt like a lie on my narrow hips. I said nothing. My twin said nothing. Ụwafụlamiro probably would've said nothing too, but that was until the crocodile bit his spirit.

In our town, there was a sacred river where the crocodiles lived. No one knew the source of the river, but we knew it never dried up, no matter the season – it sprang from the deity and it hosted the deity and that was that. No one was allowed to fish in it and, of course, no one was allowed to hunt the crocodiles – you'd have to be mad to try and kill the god's scaled flesh. The crocodiles never harmed anyone. We saw them as the keepers of the river, and sometimes Jayaike and I would climb a tree overhanging the water and just watch their dark shapes slip through the currents or rest on the banks as the morning fog rolled through the trees. The crocodiles were so old, so powerful, it felt like they had lived there since the beginning of time. On each full moon, we were allowed to fetch water from the river to take back to our homes. This water would be used for prayer, libations, anointing injuries, whatever small rituals each family needed the deity's touch for.

Ụwafụlamiro and I were by the river on this full moon with our clay pots, and I was busy trying to ignore the cool stares of girls who walked around with full chests and new hair while I was still as smooth and flat as when I was ten. They alternated between casting slow glances at Ụwafụlamiro and evil ones at me, and I felt angry blood rush to my face as I bent to fill my pot.

'Why can't they mind their own business?!' I hissed under

my breath. Ụwafụlamiro chuckled as he waded into the water and bent beside me, the muscles on his back gliding under his skin. He was like taboo fruit to the girls with his ghostly skin and moonlight hair, different and exciting and strange, so they watched him with a barely concealed hunger. The crocodiles were in the river's depths, shadows of a lurking god.

'Ignore them, Sọmadịna. They have no home training.' Ụwafụlamiro hefted his pot onto his shoulder and then, startlingly, vanished. I paused for a moment, too shocked to scream or drop my pot, and I stared at the air in front of me. He reappeared almost immediately, frowning at me in confusion. 'Why are you standing there with your mouth open? You want flies to enter it?'

'You . . . you just disappeared!'

His eyebrows pulled even closer together. 'Ehn?'

'As in, you were standing here, and then you weren't, and then you were again. You just disappeared and then came back!' He blinked and vanished again. I nearly choked on my own spit. 'You're doing it again! Look at your hands!'

Ụwafụlamiro must have reached his arms out because his pot floated from shoulder height and hovered in the air in front of him. I heard him gasp and then the pot fell, landing in the shallows of the river. When he appeared once more in front of me, he was paler than I thought possible.

'Sọmadịna,' he whispered, his voice shaking. 'What just happened?'

How did he not understand? I would have known immediately if I was him, that's how long I had been waiting and praying for something to change. I dragged up a smile and tamped down my envy, slapping his cheek lightly.

'Well done, my friend,' I said. 'You just held your gift for the first time.'

Ụwafụlamiro's eyes widened and he stared at me with that pale silver gaze I was so familiar with by now. 'I can *disappear*?'

I nodded and picked up his pot. 'You better go and register with the elders.'

It would be the last step in declaring him to be a man. He had held a gift. He was complete. How much farther, I wondered, would this pull him from me? I knew my feelings were showing in my face when Ụwafụlamiro took the pot out of my hands and set it on the bank. I couldn't bear to look him in the eye, so I looked at my feet, distorted by the water rushing around my calves. He held me by the shoulders and his voice curved around me, bouncing softly off the water.

'It's all right. I'm not leaving you behind, Sọmadịna.'

I hated how easily he could see into my heart. Quick tears pressed behind my eyelids and my voice thickened. 'You are, but it's fine. This is how it should be. Grow, mature, hold a gift, get registered. I'm the one who's falling behind, who's still a child. It's not your fault.'

He shook me softly. 'How can you be a child? Are there

not only two years between us? So if me, I'm a man, then you cannot be a child.'

'I look like one,' I whispered, miserable. 'I look like an abomination.'

Ụwafụlamiro's nostrils flared and his voice took an edge. 'Who told you that?! You're not an abomination.' He pulled me into a hug and kissed my temple roughly. 'You're not, Sọmadịna.'

I buried my face in the salt of his neck and ignored the stares of the other people who were carrying their pots past us. No doubt there would be a fresh wave of gossip about his gift, with added details of how we were being inappropriate in public. I didn't care. As if he heard my thoughts, Ụwafụlamiro pulled back slightly and cupped my face in his hands.

'Even if you look young forever, Sọmadịna, it doesn't mean you're still a small child.' He brought his face closer to me until his breath brushed mine and fixed my eyes with his. It was as if something new had been set on fire inside him with his gift's appearance, and in response, I felt my own insides slide and spark. 'Trust me,' he whispered, and then he softly pressed his lips to mine.

His mouth was cool like a fresh leaf off a mango tree, the green ones I would rip in half just to inhale the scent that broke out, waiting for fruit that wasn't ready. I felt the pads of his thumbs stroke my temples; already his hands were large enough to hold my face with nothing spilling out. The sun hit my skin in a warm wash of light, and my ears were filled with the thundering of my pulse and the water of the river. It was a stretched few seconds, and when he pulled away, I could only stare at him in trembling surprise. Ụwafụlamiro grinned at me and winked as if it was just a game, and the mischief in his face was too much for me to resist. I broke out giggling, feeling my nerves chitter a high-pitched song, and we filled up our pots quickly to start heading home. I tried to ignore the shocked glances and quick whispering that followed us, and as we walked back, Ụwafụlamiro took my hand in his.

I let fingers that did not belong to my twin wrap around mine, as if it was possible for someone else to learn the map of my skin.

CHAPTER THREE

WHEN I GOT HOME, I COULD HEAR VOICES AND LAUGHTER COMING from inside, and I knew that Mama's sister-friend was visiting her. Da Ụzụmma was a trader, a beautiful and tall woman with enough curves and body to share with three other women, as Mama would joke. Her daughter Chiotu was one of my friends – bright and popular and well on her way to becoming as full-bodied as her mother. All the boys were already salivating over her, even though she was close to Chidị and they were rumored to be courting. Chiotu just liked to smile mysteriously every time I asked her how serious it was. I never felt more like a small girl than when she swayed her woman's body next to my broomstick figure, but I couldn't wait to see her again. I wondered if she had come to visit with her mother, so I could tell her what had happened at the river. When I put down my pot and went in to greet Da Ụzụmma, I tried to push aside the memory of Ụwafụlamiro's breath becoming my own.

'Sọmadịna!'

Da Ụzụmma broke into a huge smile as soon as she saw me, and I found myself suffused in a warm hug. One thing about Chiotu's mother was that she really loved her oils, and so being near her meant being in a thick, delirious cloud of rich scents you could get drunk off. She pulled back to look at me, and I saw a quick flicker of concern cross her face, but it was replaced by her usual friendly expression. 'Ah-ahn, see how tall this one has grown! You want to hit your head on the clouds? Slow down, biko!'

I smiled back at her and caught my mother looking at me from where she was seated. Her gaze was unnerving, slow and mildly calculating.

'Did Chiotu come with you?' I asked after greeting her.

'No, she's peeling yam for me at home while complaining that it's going to make her hands itch.' Da Ụzụmma laughed out loud, and I allowed myself another smile because I could absolutely hear Chiotu protesting anything that was uncomfortable. She'd do it anyway, because she was a good daughter. We were good at being good daughters. I chatted with Da Ụzụmma for a few minutes, then begged to be excused, wanting to be away from under Mama's eye. Something made me pause outside the doorway as I left, pressing against the wall to hear what they were saying.

'Do you see what I am talking about?' Mama's voice was steady but slightly worried. 'Something must be wrong, Ụzụmma. The girl is growing in no other direction but toward the sky. The boy is the same way.'

My stomach started twisting. I didn't know Mama had noticed. It was stupid of me to think she would miss it, but she had never *said* anything.

'And no gift yet either?' Da Ụzụmma wasn't even bothering to hide how shaken she was. 'Ngọzị, I haven't seen anything like that before. This isn't . . . it's not natural.' There was a weighty pause.

When Mama spoke again, her voice sounded like it did the day Zerenjọ took Nkadi.

'Ụzụmma, biko, tell me what I should do.'

I heard Da Ụzụmma take a deep breath, and when she spoke, her voice was steady.

'Send for Ahụdi,' she said.

I heard a small sob and realized it had spilled out of my own mouth. I immediately fled down the corridor, away from Mama, away from the knowledge that there was something truly *wrong* with me and my twin. I didn't know where he was, so I hid in our bed for the rest of the evening, claiming I had a stomachache. I think Mama hoped it was the bleeding starting, because she actually left me alone to rest, instead of bullying me up to my feet like she usually would. I cried alone until I fell asleep.

I woke up when Jayaike climbed into bed with me. There was moonlight crumbling through the window as he lifted the wrapper I was using as a cover and settled his body next to mine.

'Where have you been?' I mumbled, fitting my head into his shoulder.

'Helping Papa on the farm. What happened? Mama said you're not feeling well.'

All the edges of my world were soft and sleepy. I didn't want to talk about the conversation I'd overheard. 'They're sending for Ahụdi.'

'That's good, now. She hasn't visited in a while.'

I shook my head gently. 'Mba, they're sending for her because of me.' I thought for a moment and then amended, 'Because of *us*.'

I knew Jayaike would be frowning, small lines gathering on his red sand forehead. 'But we didn't do anything.'

I sighed and shifted, placing his hand on my flat chest and cupping his smooth cheek with mine. 'Exactly.'

He was quiet for a bit, then took my hand. 'I understand.'

Of course he did. While the other boys cracked and grew wide, my brother had been left with a pure voice and slim bones. He had started working on the farm more with Papa, who was silently pleased to have him there, and Jayaike was becoming leaner and stronger. He was thin, but it was as if he was carving himself out of the body that cheated him, one defined muscle at a time. We lay together in the dim light, and as always, our heartbeats matched up and thudded together.

'Ụwafụlamiro kissed me.'

Jayaike's pulse lost its place and sounded in discord with mine. I had whispered it in a rush, unsure of how to lead up to such a new confession. I waited for the questions, the where and how and why, the something or anything.

'I saw him earlier,' said my brother, instead, in a relaxed tone. 'He said he can disappear.'

'Yes, he vanished when we were at the river.'

'Were you afraid?'

I wanted to ask him – afraid of what? Of when he disappeared or of when he kissed me like a falling leaf? Instead, I propped myself up on an elbow so I could look down at his face, at my face.

'Did I do something wrong?' I asked, feeling like a hole was spilling open between us. Jayaike blinked slowly, our thick eyelashes falling and lifting from his cheekbones. We have the same muddy gold eyes, flecked and shifting. He lifted his long fingers and ran them down my cheek, his fingernails oval shells against my skin.

'Sọmadịna.' Jayaike had a way of saying my name like it was the holiest thing to ever enter his mouth. *Let me not be alone in the world.* He splayed his fingers on the back of my neck, and his voice was an echo of mine, because we are the same person.

'Don't leave me behind,' he whispered, his small hand bones firm on my small neck bones. I thought of the fine silver hairs on Ụwafụlamiro's face, the speed of his skin approaching mine. That intimacy had had a strangeness to it, a newness of body, an outside reaching for my inside. This one was different. Jayaike was me and I was him; they just used different colors of chalk when they drew us into breathing. I leaned down and rested my forehead against his.

'How can?' I replied. 'You are with me always; I can never leave you behind.'

'I wasn't with you at the river.' He sounded slightly petulant.

Blood rushed to my face and I tried to pull back, but Jayaike's fingers flexed against my neck and stopped me.

'Don't mind me,' he said. 'Ewela iwe. I'm just being childish.'

'It didn't—'

'Don't finish that lie. Of course it did.'

I poked his ribs and tried to laugh. 'Did what? You don't even know what I was going to say.'

Jayaike smiled back at me and twisted a section of my hair with his fingers. 'I'm you, remember? It counted, it mattered, it meant something, whichever one you were aiming for.'

I tapped my fingertips on his cheekbones and watched his lower lashes in silence. The air around us was tinged with a gray sadness.

'I just want to be close to you,' he whispered. 'You're all I have.'

His voice was so soft and hesitant, it wrung out my heart. No one else could understand what we were going through, the ways we were different, not even Ụwafụlamiro. Not our parents, not Nkadi, dịbịa though she might be. It was just the two of us, like it always had been. I cupped his face in my hands. I wanted, so desperately, for Jayaike not to feel as lonely as I had when Ụwafụlamiro had disappeared at the stream. I shut my eyes and felt along our twin bond, knowing he would be at the other end, like he always was. There was a sullen gray cloud of fear and loss coming from Jayaike's end and I could feel him reaching out too, sending searching tendrils.

Sọmadịna . . .

I almost broke the link in surprise. He sounded just like Papa does when he talks in our heads.

Jayaike?

I felt him startle through the link and then it was like our spirits collided in a clash of brightness, flooding my senses with the taste of tart fruit and the smell of the earth after the rain. I was awash in all my twin's emotions, experiencing them as if they were mine. So many of them were familiar, the knotting fear that we would never be like our age mates, that something was horribly wrong with us, the drowning love he had for me, the tenderness for our family. But there were jagged deviations – a hot jealousy he was ashamed of, confusion and love for Ụwafụlamiro, and a growing restlessness he was trying to ignore. I wanted to delve deeper into these parts of my twin, but now the air was tasting sharp like hot iron, and why did it feel like there was a chasm opening up under us?

A shrill whine started up in my head, climbing in pitch and volume till it felt like a blade ripping my eardrums apart. I could feel Jayaike's pain and fright through the link, every cell of his skin below my fingertips, every particle of air in his exhale against my face. I could hear his heart as if someone was playing out his pulse on a gong, and I could hear Mama's voice rising from her bedroom as she called out to Papa in alarm.

'Olejeme! It's back, wake up, wake up! Can't you smell it?'

I was wincing from the sharp sound filling my head, but if Mama could smell the hot iron, that meant it was real.

What does she mean, it's back? asked Jayaike through the bond. I sent back uncertainty in reply, a silent shrug.

Can you feel the hole? I asked instead. *I feel like it's going to suck us down.*

There was a pause as my twin evaluated the hallucination of a chasm beneath us. I could tell it existed only in spirit, that if we looked with material eyes, we would only see our bed or the earthen floor under it.

Oh! That's not a hole, not really. He was sending me joy and surprised happiness, neither of which I understood. I checked again and felt that terror of falling forever, of death and foreboding.

What are you talking about?

His surprise focused in my direction. *You don't feel it, Sọmadịna? It's a channel, a window, a mirror. Come and look.*

I felt his spirit wrap around me, guiding me toward the emptiness until we teetered at the edge. I was flaring off sparks of terror and trepidation while Jayaike was radiating a joy I couldn't understand. I felt him urging me to look down, bubbling in his enthusiasm, and slowly, ever so slowly, I risked a look into the chasm.

Several things happened at once.

First of all, I screamed.

I still have no space in my mouth to tell anyone what I saw, the terrible power of what I felt, connected to everything at the same time, the gourd full of ashes that exploded in my cheek, the maggots crawling out of muddy gold eyes, rotten scales, a yawning jaw.

Second, our mother gasped in our doorway and dropped her lamp, breaking it. Oil splashed on the floor and fire hiccuped into the air.

Jayaike and I snapped our eyes open scant inches from each other, then whipped our heads around to look at Mama. In the brief second in between, I saw that his eyes were charcoal black, a dark smear all over, to the edges of skin. He looked possessed, and since we are one person, I knew I must have looked the same. Mama stood there, small flames stuttering at her feet, staring at us as she whispered something to herself.

The thing in the chasm roared in our heads and shot out strong waves of power, rocking Mama back a step or two. I felt its energy brush past my face, staggering in its strength, a cold beam of sheer force that hissed out one word to our mother.

MINE.

There was a world of warning packed in the single syllable, a threat, a reminder I didn't understand. I thought I saw shocked tears reflected in Mama's eyes, before Papa's hoarse voice sounded from the corridor and the chasm slammed shut. I scrambled backward until the familiar heft of the wall was pressed against my shoulder blades, my wrapper tangled in the bed. The iron taste slipped away from the air and the high-pitched whine stopped.

Everything was normal again. The night was damp and heavy, with crickets sounding outside the window. Mama was still standing with small orange flowers burning on the floor. She blinked a few times and reached for a jug of water that was on a bench by the door. I knew she wanted to smother the flames, but she was moving so slowly. Without thinking, I held out my hand and willed the fire to die. It sputtered out against the ground just as Papa walked in holding a fresh lamp, and the small pool of light it cast highlighted the terrible look that flashed across Mama's face.

'What happened?' asked Papa, his voice creaky. He was worried enough to be speaking aloud, but Mama's eyes didn't leave mine as she flapped her hand at him.

'It's nothing, the children are fine.' She took a wrapper off a hook on the wall and tossed it on the bed toward me. 'Cover yourself.'

I flinched and dragged the material up to my shoulders, trembling. I wanted her to be my *mother,* to climb into the bed and gather us to her, sing us to sleep like other mothers did to their children. I wanted to tell her about what I had seen, ask her about what I had heard, but her face was like a carved wooden door. She turned and touched my father's shoulder as she walked out on us.

'Olejeme, clean the broken lamp for me, biko. I'm going back to sleep.'

As she left, Papa frowned a little and looked at us. 'What happened?' he repeated. 'Why was there magic tasting in the air?'

It was Jayaike who gathered himself enough to answer. 'Don't worry, Papa. It was just our gifts arriving,' he said reassuringly.

I turned to stare at my twin, at his obvious and technically true answer. Papa looked relieved.

'I see, I see.' He smiled at us, but he didn't pry. 'That is good. May you hold them well, my children.' He cleaned up the lamp pieces and came over to our bed, reverting back to speaking without words. *Things will be different now,* he told us as Jayaike and I lay back and let him tuck the edge of our cover under our chins. His face was lined and gleamed like soft leather. We let him treat us as if we were five instead of fifteen because we knew that Papa had particular ways of loving.

Sleep well, he sent as he stood to leave. Jayaike and I replied in unison, speaking to him without words.

Sleep well, Papa.

Our father stopped in his tracks and broke out into a slow-spilling smile. He nodded a few times and left softly with the lamp, the puddle of light retreating with him. Once we were back to the dark, I turned my face into Jayaike's shoulder and he hugged me fiercely.

'Let's just sleep for now,' he said. 'We can unravel what happened in the morning.'

He sounded shaken, and I couldn't blame him. I didn't know if I'd be able to sleep, not after everything, but I obediently curled up against him and closed my eyes. My mother's face was waiting behind my eyelids, that frozen moment when she'd dropped the lamp and we'd looked at her. I could see us in her gaze, our arms locked together, holding each other's faces with our breaths tangling, our eyes as black as an evil night. I could see the word she'd mouthed to herself, and I knew Ahụdi would definitely be arriving soon. As if he could read my mind, Jayaike yawned and spoke in a whisper.

'What was that first thing Mama said when she entered just now?'

I waited before answering, heard his chest settle into a

deep, regular sleep breathing, and wondered if he would hear my answer.

'Abomination,' I whispered, feeling a new shame. The word was a world of grief stuffed inside my mouth. 'She called us an abomination.'

CHAPTER FOUR

I DREAMED OF ENDLESS CHASMS AND A MAN I'D NEVER SEEN before.

His face was unremarkable – he could have looked like anyone in my town, except for his eyes. They were dark pools that stretched almost over the whole surface, leaving only a ring of yellow cornea visible. He stank of hunger. It didn't show on his flesh, but I could tell his spirit was starving, greedy like a deprived leopard. When he appeared in my dream, he wore blue cloths in a shade I had never seen, dark like the sky before it tipped fully into night. He swiveled his head like a hunter, his nostrils flaring as he sniffed the air. I tried to press myself into the shadows so he wouldn't see me. I didn't know why, but it felt very important that he did not see me.

'Who is calling a god?' he asked out loud. His voice was a river crashing against rocks. 'Show yourself.'

I held my breath, but next to me, Jayaike turned over and sighed, still asleep even in the dream. The man's head whipped in our direction and his eyes landed on my twin. I saw the hunger flare in the stranger's face, but I was too terrified to move, to seize my brother and run.

'There you are,' the man said, his gaze focused on Jayaike. 'What a pretty child!'

I was cloaked in shadow, pressed into darkness, but a warm light glowed over my brother. The man walked closer and crouched next to us, still not seeing me.

'So much power,' he marveled out loud. His eyes flickered and I didn't even dare to breathe. For a moment, he looked confused. 'It's as if I know you already,' he whispered to my twin, right before his confusion cleared into something sharp and greedy. 'Don't worry. I will find you, and you will come to me, god or no god.'

The man reached out his hand and I opened my mouth to scream, but no sound came out as I watched this hunter stroke my brother's head. I fought to move, to stop him, but then I was hurtling awake in our bedroom, sweat clinging to my armpits and my twin snoring lightly beside me. I waited for long, terrible minutes, as if the stranger would reappear, but nothing happened and the night stayed the same.

It took me a long time to sleep again.

CHAPTER FIVE

MAMA ALWAYS HATED THAT AHỤDI LET US CALL HER BY HER FIRST name as well as calling her Grandmother, but then again, Mama and Ahụdi never really got along. Mama thought my grandmother was too free. When she said this, I told her that I didn't understand how freedom could be something you can have too much of. Mama got angry and told me I was too young to understand.

'I can't stop your grandmother's behavior,' she added, 'but if you or your brother ever open your mouth to call me by my given name, you will know yourselves that day!'

I knew she was just saying that, but the idea stuck to me. Did we know ourselves? How could that be framed as a threat? I thought I already knew myself, but I guess not yet, not all of me. I asked Jayaike if he knew himself yet and he looked at me with a serious face.

‘What kind of a question is that, Sọmadịna?’ he said. ‘If I don’t know myself, who is it that will know me?’

I wish I had that kind of clarity. I remembered a day when I was sitting in a mango tree with Chiotu as stickiness dripped down our chins and in between our fingers. ‘Your mother doesn’t like Ahụdi because of her wife,’ she had said, picking a mango fiber from between her teeth.

I frowned, trying to put together the pieces. After my grandfather Kesandụ died in the Split, Ahụdi had remarried several years later, when Papa was around my age. ‘Because of Da Ọlụchi? How?’

Chiotu grinned at me mischievously. This was before her body had exploded out, but even then, she had a slink to her, like her every movement was a purr. ‘Don’t you know what Da Ọlụchi does?’

I tried to look both nonchalant and confident. After all, this was my grandmother’s wife she was talking about.

‘Of course. She runs a boardinghouse for young girls. It’s like a school or so.’

Chiotu chuckled deeply but was nice enough to not laugh in my face. She knew how sensitive I could be. ‘Sọmadịnaaaaa, ahn! Who told you that story?’

I shrugged uneasily. ‘I don’t remember.’

‘It must not have been Da Ahụdi, she wouldn’t tell you a half-truth like that.’ She shook her head at me. ‘Da Ọlụchi is a retired courtesan, my dear. Her boardinghouse is where she mentors young courtesans, the best of the best. I'm thinking of attending.'

I watched as she peeled off a slice of skin from the fruit and popped it into her mouth, licking her fingers slowly, watching me with bright eyes.

'Why would Mama have a problem with that?' Being a courtesan was a respectable profession – not a common one, but certainly not scandalous enough for Mama to dislike Ahụdi based on that alone.

Chiotu rolled her eyes. 'Ehn, it's not that Da Ọlụchi is a courtesan that is the problem, Sọmadịna. It's the *type* of courtesan she is, and the fact that your grandmother married her. Publicly, even!'

I thought for a few minutes, sucking on the seed of my mango. That made more sense. Courtesans were supposed to be discreet and unobtrusive, refined and delicate in behavior like a well-bred flower. Most courtesans would never do anything as open as discussing or even admitting to their profession in public.

Da Ọlụchi was nothing like that.

She was refined and delicate, true, but in much the same way that a razor blade is refined and delicate. She also had no problem discussing what she did in public, she was extremely open in her affections toward other women and men, and she did seem to derive a twisted pleasure in making Mama uncomfortable. After all, Mama would have made a magnificent courtesan herself, as naturally beautiful and secretive as she was. Instead, she had focused her energy on becoming a respectable farmer with a family she wanted nothing more from than to be ordinary. She was not lucky in that, not with twins, not with a dịbịa father and daughter, and certainly not with a mother-in-law married to a legendary courtesan with a big mouth.

Ahụdi didn't make things any easier for Mama. She completely refused to tell her wife to tone it down when they visited, and Papa was forced to ask her to sometimes come without Da Ọlụchi, just so that Mama could have some peace of mind. I swung my legs from my branch, wishing Mama got along better with Ahụdi, then something Chiotu had said suddenly registered.

'Wait, *you* want to be a courtesan?' I asked her.

'Why not? Do you know how rich I could be? And I have the face for it.' She posed for me, angling her face to catch the rays of light filtering through the leaves. No one could argue with her on that fact. Chiotu's face was extravagant in its beauty. Her lips were wide and full, her cheekbones were sharp like cutlasses, strong as a shelf, and her eyes were weighed down with thick lashes.

'You talk too much to be a courtesan,' I told her. 'You will tell too many secrets and then they will force you to retire somewhere where no one can hear your chattering.'

She turned serious in a flash and fixed me with her eyes.

'All you people pay so much attention to what I am saying, you don't ever notice the things I don't say. Everyone has secrets, Sọmadịna.'

I had brushed her off then, but her words came back to nudge me the morning after Mama broke the lamp, the day Ahụdi was supposed to show up. Jayaike had left the bed before I woke up, so I lay alone, reluctant to get up and deal with everything from the night before – the vision, the dream, the power that had given my twin and me our gift. I wondered if I had imagined what I saw in the chasm, or the look on Mama's face and the voice that spat at her from empty air. She was probably going to use her power to travel to Ahụdi two towns away, and then bring her along when she traveled back. The trip would take her only a few minutes each way, but Ahụdi probably wouldn't be here till midday. Mama's traveling was strongest when the sun was high.

I sighed and swung my legs off the bed, rubbing my hair where it had flattened. It was still early; I could leave the compound and say I was going to fetch water at one of the streams. I quickly knotted a clean wrapper around me, settling my waistbeads on top, and picked up my water pot from the corner of our room. As I balanced it against my hip, Jayaike came in holding his own pot.

'Good, you're ready,' he said. 'Let's go.'

'Go where?' I asked.

He looked at me like I was being deliberately slow. 'To fetch water. You're even holding your pot. Hurry up. We have a few hours before Ahụdi gets here, and I took food for us.' He showed me a small cloth bundle, which he stuffed into his leather bag, then he looked at me expectantly. I shrugged and followed him out the door and across the compound.

We walked in silence past the farms, into the early morning cool of the People's Forest, down the worn red path to our favorite spring. I glanced over at Jayaike a few times, but he was humming to himself, looking ahead and relaxed. We passed a few other people and exchanged polite greetings, then headed to our spot, a quiet section of the stream bank. Jayaike put down his pot and sat at the edge, sliding his red legs into the water. I sat next to him and rested my head on his shoulder, running my fingers through wet sand.

'So,' he finally said. 'Tell me what you saw yesterday, when we looked down.' My chest tightened a little, but I kept my voice light.

'Tell me what you saw first,' I retorted. 'Because I doubt we saw the same thing.' It felt strange to say that, since we were so used to being one person, but then I had kissed Ụwafụlamiro and Jayaike had not. Then I had looked into the chasm and seen horrific things, while he had been delighted. We were splintering apart into two people and I didn't like it.

Jayaike leaned his head back and the sun wept on his closed eyelids.

'I saw *life,* Sọmadịna. I saw a bursting and a budding and

a blossoming, I felt an immense love that humbled me.' He turned his head delicately and opened his eyes to look at me. 'I saw us.'

My brain flashed to the gold eyes I had seen, the wriggling worms crawling out of them like tears, the dead scales.

'That is *not* what I saw,' I muttered.

Jayaike looked surprised. 'Really? What did you see?'

I chewed the inside of my cheek, trying to think of words that could hold all the horror of what I had seen within them. There weren't enough, or any. I touched my twin's cheek with my fingers and closed my eyes, connecting to the old bone bond between us. It had always been there, but it had been passive all our lives, a sleeping link. The previous night was the first time it woke up, the first time I was able to feel the full range of Jayaike's emotions, as if a gate had been opened. This was beyond speaking without words; this was something different. Maybe something only twins could do – I didn't know. We would have to ask Ahụdi.

As I connected to the bond with intention, it awakened as if it was listening, waiting. Jayaike joined me there and the bond hummed with life, an open channel. We took a few breaths together, balancing against the intensity of the link and the rush of the other's emotions that came with it.

This is not what Papa does, Jayaike sent. I chuckled to myself – of course he was noticing things just as I was.

I know.

It felt easy, though, instinctive. I sent him a quick impression of what I'd seen in the chasm, the smell of decay, the rotten and knowing eyes, the bloody, smiling jaw. I couldn't help tacking on an impression of the hot fear that had sliced through me. Jayaike recoiled and pushed my hand off his face.

'What was that? That's not what I saw!' His voice shook and he seemed more upset than I had expected. 'I don't understand . . . What I saw was beautiful. Why did it look like that to you?'

'I don't know,' I answered unhappily. 'Can we talk to Ahụdi about it when she gets here?'

Jayaike nodded, but he was still disturbed. 'That's not right,' he murmured, almost to himself. 'She's not supposed to look like that . . .'

'Who's not supposed to look like that?' I asked.

He blinked a few times and looked up at me. 'I don't know. The deity, perhaps? Ala. That's who gives us our gifts, no?'

There was no comfort in that. 'I don't think we should be having visions from Ala,' I said carefully. 'Is that not dịbịa business?'

We stared at each other. I didn't ask Jayaike to show me what he had seen. I didn't want more evidence of this drift that was starting between us, but I also couldn't find the mouth to tell him about my dream, about the man who had looked at him with so much hunger. It was just a dream. It wasn't real, and we had bigger things to worry about. It didn't matter. Maybe I wasn't being brave, but I just didn't want trouble. There was nothing wrong with that.

I picked up a stone and flung it into the spring with frustration. It splashed. 'What is happening to us?' I flopped back on the bank and lay looking up at the sky. 'None of this makes sense.'

Jayaike thought for a minute. 'The way you just showed me what you saw, is that a gift?'

I sat up immediately, disliking the implications of what he was saying. 'It might just be a twin thing,' I replied. 'We just found out we can speak without words, so that's already one gift. And it's from Papa's side.'

What I didn't say was that I *needed* it to be just one gift. Any more meant you were a dịbịa, meant the Sacred Forest and a life you could never come back from.

Jayaike gave me a hesitant look. 'I saw what you did,' he said. 'Last night.'

My heart stumbled. Did he mean the dream? Had he been awake inside it?

'I didn't do anything,' I countered, and it tasted bad in my mouth. I was a liar. I was a keeper of secrets. I was breaking us in two even as I hated doing it. I had let the stranger touch his head and I had done nothing to stop it.

'The fire by the door. You put it out with your mind.'

Jayaike hugged his knees and his eyes turned sad. 'That's another gift.'

He didn't need to count it out loud. Nausea churned in my stomach and tried to fling itself up my throat.

'No,' I said. 'I don't want it.'

My twin sighed. 'I don't think that's how it works.'

We sat there and didn't say anything for a while. The birds sang wildly around us, as if competing with the rush of water shouting from the spring.

'Will Zerenjọ come for us?' My voice was small and scared. Deep inside my heart, I already knew there was nothing normal about being able to send emotions and images through our minds. We already had more than one gift. We were already marked.

My twin held my hand and squeezed it tight.

'Maybe,' he said.

'I don't feel like a dịbịa.'

Jayaike's mouth twisted. 'I don't think that's what we are.'

I turned my head to look at him. 'How do you know?'

He shrugged. 'I just feel it. It doesn't feel correct.'

I hoped he was right. Mama would hate it if we were dịbịas. Mama might hate *us* if we were dịbịas. 'I hope Ahụdi will be able to answer these questions.'

Jayaike grunted and reached for his bag. 'She'll know what to do. It's Ahụdi – she's the expert on holding gifts.' He pulled out the bundle he'd brought and unwrapped the cloth to reveal a small random pile of akara, guavas, and balls of garri rolled sticky with coconut water and palm sugar. 'Until then, let's not worry too much about things we can't control, ehn? Come and eat with me.'

I sat up and washed my hands in the water curling around my legs before joining him for food.

'Should we tell Ụwafụlamiro?' I asked.

'He's traveling with his parents,' my brother answered. 'One of their trading trips.'

'But I just saw him yesterday!'

Jayaike glanced at me. 'They left this morning.'

I bit my response back, trying not to feel a sting that Ụwafụlamiro had told him and not me. Before the kiss at the river, it wouldn't have mattered. Telling one of us was as good as telling the other, but that was *before.* He'd kissed me and left town immediately after! How was I supposed to feel about that? Clearly it didn't mean anything to him – I should have known from how he was joking afterwards. Or maybe it was because his gift had arrived. There was no real way for me to know, so I said nothing.

Jayaike and I bathed quickly and fetched our water closest to the source, before heading back home, balancing our pots on wads of cloth on our heads. Our home compound was quiet when we arrived. We emptied the water into the larger main pot by the kitchen and put our own pots away.

'Where's Papa?' I whispered.

'He must be at the farm already; his cutlass is gone.'

We walked softly into the kitchen, slightly afraid of running into Mama. But the person sitting on a low stool and peeling yams was too tall to be Mama, and her braided hair was unmistakable. I squealed in excitement and ran over to her.

'Ahụdi, you arrived already!'

I wanted to embrace her, but she laughed and fended me off.

'Give me a moment, my daughter. Let me wash this yam off my hands before you end up itching for the next three days!'

She scrubbed her arms with clean sand and poured water over her skin, wiping it dry on her cloth. I giggled as she snatched me up into her arms, pressing me to her. I was much taller than the last time she had seen me, and I felt her staring at me when she released me, as I bent quickly to brush my fingers across her toes. Her gaze shifted to Jayaike, who was smiling shyly at her. His change must have been more marked than mine, not only was he taller, but he was also sinewy with farmwork muscles, with none of the delicate childlike softness he used to have.

Ahụdi gasped softly and walked over to him, incredulous. 'Is this my son?'

'Ahụdi.' Jayaike dropped to one knee to touch her toes, and she lifted him up by his shoulders.

'Ah-ahn. You have both grown up so much since I last was here.' She laid her hand against his face and smiled easily. I saw him relax into her caress and I was glad that she didn't even seem to notice his lack of facial hair.

'Where is your wife?' he asked, wrapping his hands around her wrist.

'That woman! I show up and everyone wants to know about her instead. I don't blame you!' Jayaike flushed and looked down, and Ahụdi laughed. 'She's here, child. She's tasting the air in your room.'

Da Ọlụchi's gift was that she could detect energy as if it was a flavor in the air, even residual energy left behind after an incident. It made it easy for her to manipulate people, since she could always tell what their moods and emotions were. Sometimes, she could even predict the direction in which their energy was going to shift. Her gift served her well at her job.

'Where's Mama?' I asked. 'She brought both you and Da Ọlụchi?'

That was rare. My mother disliked transporting multiple people when she traveled – I was surprised that she agreed to bring her least favorite person along.

'Your mother is sleeping. The journey tired her out, but given what she described to me, it was in your best interests to have both Ọlụchi and me here.' Ahụdi pushed her braids off her face and looked seriously at us. 'Speaking of which, let's sit down so you can tell me what happened. Your mother kept going on about possession and voices coming out of the air, I could barely form a correct picture in my head.'

We followed her into the main room and sat cross-legged at her feet as she settled herself into her favorite chair, the low one with the leopard skin slung over it. The story was that it was the first kill Papa made when he was young, but Papa never liked to talk about it. I got the sense that he never really liked hunting – he preferred to grow life, not take it.

As soon as our grandmother settled, she looked at us expectantly. Jayaike and I exchanged glances.

'We think our gifts arrived,' he said. 'We can speak without words like Papa, but we can also send each other what we're feeling or things we've seen.' He gave me another look and I nodded slightly. 'Sọmadịna put out a fire with her mind. We saw a vision, but we saw different things. I saw life and she . . . she saw death.'

'Our eyes changed color,' I added, trying not to notice my twin's brief hesitation.

Ahụdi drummed her fingers against the patterned fur. 'Is there anything else?'

Jayaike took a deep breath. 'There was also a voice that spoke to Mama from the vision. I heard it like a roar, but I couldn't understand what it said.'

I turned slowly to stare at my twin. 'You heard that?'

He hadn't said anything about it before. Neither had I, but I thought I was the only one keeping secrets.

He looked surprised. '*You* heard it? I thought it was only in my head.'

'Why didn't you say anything?' I didn't mean to sound accusing, but the words came out like that anyway.

Jayaike flinched. 'Why didn't *you*?' he shot back.

I didn't have an answer. Betrayal tasted like rancid oil in my mouth, but I knew it was mine, not his. We should have become so much closer once the bond woke up, so why did it feel like it was also pushing us apart? Why couldn't I just *tell* him about the dream? Just days ago, I wouldn't have thought it was possible for us to keep things to ourselves, yet here I was, clutching a knife of secrets by the blade, unable to let go even as my hands bled. I blinked and for a quick moment, the man in blue smiled at me. I stifled a gasp as Ahụdi leaned forward and Jayaike gave me a questioning look.

What is it?

I shook my head. *Nothing,* I lied. *It's nothing.*

'What did the voice say?' Ahụdi asked.

I pulled myself together. 'It felt angry at Mama. All it said was "Mine," as if we belonged to it? I don't know. I don't understand what it was talking about.'

Ahụdi hummed to herself, looking at both of us, then raised her head to look at the door a few seconds before her wife entered. Da Ọlụchi walked like liquid metal, just like the hot, gleaming slide I'd seen at the blacksmith's forge. She had indigo patterns all over her skin, even on her face, and they showed up beautifully against her skin. Ahụdi told us she had gone gray at an early age, and she always refused to stain her hair, so it remained silver, and she wore it sculpted into a ridge that ran from her forehead to the nape of her neck.

Jayaike and I scrambled up and hurriedly brushed her feet with our hands before entering her hard embrace. Da Ọlụchi didn't like physical contact as much as Ahụdi, so she held us tightly but released us quickly, then took our chins in her firm hands and held our faces still. I could feel her tasting our emotions. Her gift felt like small, dry licks of air against my skin. When she had collected what she needed, she stood back and gave us a thorough looking-over.

'So,' she said, gesturing to our bodies. 'Nothing is happening, ehn?'

I gasped and Jayaike stiffened beside me.

'Ọlụchi!' Ahụdi sounded amused and scolding at the same time. 'You're embarrassing the children!'

Da Ọlụchi kissed her teeth contemptuously. 'Nonsense. They need to face what's happening to them, or in this case, *not* happening to them. Do you think it helps them to have everyone whispering about it and no one talking directly to them?'

Ahụdi threw up her hands and sat back in resignation as Da Ọlụchi turned her attention to us.

'You aren't developing physically, other than your height, but you've started developing gifts, correct?' We muttered an affirmation and she nodded. 'Well, Ahụdi will tell you that's highly unusual, but you already knew that. Why don't you let her examine you, and then we can sit down and discuss from there?'

Ahụdi was already unrolling two mats onto the floor. Jayaike and I lay down on our backs and closed our eyes. It wasn't the first time Ahụdi had examined us – she checked up on us at least once a year to make sure we were healthy. She liked to examine us at the same time because we were twins; she said it gave her a rare chance to directly compare people so similar to each other. I felt her begin the scan from the top of my head – a wave of gradual heat dragging through my body. This time, she moved slower than usual, the wave traveling through my head and neck, searing my collarbone, spine, ribs, belly. I made sure I didn't move a muscle and kept my body relaxed, listening to the chickens outside and the occasional complaint from one of our goats. In fact, I nearly drifted to sleep in the few minutes it took her to complete the scan. I hadn't felt that secure in a while. Jayaike and I were clambering to our feet when Mama walked into the room, her face creased from sleep.

'You picked the right time to wake up,' said Ahụdi, rolling up the mats again. 'I just finished examining the children, and Ọlụchi has tasted their room. Sit down, Ngọzị.'

Mama sat on a bench and leaned against the wall, avoiding eye contact with us. I felt my heart wrench and a small voice whispered *abomination* to me. We were her children, but she was scared of us, or disgusted. I wished I knew which one it was. I wished she would *look* at us. The small turn of her head away felt like a sign that bad things were happening, and it made me afraid.

'First of all,' continued Ahụdi, 'the children are holding gifts.' She paused and dropped the next sentence like a stone into a well. 'They are holding more than one gift each.'

'Chei!' Mama clutched her chest. 'They are dịbịas?!' The horror in her voice felt like she'd reached out and slapped me across the face. When she heard the news about Nkadi, it had felt like a loss, but this? This felt like a rejection.

Ahụdi stopped her by raising a hand. 'That's the strange part – they're *not* dịbịas.'

Relief. I gasped from the weight of it, and next to me, Jaya-ike let out a shaky breath. We exchanged a hopeful look. This meant we wouldn't be sent to the Sacred Forest.

Da Ọlụchi looked confused. 'How can they hold multiple gifts and not be dịbịas?'

'Truly, I don't know,' answered Ahụdi.

It was such an unexpected answer that the room fell silent. Ahụdi was the greatest healer we knew. She always had the answers. My relief drained away, replaced by a creeping fear.

'What are they, then?' Mama asked. 'What are my children?' I winced at the question.

Ahụdi shook her head. 'I don't know. Some of their gifts

are dormant – I can't read them clearly and I can't predict when they will develop. There is also a strong imprint of ala mmụọ on the children themselves.'

'The spirit world?' Mama was starting to sound angry. Everyone knew she resented the spirits because of Nkadi, because of how many times they had sent her to Mama, then taken her back, laughing as Mama buried child after child after child.

'There was a heavy residue of the spirit world in their room as well,' added Da Ọlụchi. 'I believe a channel was opened recently.'

Jayaike and I stared at each other with wide eyes. *The hole,* I sent.

The mirror, he agreed.

'Wait,' said Mama. 'Are you trying to tell me that there was a channel to the spirit world open in this my own house?!'

'It's not only that,' said Ahụdi. 'I believe that the voice you heard came directly from there.'

Mama's face didn't flicker at all. 'What voice?' she asked, deadpan.

Ahụdi rolled her eyes into the back of her head. 'Ngọzị. Don't try that with me. The twins heard it.'

Mama looked at us for the first time, and I grabbed Jayaike's hand because her face was furious now, raging.

'They don't know what they're talking about,' she spat out.

Ahụdi didn't even bother arguing with her. 'I'm sure that's

not true, Ngọzị. Let us look at this problem correctly. You have two children who are developing gifts but nothing else, an opening into the spirit world, and a voice speaking to you from there. You know that this thing has now passed whatever I as a healer can do for you. We are playing with fire when we look at the business of spirits. You need a dịbịa.'

I could see Mama rearing back in anger the moment she realized where Ahụdi was going with this. 'Don't even—'

Ahụdi cut her off ruthlessly. 'You need your father.'

Mama was glowing with rage. 'No! That . . . that man will not enter this compound and lay his hands on either of my children! Tụfịakwa!' She drew quick circles around the sides of her head with her hands, snapped her fingers, and spat on the ground in rejection. I felt a brief warmth that she was being protective of us, that we were *her* children and she would stand between us and her father.

Da Ọlụchi clicked in her mouth and shook her head in reproach. 'Don't be a fool, Ngọzị.'

Mama whirled at her and pointed a long finger insultingly. 'Nobody has asked you to put your mouth in this, Ọlụchi.'

I froze. It was absolutely out of line for Mama to speak to an elder in such a tone, especially her husband's second mother. I watched as Da Ọlụchi's face crystallized into a hard smirk, and the air went cold. Ahụdi slowly stood up, her anger pushing off her in slow, throbbing waves.

'What did you just say, Ngọzị?'

Mama looked uncertain but defiant, and I realized she might actually be stubborn enough to not retract her insult. I pulled on Jayaike's hand. *Let's go,* I sent.

Ahụdi is about to tear Mama apart! He sounded fascinated. We had never really seen Ahụdi angry before, but I felt certain that this was not the time to stay and watch. All of this was about us and, yet, not about us at all.

She won't hurt her. Let's go, I insisted. My skin was crawling at the tension escalating in the room and I suddenly needed to be far away from all of them, from imprints of spirits and from walls and thatch roofs that felt like boxes and coffins.

I dragged him out of the house and into the compound, then ran my hands through my hair, agitated. The sun beat down on us.

Go and get Papa, I sent.

Jayaike turned automatically, then hesitated and looked at me. *Are you not coming with me?*

Time slowed down for a moment and I could see the picture in my mind so clearly. Both of us standing in our home, wearing close to the same face, but with our spirits separating. I was sending him away so I could be alone, because I *wanted* to be alone, and he was looking at me with absolute trust, just like he always had, wondering why I wasn't by his side.

I shook my head in response to his question. *You can run faster than me. I'll wait here for you and see what happens.*

He looked worried but turned back around and broke into

his graceful run that ate up the ground. I scuffed my foot against the earth and wrapped my arms around myself. I felt like worms were crawling under my skin and I was seeing flashbacks of the face in the hole. A spirit, Ahụdi had said. Why would a spirit be shouting at Mama? Could it be the deity, like Jayaike had said?

The voices in the house spiked in volume, and I could almost see the anger pushing through the walls. I didn't want to be near my family anymore, not for another moment. I tried to wait a little, but I found myself walking out of the compound, slowly at first, and then in a jog that turned into a desperate run. I wanted to be back in the People's Forest, back at the spring, lying in water that could wash away everything.

I ran like a homesick wind and I left everyone behind me.

CHAPTER SIX

I KEPT MY FEET MOVING UNTIL I LOST MY BREATH IN THE STEPS BEhind me and my side started hitching in pain, then I stopped and doubled over, sucking in huge gulps of air and bracing my hands against my knees. How long had I been running? Dust was caked on my feet and ankles, and sweat ran down my spine. I took a few deep breaths, straightened, and looked around me. The air was sticky and humid. I was close to the border of the People's Forest, right around where Da Ụzụmma's farm was. With a tired sigh, I started walking in that direction. I knew she had a small hut in the center, where they would share food and sometimes rest on the mats that were stored there. I just wanted to lie down in the shade for a little while, before heading home to deal with my family. Hopefully, Papa would be home by now, making peace between Mama and Ahụdi.

I liked being on an empty farm when no one was working,

when it was just me and the crops. I could almost feel the impressions of the people who had sculpted the land into growing green things aching for the sky as I squeezed the earth between my toes, thinking about the day I'd gone to the farm with Papa, when I was much younger. He let me play with the soil he was working in, pouring water in it, making mud, and patting it on my arms.

'Look, Papa!' I'd shouted, enthused. 'It's like my skin!'

Daughter of Ala, he'd sent, smiling. *Everything will grow from you.*

I smiled to myself at the memory, and then suddenly, my foot sank into the earth as it softened and crumbled below me. I stumbled and fell onto my hands and knees, crying out in surprise. I could see the hut – it wasn't far from me; a little bit longer and I would have been inside, in the shade, maybe safe. Out here, the soil was shifting beneath me, and the air was full of hot iron again, full of a hungry whine, and my skin was wriggling over my flesh.

I could feel a steady pulse in the earth below me, getting closer and closer. I tried to crawl away, but my body wasn't listening to me anymore. The pulse slithered through the ground and filled me up like lightning, but just before I lost myself to it, I saw a glint from the earth in front of me.

It was a bead, worn shiny from use, a yellow bead that I recognized easily. I had seen it, and all the others like it, strung around Chiotu's waist for the past few years. She loved her waistbeads, how they adorned her hips and the smooth curve of her belly, and while most girls wore red beads, including me, Chiotu had chosen yellow, like small suns against her skin. Everyone watched how her hips rolled as she walked, how the beads glowed. Now they were scattered on her mother's farm, some trampled into the earth, more and more catching my eye in little yellow shocks.

The pulse shot through me, assuming command of my muscles and bones. I smelled the river. My skin folded into rough scales and I could feel the pull of that horrible chasm again as the pulse dragged me into a half crouch and propelled me forward jerkily, my body swinging unevenly and stumbling toward the hut. I was a toy, a swinging sack of flesh that no longer belonged to me. My jawbone felt both loose and too strong. As I got closer to the hut, an ugly knot formed in my stomach. I could see legs sticking out from the doorway of the hut, long dark legs that I had run alongside, that had dangled from mango branches with me, that were now kicking frantically against the ground, kicking up loam like my crawling skin.

'Chiotu!'

I said her name hoarsely as the pulse surged up my throat, and then I started coughing, my tongue swelling in my mouth. My teeth felt like they were slicing through my own gums. I staggered closer to the doorway, and that was when I saw Chidị.

He had the broadest shoulders in our age group, the biggest

chest, bulked up by working at his father's forge. He was wrestling Chiotu to the ground, broken beads scattered around them, and he had hit her in the face – one of her eyes was swollen and discolored. She was screaming, but no sounds were tearing out because he had stuffed her mouth with a piece of cloth. Her small wrapper was flung to the side, and he was trying to get control of her arms as she flailed and fought at him.

The pulse in me roared up and I was lost. The river roared around my body. The voice that had shouted at Mama came back, hissing in pleasure.

Mine, it crooned.

I sobbed within myself, and my flesh responded to the voice without me, straightening and calling Chidị's name. I didn't sound like myself – my throat was not my own. Whatever had taken hold of me was shaping me, directing me with an unfamiliar purpose. Chidị looked up and snarled, moving toward me swiftly and with forceful intent. Almost lazily, I felt the pulse lift my arm, stopping him in his tracks. I could see the muscles in his neck working as he tried to speak, but the magic – by the river, this was *magic* – had shuttered his throat closed.

Mine, the voice whispered, and this time it was harsh, a hammer breaking justice open against bone, a claim of what had been given and what could be taken away. It showed me then what a person's vital force felt like – it let me hold Chidị's life like a small bird fluttering against my palm. Everything each cell in his body was doing meant nothing; it was just a flicker of heat, a small bubbling life. *Mine,* explained the voice, and I understood.

I understood the sin. I understood the judgment. I understood that what cannot be salvaged must be thrown back. I understood how to obey. The whole world was yellow.

'Stop.'

The command was so simple, just one word. I could not recognize my own voice, as low and guttural as it was, but all it took was one word. One push of will and the flicker in my palm was no longer there. Before me, Chidị's skin turned ashen, his eyes rolled into white, and he dropped to the floor, dead.

Chiotu ripped the cloth out of her mouth and screamed, a long, full, heavy cry that shook the walls of the hut. I felt the pulse in me bloom and exult, then it was gone, rocking my body from the force of its withdrawal. I fell to my knees, shaking and vomiting the food my twin had shared with me. Chiotu was backing away from me as fast as she could, her eyes dilated and her mouth dripping wet and red, screaming and screaming. My head felt like hot coals had been scraped throughout my insides. I was shaking as if cold water had replaced all the blood in my body, and through the shock, I could suddenly feel my twin bond again. I hadn't even noticed it was gone.

Jayaike was sending frantically to me, *Sọmadịna! What happened? Where did you go? Sọmadịna!*

I collapsed forward, feeling my cheek hit the ground, Chiotu screaming in my ears and my brother calling in my head.

Wake up, Sọmadịna. Nwanne m. Biko, open your eyes.

Jayaike was reaching for me through the bond. I wanted to send him away, to protect him. We were no longer one person. He needed to step back – he had no idea what horrors had come forth from my right hand. But I was afraid and I did not want to be alone anymore. I forced my eyes to open and saw their muddy gold staring right back at me from Jayaike's face.

'She's awake, Papa,' he said, embracing me quickly. 'Thank the deity.'

I let him help me to a seated position, trying not to vomit again from the pain in my head. We were sitting against an outside wall of the small hut, still on the farm. Papa stepped into my field of vision and squatted in front of me.

Nwa m. You are here. He took my hands and squeezed them tightly, then stood up again and walked over to Chiotu. I turned my head to look at her. Someone had wrapped her in a worn red cloth, and she was sitting with her back against one of the palm trees, hugging her knees and pressing her face against them. I struggled to drag my voice up from wherever in my stomach it had run to.

'How is she?' I asked.

Jayaike sighed. 'She's there. He beat her up badly. Papa wants Ahụdi to look at her.'

It was then that I saw the body.

The corpse that used to be Chidị was covered in palm fronds, and it had been moved to the side. My stomach surged and I started retching, spitting up nothing but bile and saliva. Jayaike stayed next to me and rubbed my back, murmuring softly to me, 'Ndo, ndo. It will be fine.'

I wanted to scream at him. How could he be so wrong? *Nothing* would ever be fine again. Murder was a taboo against our mother deity Ala, and the punishment was death. Even if you could prove it was accidental, you would be banished nonetheless. I had ruined us all. I had destroyed my family and I couldn't even tell them how or why it had happened. Something had entered me, used and ridden me, then it had thrown me away next to Chidị's body. He couldn't be dead. He was wicked, but he couldn't be dead. How could Jayaike be so *wrong*?

My brother put his arms around me, but I felt no comfort. He smelled like salt and sweat. I smelled like death, like rot and decay – didn't he notice? Didn't he see how my hands had been stolen and returned to me? I was not Sọmadịna anymore, I was something discarded, something different. I could hear Papa speaking quietly to Chiotu, the wind moving in the trees, and the silence from Chidị's body.

When Mama arrived, she was walking fast, holding her

wrapper to free up her knees. Ahụdi was walking behind her in a measured, strong stride, her thick braids bound on top of her head in a rough knot.

'What happened here?' Mama's voice was sharp. Papa came up to her and led her to one side, lightly holding her elbow. They stood with their heads bent together, and Ahụdi came over to me, touching my face with her hands.

'Your father said there was an accident,' she said. 'Ọlụchi had to leave to take care of some business, but your mother and I came as fast as we could.'

I gave Jayaike a pleading look, and he nodded.

'I'll tell you what happened,' he said to our grandmother. 'Can we step aside? I want to give Sọmadịna a little space to breathe.'

Ahụdi squeezed my shoulder and smiled sadly, then they moved aside and I heard Jayaike's voice whispering fast, a small bird with beating wings. Mama's voice broke over like a flood, suddenly loud and foaming.

'You said it was an accident! Why should I not have told them?'

Papa was frowning at her and shaking his head, clearly upset but refusing to speak aloud. It made Mama look like a madwoman, as if she were having an argument with herself.

'They are his parents! Their son is dead and they don't even know because you decided to leave out that piece of information! What is wrong with your head?'

Papa's face was mutinous. Mama threw her hands up and walked a few steps away from him, then turned to glare at him, her hands on her hips. 'You have no right to deny that family information about what happened to their son,' she hissed.

It provoked Papa into using his voice. 'You think it is wise to bring them here?' he croaked. 'Where their son was killed by our daughter? With Chiotu in that state? Did you send for Ụzụmma, even? Have you even checked on your own daughter?'

He broke off coughing and clutched at his throat. Mama drew back and stared at him in hurt shock.

'Of course I sent for Ụzụmma.' Her voice was soft and betrayed. She looked over at Chiotu, who was keening softly to herself, moaning in ragged sobs. Ahụdi hurried over to her and crouched by her side, talking to her in calming tones, taming her simmering panic. I tried to pretend that Mama wasn't avoiding me, avoiding my eyes, my face, my treacherous hand. I tried to forget how she had ignored Papa's question about checking on me.

'He was forcing that girl,' Papa growled. 'Look at the child's face! My concern is *not* the well-being of his family.'

Mama looked at the bundle that used to be Chidị, and her hand drifted up to touch her collarbone.

'He was someone's child,' she murmured.

Papa threw a harsh look at her. 'Look to your own children, Ngọzị,' he rasped, turning on his heel and walking away from her, coming toward me. He sat down on the floor next to me and rested his hand on my head.

My child. His voice was clear as a bell in my head, without the jagged edges it had when it came out from his mouth. *Don't mind your mother, ehn.*

I waited for him to give some kind of explanation for her behavior, her coldness, her withdrawal, but when he remained silent, I realized that he had no explanation. He was as lost as I was.

Jayaike came over and sat on my other side, and I knew he was avoiding Mama. We heard heavy breathing and the sound of someone running, then Chidị's father burst into view a few moments later. The blacksmith was a short man, but stocky, with a thick beard and hairy arms. His eyebrows were twisted in a snarl of anger that deepened when he saw me and Jayaike. I had forgotten that he hated twins, still followed the old thoughts that said we were evil and unlucky.

'Where is my son?!' he bellowed. We all stared at him for one dreadful moment, then Ahụdi came over and spoke softly to him. I knew the moment it sank in because he looked as if he wanted to hit Ahụdi. She was an elder, though, so it was unthinkable, but his fists clenched and his face hardened even as his eyes took on a sheen. When he spoke again, his voice was like glass. 'Where. Is. My. Son.'

Ahụdi stepped to the side so that he could see the palm bundle laid out. He walked stiffly over to it and knelt down, running his scarred hands over the fronds. Mama covered her mouth with her hand and turned away, while Papa took a step to block Jayaike and me from the blacksmith's view. Ahụdi was now by Chiotu's side, rubbing her back in smooth, firm circles. My friend's yellow beads were still scattered around, stepped on and muddy.

'Diọkpara m.' The blacksmith's voice was flat as he addressed the body. He was angry – oh, he was so angry – but he was controlling it, even though it was burning white-hot inside him. He rested his hand on his son's chest, shut his eyes, and took a deep breath. When he released it as he turned to us, his eyes were red and his neck was veined. He pointed straight at me but looked at Papa as he spoke.

'That girl will die for murdering my son,' he stated.

'It was an accident!' I surprised myself by shouting back. 'He was attacking Chiotu. I only wanted to stop him!'

Chiotu's head snapped up, and her wild eyes fixed on me. 'You killed him!' she screamed. 'You raised your hand and he died – you killed him as if he was an ant! What kind of witch are you?'

Chidị's father did not even spare her a glance. He had completely ignored her ever since he arrived, as if she was not part of the story, as if nothing had happened to her. I was shocked at her outburst. Everything that had happened to me was because of her, to save her. I couldn't tell them the terror of having something else move my body, whatever had put Chidị's life into my hand. His father wouldn't believe me and wouldn't care.

'Your son was a beast.' This came from Jayaike, who spoke from between clenched teeth. Ahụdi hissed in disapproval and Chidị's father took a step forward, his fists beginning to rise. Papa took a step forward as well, looking calmly into the man's eyes. The moment was taut, so much so that it shook. Chidị's father shook his head and glanced at his son's body on the ground.

'You allowed these abominations to live,' he hissed. 'And now my son is dead.'

Mama looked at us then, agonized, and her face was a snarled mess of grief and fear. I remembered the look and whisper when she saw Jayaike and me in our bed, and it hit me like a shock of cold water that my mother, some part of my mother, truly believed she had given birth to abominations. My heart crashed in my chest and my fingers searched for Jayaike's hand. Mama saw the gesture and turned away from us. Chidị's father unwrapped the body and lifted his son into his arms. Ahụdi tried to protest the unwrapping, but he brushed her aside.

'Let everyone see what she did to him,' he insisted, setting off back toward the village. Mama started walking behind him, and Ahụdi gently helped Chiotu to her feet, persuading her in a low, steady voice. We all walked away from the farm and the hut, the yellow beads glinting behind us like droplets of light on earth the color of my skin.

CHAPTER SEVEN

I WILL NEVER FORGET HOW CHIDỊ'S MOTHER'S VOICE TORE PAST her throat and scattered her teeth when she saw her child draped over her husband's arms. She screamed like a dying sun. She tore at her hair and beat her hands against her chest. The blacksmith laid the body at the threshold of their house, and his wife wept over their son, calling his name and begging him to open his eyes.

'Anwụọla m ooo!' she wailed. 'I have died! Chidị! *Chidị!*'

I looked away, because all I could see was Chidị's mouth in that triumphant sneer of power as he held down Chiotu in the hut. It was grotesque to watch his mother's grief and think of Chiotu's swollen face. I could not escape the way his eyes had gone dark when the pulse in me snuffed out his life. It played in my head over and over, a nightmare that wouldn't give up.

‘Let us step outside the compound,’ said Ahụdi. ‘We should not be here.’

Papa nodded and steered Mama outside, where a crowd was already gathering. Jayaike held my hand in a clamped grip. He had been silent since we left the farm. I wondered what he was thinking, and I would have asked him through our bond, but somehow the silence was enough. *I am here,* it seemed to say, with his sweaty palm clenched to mine. *I am here. I will always be here.*

Papa was trying to manage Mama’s emotions while being concerned for me, and Ahụdi was more healer than grandmother right now. I didn’t blame her. Chiotu needed a healer more than I needed my grandmother. Besides, I would never need anyone as much as I needed my twin. As long as I had him, I would be fine. I squeezed his fingers and he squeezed back immediately. We didn’t even need to look at each other. I might be damned but I didn’t have to be alone.

The growing crowd was giving a wide berth, and I could hear their voices like leaves rustling in a tree. Da Ụzụmma broke through them, her eyes wild with worry. She gave a sob when she saw her daughter and clutched her close.

‘Gịnị mere?’ she asked, her mouth pressed close to Chiotu’s hair. ‘What happened?’

Safe in her mother’s arms, Chiotu broke down utterly. The crowd watched in fascinated shock.

'He went mad, Mama,' she wept. 'We were just meeting to talk at the farm. I had told him I didn't want to continue again, and he said he just wanted a chance to talk to me, just for a little while.' She hiccuped and Da Ụzụmma stroked her hair gently, tears tripping over her lower eyelids. 'But then he got so angry, Mama. He got so angry and I tried to leave, and he hit me.' A murmur rippled through the crowd, all shamelessly listening in.

'He knocked me down and dragged me to the hut. He kept saying that no one can just leave him like that, that who did I think I was, that he would show me pepper. And then he . . . he tore off my beads . . .' Chiotu dissolved into fresh sobs and the crowd gasped.

'Chineke!' exclaimed a woman nearby, her hands reflexively going to her waist.

Waistbeads were so special that the thought of someone breaking them off a body was a deep violation. They were given from mother to daughter when the girl turned fifteen and they became a part of the person who wore them. We never took them off, because our beads were a sacred thing. Da Ụzụmma was livid.

'Where is he?' she shouted. She looked torn between holding her child and going after the person who had hurt her. There was a hesitant silence as people looked at each other. It was clear that Da Ụzụmma still didn't know what had happened.

Mama was the one who came up to her, dark circles smudged under her eyes. A part of me marveled at how I had aged my mother in the span of a hot afternoon.

'Chidị is dead,' she said.

Da Ụzụmma's face wavered. 'Eh? Where is he?!'

Mama shook her head and placed a hand on Da Ụzụmma's shoulder. 'He is dead, Ụzụmma.'

'Dead?' Chiotu pulled away enough from her mother to spit in my direction. 'She killed him!'

Her mother looked genuinely surprised now. She looked at me, puzzled. 'Who? Sọmadịna?'

Chiotu was glaring malevolently at me. 'Yes! She just opened her hand and when she closed it, he fell down, and then she *smiled*!'

Her voice curdled sour and ugly on that last word and I took a step backward. That part I did not remember. The eyes of the crowd were on me, suddenly suspicious and unfriendly.

Don't listen to her, sent Jayaike. *Whatever happened there, it wasn't you, Sọmadịna. You need to remember that.*

I didn't believe him. He hadn't been there. He hadn't seen me.

I smiled, Jayaike. I killed someone and then I smiled. No wonder Mama looks at me like I'm a stranger now.

It wasn't you! Jayaike was insistent, but I felt a hopelessness settle on me like a soft vulture on the back of my neck. Mama was right. Chidị had been somebody's child, and I took his life as if it meant nothing. What was worse was that in that moment with all that heat of power burning through me, could I even say what his life had meant? What had it been other than a small flicker among millions of other flickers? Who notices the loss of an ant on an anthill?

In the next moment, I loved Da Ụzụmma fiercely because while everyone was evaluating the accusation and raking their stares over me, as if guilt would show up like pimples on my face, she straightened her back and looked me deep in my eyes.

'Thank you for saving my daughter,' she said.

I didn't know what to say, so I managed a small nod, and it seemed as if that confirmed everything. Someone asked if I really did it, and I could hear the rumors germinating from under their tongues, quick, dirty shoots springing up. Their voices sounded like locusts coming over the sky. Ahụdi sighed in exasperation and seared them all with a scorching glance. They subsided into a muttering silence, but I could tell that things stood precariously for me, hovering on a thin edge that could easily fall on my neck. Chidị's father walked out of his compound, haggard and drawn, but his reddened eyes were glowing with a cold righteous anger. He felt like a furious priest, like the son of thunder.

'Go to your own home,' he said to us. 'We have had enough of your evil on our doorstep. We will call a meeting of the elders, and your daughter will answer for her wickedness.' He looked straight at me as he spoke, and I wanted to say something, anything – did he not understand what his son had been doing? Instead, I wilted under the blaze of his hate and clung to my brother. The elders terrified me. Their decisions were law and I didn't feel good about my chances in front of them. For a moment, Ahụdi seemed like she was about to speak, but then Papa touched her elbow and shook his head slightly.

Let us go, he sent to all of us. Mama and Da Ụzụmma touched their foreheads together in a short farewell embrace. Jayaike and I put our arms around each other's waists and walked in a matching step toward home. Many eyes followed our backs as we left.

The elders met that very night, in the square under the iroko tree. I think everyone from our town was there, gathered in a vibrating crowd, craning their necks to look at me and Jayaike. My brother had refused to leave my side, as if he had been accused along with me, as if he had raised his hand beside mine back there on the farm. It was almost as if nothing had changed and we were still one, but I knew better. If my secrets had not proven it before, those boiling moments it took to snuff out Chidị's flame had set it in stone. I was separate from my twin, even if he refused to let me go. I was a killer; I was death. I wasn't brave enough to save him from myself. I wasn't even brave enough to talk about the man in blue from my dreams, who barely seemed real now anyway.

The elders gathered in a solemn line, sitting on their ceremonial stools with their attendants standing behind their left shoulders, holding long white horsetails. The iroko tree towered over them, its wide branches breaking up the moonlight that was streaming from the sky. The titled men and women of our town all had prominent seats; some had spread skins on the floor while others had also brought low stools and even a few benches. I looked to my left and I saw Da Ụzụmma was standing with her hands on Chiotu's shoulders. They had applied a salve to her swollen eye and bandaged her wrist, and she was cradling it in her other arm. Da Ụzụmma's eyes were pleading apologies at my mother, and I realized that Chiotu would not be testifying in my favor. She wouldn't even look near my face.

I shouldn't have been surprised, I suppose. Even though Chidị had beaten her and torn off her beads, he was still the boy they had expected her to marry at some point. She had loved him, and I had struck him down in front of her. Jayaike kept telling me that none of this was my fault, but even he could not understand how that force had leaped up and taken me. No one understood Chiotu's story, even though they believed it. How could I have killed Chidị just by raising my hand?

Ahụdi insisted that there was spirit involvement, and although that was obvious to me, my parents were pushing against it. They worshipped the ancestors and the mother deity Ala like everyone else, but what they had experienced from the spirit world was the torture of watching infant after infant die in their arms. Mama had gone through five pregnancies for nothing, until they had managed to make Nkadi stay. My parents did not want to deal with spirits influencing their children, not anymore.

'You have to call Zerenjọ,' Ahụdi had insisted before we went to the square. 'You need to let him know what's happening. Don't enter this spirit business with your eyes closed.'

Mama had been pacing up and down our main room, her soles slapping against the smooth floor. She was chewing on a fingernail and kept her head bent. Papa's eyes followed her back and forth.

Perhaps we don't need Zerenjọ, Papa suggested to us. *The children's gifts could just be malfunctioning. You know much about gifts.* He had looked up at his mother, and there was this hope in his eyes that this could all be smoothed over, like water rubbed on clay, filling in the imperfections.

'I am telling you that this has passed what I know,' said Ahụdi, as gently as she could. 'We need a dịbịa.'

Papa shook his head. *I don't know if that is a basket I want to open.*

'Now is not the time for doubting,' cautioned Ahụdi. 'What if someone else gets hurt?'

'Get killed, you mean,' said Mama from behind her teeth. I couldn't help myself; I spoke up from where I was sitting.

'It was an *accident*!' I shouted, but she didn't even glance my way. She continued her pacing uninterrupted. I raised my hands and let them drop on my thighs in despair. 'Why won't you even look at me?' I asked, my voice breaking.

She stopped walking but didn't raise her head.

'I do not know who you are anymore,' she answered, her voice flat as a board. Before I could respond, she slowly walked out of the room, her head still bent. It scooped out everything in my chest, leaving me bloody and hollow.

She's in shock, said Papa. *Sọmadịna, she will come around.*

I wasn't so sure – there had been such finality to the droop of her back. I needed her to forgive me for everything, for killing Chidị, for existing as myself. Whatever she wanted, if it was in my power, I would have laid it at her feet, just to get my mother back. I couldn't talk to my twin about it. He wouldn't let go of my hand and I could feel the grief pouring off him, the confusion around her rejection, the way he was hoping the next sunrise would fix everything. I couldn't do anything except hold his hand back.

To my surprise, my mother came to the town square. When Chidị's family arrived, they were ready to call the meeting to order, and all the chattering conversations mellowed out into a quiet hum. The priest of Ala was the one who stood up to bless the gathering. He was the person who guided us as a community in the rituals for the deity; not as powerful as a dịbịa, but important because he lived with us instead of in the Sacred Forest. He was thin and angular, the color of pale sunlight in the early morning, and his voice was like a bell. He kept the prayer short and broke the kolanut, bringing life, as we say. Once the rituals were observed, the elders called for testimonies. Our justice procedures were simple – everyone had a chance to tell their sides of the story, witnesses spoke, and the elders passed down a decision after consulting with the priest. In my case, the proceedings wouldn't take very long since only Chiotu and I would be speaking.

They called her first and she came up without her mother. I think she was drained of tears at that point. She spoke calmly about how he had attacked her, and when she started speaking of me, her voice became as brittle as a thin stick. Her mother must have cautioned her, because Chiotu didn't call me a witch or anything like that. She simply told them what she saw. I tried to ignore the stares of people on me as she described how the pupils bled black over the rest of my eyes, how I smiled, and to her credit, how I collapsed afterwards. The people gathered remained silent, unlike the crowd outside the blacksmith's compound – the seriousness of calling the elders together had disciplined their usually flapping mouths.

When my turn came, I tried to calm my wobbling nerves, and I told them what had happened as simply as possible. I told them about the pulse that had bubbled up from the soil and entered my body, moving it against my will. I tried to convey the powerlessness I felt, but I also kept to the facts because I truly didn't know if what Chidị had done justified what I did to him. I told them about feeling his life, and when I said how I stopped it, a low murmur passed through the people at my confession. I fell silent and looked at the faces of the elders. Most of them didn't look as horrified as I thought they would. If anything, they seemed interested, curious even. They had seen so many things in their lifetimes, maybe this was just another item on a strange list. After all, they had been alive back when there were people without gifts, and no one in my generation could even imagine that now.

The elders conferred briefly among themselves, and the priest joined them after giving me a slow, thoughtful look. My skin was clammy and cold – I couldn't even feel my fingers in my brother's grip.

Have faith, Sọmadịna.

I ignored my twin's message and he kept silent after that. When the elders were done, it was the priest of Ala who stood up to announce their decision. The crowd almost vibrated in their eager silence. He did not draw it out, which might have been kind of him.

'While it is clear that there are forces beyond a human nature at work here, the fact remains that the boy Chidị was killed at Sọmadịna's hands. She has confessed to the crime and under the eyes of Ala, this is an unforgivable taboo, punishable by death. Where a life is stolen, the payment is a life. That is the judgment of the Council.'

Jayaike let out a low moan, but it took several moments for the words to register in my brain. The people around us had already broken into commotion. I didn't understand what was going on. Papa's eyes were shocked and his skin was gray. Mama's face was utterly blank. She looked at nothing, least of all me. The blacksmith looked triumphant, and in the cold smirk on his face, I realized that my people had just decided to execute me. My legs dissolved, but before I could collapse against my twin, another voice cut through the crowd like a gong.

'I rebuke that judgment!' it declared, and the words echoed eerily over everyone's heads.

The priest threw his cloth over a shoulder and barely suppressed a sneer as he looked around to see who had spoken. 'On whose authority?'

The crowd parted and an old man in deep red cloth stepped out, power clinging to him like the fog of a morning. I had not seen him since he came to take my older sister away.

'Grandfather,' I whispered.

'On *my* authority,' my grandfather said, his eyes piercing the priest.

I heard Mama draw in a quick, sharp breath, and as if he heard her from across all that space, Zerenjọ turned his head and looked directly at his daughter. A rush of relief swept through me, strengthening my legs. It peaked into a sweet crest when I caught sight of the apprentice walking behind him. I nudged Jayaike. *She's here!* I sent.

I know, I see, he replied, glowing in her direction. The golden leopard was covered in chalk, her head shaved.

Our sister, Nkadi, had come home again.

CHAPTER EIGHT

TILL TODAY, I WONDER IF THE COUNCIL WOULD HAVE KILLED ME IF my grandfather hadn't arrived to stop them. The priest served the mother deity, but priests were just normal people with a single gift. They didn't have the power that dịbịas had. If priests were the deity's servants, then dịbịas were their anointed, their favorites, with the multiple gifts to prove it. The older a dịbịa, the more powerful they were, and Zerenjọ was the oldest dịbịa alive, one of the few surviving from the Split. He had the authority to challenge the Council's ruling because he was above human decisions; he answered only to the deity. This wasn't a freedom for the dịbịas. If they transgressed, mercy would never be an option. The deity is harshest with her own.

The priest was visibly irritated at my grandfather's presence, but he was trying his best to conceal it and appear gracious.

He bowed as he greeted Zerenjọ, and the corner of my grandfather's mouth twitched up briefly.

'We were not expecting to have a dịbịa attending,' the priest said politely.

'I was not expecting a priest of Ala to ignore the hand of a deity when condemning a girl to death,' responded my grandfather coolly. The priest tightened his jaw at the jibe – to accuse a priest of making a misstep was something only a dịbịa could get away with.

'Sọmadịna killed a man. This is justice.'

Zerenjọ put both his hands on his tall staff and leaned his chin on them. 'How?' he asked.

The priest narrowed his eyes. 'Ehn?'

'How did she kill him?'

One of the elders spoke up. 'She confessed to it, Zerenjọ. It's murder. We don't understand the how of this, but does it matter?'

My grandfather pursed his lips and tilted his head from side to side in reply. 'When it is a deity working through her, then yes. It matters.'

His words left me stunned as everyone broke out into a clamor and Chidị's father stepped forward, anger radiating from him.

'There is no god working through that small girl! It's only because she's your granddaughter that you're saying that. You will not deprive my family of justice!'

Zerenjọ raised an eyebrow at the blacksmith and ignored the insult. Accusing a dịbịa of partiality was inconceivable. 'Ask yourself if you are willing to stand in the way of a god. Do you wish to counter the will of Ala? Will you dare to command the crocodile?'

The blood left the blacksmith's face and his shoulders slumped. No one was foolish enough to stand between a god and anything. I felt discomfort gather around me like a cloud, and I wanted to run far, far away from here. Zerenjọ turned to the elders as the man stepped back with a bent head, shame and anger tight in his neck.

'None of you wondered how a girl was capable of striking down another person? Not even after she described clear signs of possession?'

Another of the elders shrugged. 'To tell you the truth, Zerenjọ, if she has the power to take life that easily, our judgment is even more necessary, possession or not. How can we register someone like that? We have never seen such a thing, and it's not something we want to risk in this community.'

'So you decide to have her killed instead.'

'She *killed* someone, Zerenjọ!'

'A god's harsh justice,' he said, waving a hand dismissively. 'There is no trouble. You do not have the full facts at your disposal, so I cannot blame you. Allow me to call a new witness.' He beckoned in Mama's direction. 'Ngọzị.'

'Your own daughter?' The elders looked skeptically at him

but were wise enough to not make as bold an accusation as the blacksmith had.

Zerenjọ smiled without a shadow of amusement.

'I am a dịbịa before I am a father.' His voice took on eight shades of sadness. 'That is a truth that plunges a cutlass in the back of my family. You will not bring it up again.'

Chastised, the elders turned expectantly to my mother. Mama gritted her teeth but stepped forward obediently. I was wringing my hands together, pressing my thumb into my palm like it could center me.

'Tell them about the twins' gifts,' commanded Zerenjọ. Jayaike and I looked at each other, surprised.

How does he know? asked my brother silently. I shook my head, perplexed.

I told him. The voice was new to our heads, but as familiar as our hands. We both stared at our sister, shaven and draped in red. Nkadi smiled reassuringly at us. *Some gifts do run in the family,* she sent.

But how did you *know what happened?* I asked.

She shrugged. *I kept seeing you both glowing with too much power in a dream, night after night, days before now. When I told Grandfather, he realized it was a vision, and he interpreted what it meant. We started traveling immediately.*

I wanted to ask her more, but Mama was giving her testimony now, narrating what she had seen that night in our bedroom, the iron taste of magic, the voice that had hit her, and her children with charcoal eyes. She told them about calling Ahụdi in and what our grandmother had discovered when she examined us. When she had finished, she looked coldly at her father and he nodded, giving her permission to step back. Zerenjọ handed his staff to Nkadi and approached the Council, spreading his hands open.

'It is unusual for any child to have direct contact with the spirit world when holding their gifts for the first time. Even though Sọmadịna carries the blood of dịbịas from myself and the late Kesandụ – may his spirit be at peace – it is unusual for anyone to have multiple gifts and not be a dịbịa, let alone have those gifts lie dormant. As such, I have performed the necessary divination and sacrifices to speak to Ala and ask for her guidance.'

The priest huffed. 'Ala's taboo is clear,' he insisted.

'What did the deity say?' asked an elder, ignoring the priest.

Zerenjọ seemed reluctant to share what he knew, but the words came out of him anyway. 'The twins *belong* to Ala.'

There was a slow uproar among the elders. 'How can that be? They were not born at her shrine,' countered one of them.

'They are not dedicated!' argued another. I stood there, stunned. The practice of children belonging to the deity was as old as the taboo against twins, and almost as forgotten. Just stories, ancient stories. How could it have anything to do with me and Jayaike?

The elders' questions and shouts overlapped until Zerenjọ had to raise his voice to get silence.

'The ways of the deity are not for humans to understand. We cannot draw shapes in the sand and expect a deity to remain inside. You cannot tell the crocodile which direction to swim in.'

People nodded in agreement. That much we all knew was true.

My grandfather continued. 'The twins were a gift to Ngọzị from Ala, after my daughter prayed for her spirit child Nkadi to remain. They should have been taken to a shrine for the appropriate sacrifices to be made. They were not.'

Mama pressed a hand to her mouth and from the shamed guilt on her face, I knew this to be true. Ala controlled fertility – she would have been the one Mama came to, begging for her children to stop dying. Was this what Nkadi meant when she told me once that I had no idea how much Mama had wanted us? It seemed like Jayaike and I had been the only ones kept in the dark about how we got here, what deals were made with a deity over our heads. Zerenjọ looked directly at my mother as he kept talking.

'When Nkadi did not die, Ngọzị resented the suffering she had been put through. She did not thank Ala, despite the gift of twins. Now the mother deity has claimed the twins for her own. They will be her hands. They will never reproduce. They will be the children of the crocodile, something we have not seen in generations, with gifts beyond those of a dịbịa.'

His voice was a storm tearing my whole life apart, the words beating like a gong against my bones, yet my grandfather had to speak louder and louder over the uproar rising from the elders and crowd, the sound boiling up under the moon. Jayaike and I looked at each other, both reeling from the revelations being shared. We were being exposed, stripped to the spirit in front of the town, made naked to their eyes and their judgments. I hated our grandfather for doing this so publicly, even if he was saving my life. Chidị's father came forward again, his voice a booming drum.

'So my son must go unavenged?! What kind of justice is this?'

Zerenjọ whirled on him and his eyes sparked. 'Your son was violently assaulting a young girl when Ala decided to strike him down. This council cannot help you. The judgment of a god stands above all. You would do well to make amends to Ala and to that young girl for your son's crime. Begone!'

The blacksmith swallowed strongly, his face a rictus of pain and fury, but he turned around and stormed out of the gathering, taking his family members with him. Several of them cast evil glares at my family as they left, and I saw Mama flinch.

'Zerenjọ, we cannot have children more powerful than dịbịas just walking around dispensing justice as they see fit. What will happen to the system? There will be chaos, no order. How do we register people with gifts like that?' The elder who spoke looked genuinely worried. 'The girl murdered someone. The law is very clear on that.'

'Is the law greater than a god?' Zerenjọ posed the question gently and watched the elders dissolve into arguments.

'At least banish her!' shouted one of them.

'You want to banish a hand of Ala? What curses do you want to bring to our land?'

The debate raged hot and even the audience was aflame; everyone was looking and talking about us. Nkadi walked over, greeted our parents in a quick embrace, and touched Ahụdi's feet.

'We are not needed here anymore,' she said. 'Grandfather will manage it with the elders, but the people are unhappy and afraid. We need to go back to the house.'

Ahụdi agreed and so we pushed our way through the crowds, enduring the deliberate bumps and slights delivered by several people. It was the rich dark of night as we walked home, crickets singing on the side of the paths and fireflies dancing around our knees. Mama walked several paces behind us, and after a while, Papa fell back to walk with her. As soon as we arrived home, Ahụdi told everyone to go to bed.

'Zerenjọ has given us a lot of information and this has been a long day,' she said. 'Sleep and we can come together as a family tomorrow to discuss what our options are. Ka chi fọ.'

In any other circumstance, Mama would have argued with her, but this time she kept silent and let Papa lead her away. He gave Jayaike and me a consoling look as they left.

All will be well, he promised. I didn't believe him, but I gave him a smile anyway. Nkadi touched our heads.

'It's good to be back,' she said. I noticed she didn't say *home,* but she went to sleep in her old room. Ahụdi kissed us good night and left Jayaike and me at our doorway. We stepped into our room and Jayaike closed the door firmly behind us. His eyes were bright.

'Did you hear what one of the elders called you? The hand of Ala.'

I scoffed, sitting on the bed. 'Biko, they should come and take it back. I don't want this.'

My twin frowned. 'It's a blessing, Sọmadịna. We've been chosen by a god. Nothing that happened on that farm was your fault.'

'Are you mad?' I couldn't believe he had just said that to me. 'You think that was a blessing? To watch someone *die* at my hand?'

Jayaike flinched but pressed on. 'But it wasn't your hand, that's what I'm saying. It was hers. It was really hers.'

I shook my head in disbelief. I kept my voice low, because what I was saying felt as blasphemous as it did true. 'You don't understand. It doesn't matter if she moved me, it just makes it worse. She *used* me. She made me a *murderer.* I can't forgive myself for it, even if you so easily can!'

My twin stared at me with confusion and grief in his eyes. Of course he didn't understand. He wasn't the one the deity had chosen to do her dirty work.

'It's fine,' I choked out. 'Let's just go to sleep.'

My brother kept looking at me, now solemn. 'I love you, Sọmadịna. You are a good person. This was not your fault.'

I tried to smile but gave up. 'It doesn't feel like that right now. I don't believe it's true.'

'That's okay,' he replied. 'I can believe it enough for both of us.'

I dreamed of the hunter in blue again. We were all by the stream and Jayaike was lying in the water, his face turned up to the sun.

'He is perfect, isn't he?' The man in blue was standing next to me, his robes gently moving in the breeze.

Terror seized me immediately and all my muscles locked in place. The man looked down at me with his tainted eyes and chuckled. He smelled like dry pepper, clean and sharp.

'Oh, I can see you now, little girl. You remind me of someone I knew a long time ago. You're as beautiful as your brother, but don't worry. Don't run. I can only take one of you.'

I forced myself to speak. I wouldn't let Jayaike down again, not like this. 'Don't take him,' I said. 'Take me instead if you have to take someone.'

His eyes widened even further, making him look more creature than human. 'The deity has already touched you,' he said. 'I'm not fool enough to take you like this.' His eyes wandered back to my brother. 'Besides,' he added, almost dreamily, 'it doesn't matter.'

'What do you mean?' I asked, trying to stop my teeth from chattering in fear.

'Because you'll come straight to me when I take him. You can't help it.' He shrugged and didn't even look at me. 'I'll get you anyway.'

I couldn't answer. By the river, he felt so *wrong*. It would have been better if he looked the part, if he didn't look like someone I could pass by in town if not for his eyes. I couldn't even be sure I hadn't met him before, dressed in something else, not the blue robes. I would remember the robes. I would remember the eyes. I wouldn't remember his nondescript hands or face. When I tried to recall the details of him, they blurred away. The only things left were the colors, the blue, the endless black, the murky yellow.

'What do you want from us?' I asked. 'Why are you here?'

The hunter crouched at the bank of the stream and passed the tip of his tongue over his lips. 'You both made such a ripple in the spirit world the other night when the god came to see you,' he said. 'It was easy to find you – well, it was easy to find your brother. You? You hid for a little while, but then she moved you and there you were. So much power. So young. I will eat you both alive, little girl, all in good time.' He twisted his neck to grin up at me. He looked like a wild animal, waiting before it pounced. 'I want my freedom and you both will give it to me.'

I woke up with a scream behind my teeth.

My hands scrabbled in our covers until I found the reassuring bulk of Jayaike next to me. He turned restlessly in his sleep and I nearly wept in relief. He was here. He wasn't going anywhere. I lay back in bed and stared at the ceiling until my stomach rumbled. I hadn't eaten since the stream, and I'd vomited all that back up. Jayaike was still restless next to me, so I slid off the bed carefully and went to see if we had any food in the kitchen.

When I passed our parents' room, I heard Mama's voice pitched low but intense. I couldn't resist pressing myself against the wall and inching closer to listen.

'I did not owe Ala anything!' Mama sounded like she was on the verge of tears yet furious, all at once. 'How can you even *say* that when you saw how many children we put back in the ground? You *know* how much I bled and suffered to bring them into this world only to have her take them back, and now she mocks me by giving those twins unnatural gifts? I do not want small gods under my roof!'

Papa was deeply upset. I could tell because he was using his voice, cracked and rusty. 'They are our *children,* Ngọzị. If we do not protect them, who will?'

'Protect them? From what?' She scoffed at him. 'We are

the ones in danger! What if Ala decides she will have her vengeance through them and we die at the hands of people we brought into this world?'

'You should have made the sacrifices when they were born! I trusted you to carry out women's business – you know men are not allowed to perform that rite at the shrine. You brought this down on us, Ngọzị, with your spite and bitterness and ingratitude. Ala gave us Nkadi!' Papa's voice cracked and he broke into a cough.

Mama spat loudly in contempt. 'It was not you who pushed those children out of your body, Olejeme.' Her voice was like crushed bitterleaf. 'Ala gave me pain and a child who was destined to forever leave me. I will not hear talk of the gratitude I owe her.'

'She gave you two more children, Ngọzị,' rasped Papa.

Mama's voice snapped like a whip in response. 'She gave me abominations.'

I felt like I had been turned into chalk, flaking off with every word Mama said. I backed away slowly and then fled toward my room, bile swirling up from my stomach. My teeth chattered against each other and my hands were shaking. How would I face her again? How could she throw us away? Had she *ever* loved us?

I burst through my door and called out to Jayaike, tears blinding my way toward our bed. He didn't reply, and I tore the covering off the bed, expecting to find him still tossing in his sleep.

The bed was empty.

The hair on my neck prickled and I suddenly noticed the emptiness in the air around me. I didn't need to look around the room to confirm the knowledge punching me in the stomach. After a small lifetime of being able to feel Jayaike's presence close by, steady and constant, its absence was glaring, loud as a gong. I called his name as if that could summon him back, as if I didn't know the truth by now, in the collapsing pit of my stomach.

My twin, my brother, was gone.

CHAPTER NINE

EMPTINESS WHISTLED AROUND MY EARS IN A WHIRLWIND, DRAGging air out of my lungs. I turned in a slow circle, as if that would change anything.

'Jayaike?'

Even my voice sounded hollow. I closed my eyes and tried to find my twin through our bond, but all I could see was a thick gray fog. I tried to push past it and a sharp pain spiked through my head, snapping my eyes open as panic climbed up my throat. Was this how Jayaike felt when he lost contact with me while I was on the farm, or was my brother dead? Is that why I couldn't reach him?

The space around me stretched out and it felt like the ground was melting below my feet. Panic boiled up uncontrollably in my chest and my fingers began to sizzle as a white haze fell before my eyes. I was falling apart – I knew I was falling apart but I didn't know how to stop it. I closed my eyes and felt someone's cool fingertips press against my temples.

'Breathe,' commanded Nkadi. 'We can't have you knocking down the house.'

I hadn't even heard her enter the room. I forced air into my lungs and the panic sobbed itself down. 'Jayaike is gone,' I choked out.

'I know,' she replied. 'Come and sit down.' She led me to the bed and rubbed my back as I drew in ragged breaths.

'I can't find him with our bond.'

There were no words for how that felt, like the ground had been snatched up from under me and thrown somewhere far away.

'I know.' Nkadi's voice was steady. 'I tried to divine his location, but he's been veiled.'

I pulled away from her, my fingers digging into the bed. 'I have to go and look for him.'

Nkadi shook her head gently. 'Not right now,' she said. 'We need to wait for Grandfather.'

'What?' I stared at my sister. She had never looked more like a stranger than in that moment. 'He's your brother too! How can you even *say* that when he's missing?'

Nkadi twisted her mouth as she placed three fingers under my chin, spreading the palm of her other hand over my forehead.

'Grandfather warned me, but I didn't understand before. What it means to be a dịbịa first.' Her skin was warm and there was a hint of apology in her eyes. 'Go to sleep, Sọmadịna.'

A jolt rocked through my skull and my vision blurred, the room tipping back as I slid into darkness.

When I opened my eyes, it was morning and sunlight illuminated a room that was painfully empty. I scrambled quickly to my feet, my chest thudding. The skin on my forehead was still warm from Nkadi's touch, and I fought back a wave of betrayed anger. She had *stopped* me from going after my twin. She had used her magic to force me to sleep and I had lost *hours.* How much farther away was Jayaike from us now? Nkadi had no right to make decisions like that for me, whether she was a dịbịa or not! I rubbed my face as I went into the main family room, my steps harsh and quick, trying to ignore the soreness in my chest that was shaped like my brother.

Zerenjọ was sitting on a low bench with Ahụdi, and they were speaking together with urgent hand gestures, a large bowl of yam pottage forgotten between them. Mama wasn't there, but Papa was standing by the doorway with his chewing stick moving in small circles in his mouth, his eyes anxious. I jumped when Nkadi tapped me on the shoulder to hand me a bowl of pap.

'Ewela iwe, Sọmadịna,' she said immediately, trying to fend

off my anger. 'You needed to rest last night, and I knew you wouldn't agree.'

I ignored the food she was offering. She had lost her mind if she thought I was going to eat when Jayaike was missing. 'Where is my brother?'

Nkadi flinched. 'Don't be like this, Sọmadịna. He's mine too.'

I had to bite back a snarl. She was talking like a dịbịa, like she had all the answers and I just needed to trust her, but she didn't know anything. She didn't know the man in blue had made me promises and, worst of all, that he had kept them.

'Where is he?' My voice was taut and furious.

The rest of our family looked up, but Nkadi shook her head slightly at them and leaned in toward me, taking my hand in hers. I wanted to pull away, but her fingers were strong. She had applied fresh chalk on her shaved head and she didn't look like the leopard I'd known all my life.

'I divined that a gateway to the spirit world opened last night. We think that's what took Jayaike.'

My vision blurred for a moment. The hunter had really done it. He had stepped out of my dreams and he had taken my brother out of this world, stolen him into the spirit world while I was eavesdropping on our parents. I had heard nothing, smelled nothing, felt *nothing.* How could Jayaike have been taken without me noticing? It had been so loud the last time, all that hot iron in the air.

‘I would have known,’ I said, shaking my head in refusal. ‘I would have known if something like that happened to him.’

Across the room, my grandparents exchanged weighted looks.

‘We only know what the deity permits,’ Zerenjọ said, leaning against his staff. The carved wood was filled with symbols that I couldn’t understand. ‘Nkadi and I will search for him.’

My spirit recoiled at his words. I knew I was supposed to listen to him. I was supposed to be obedient because they were my elders. They were supposed to know best, but they didn’t understand. I hadn’t told them about my dreams in time. They couldn’t search for him properly if they didn’t know about the hunter, and I couldn’t just sit still and hope that the dịbịas would find Jayaike. There was only one thing I knew to be true, as clear as the sun slicing through a thick cloud.

‘I have to find him,’ I said.

They all stared at me, worry mirroring in their eyes.

‘We’re going to look for him,’ Nkadi repeated. ‘Don’t worry.’

I shook my head. She didn’t understand anything. ‘I had a dream.’

‘It’s too dangerous when the spirit world is involved, Sọmadịna.’ My sister spoke as if I were a terrified animal she was trying to placate. ‘You will stay with Ahụdi and we will bring him back to you.’

‘He said he would take Jayaike and eat him alive.’

Nkadi paused. 'What?'

'*Who* said that?' Ahụdi's voice had gone tense. I met her eyes reluctantly, guilt searing inside me.

'I should have said something sooner. The hunter said we would come to him.' I knew I wasn't making sense to them, but all I could think was that he had been right. I *would* run right to him if that would lead me to my brother.

Ahụdi rose from her seat to crouch in front of me. 'Sọmadịna. Tell us everything.'

This time, I did. Their eyes widened as they listened, and although Nkadi tried to hide it, I saw fear flash over her face. Papa had been silent this whole time, but now his skin was gray with his own fear.

'Another dịbịa?' Nkadi murmured the question to Zerenjọ, and our grandfather's mouth tightened.

'It's possible,' he said. 'But the description matches no one I know.'

Ahụdi stood and whirled away, her hands fluttering in distress. 'This changes nothing,' she said. 'Sọmadịna will stay with me while the dịbịas look for Jayaike.'

I had no intention of staying with her, but something was wrong in how she had said it. 'Why would I stay with Ahụdi instead of here at home?' I asked.

A tense silence fell over the room. I looked at my sister, but Nkadi's eyes slid away from mine. The hairs on the back of my neck rose slowly. I looked over my family, stopping on my father's face. His eyes were glassy with tears, and a horrible foreboding uncurled in my stomach.

'Papa? What has happened?'

His throat worked, but the silence didn't shift, and it was Nkadi who finally spoke.

'Mama has gone a little mad,' she said.

'What are you talking about?'

There was no such thing as going a little mad. Either you went mad or you didn't, and it was nothing to joke about. Some people said that it was a punishment from the deity, crocodile teeth tearing at your mind, and the foreboding in my stomach thickened as I remembered what Zerenjọ had said during the Council – that Jayaike and I belonged to Ala, that Mama had broken a promise when she failed to dedicate us. I didn't want to think about it, or the fight I'd overheard between her and Papa. Was she being punished by the god?

My sister was talking, but I hadn't heard a word. 'Biko,' I interrupted, 'say what you said again.'

Nkadi glanced at me, worried. 'I said, Mama doesn't want to look for Jayaike.'

Something inside me cracked apart.

Abomination.

Should I have laughed or cried? Should I have screamed, or beaten my head against the ground? What was the correct way to react? I just sat there, my mouth soft and open as the words bounced around in my head. Nkadi rushed to fill the silence.

'But there's something wrong with her,' she continued. 'That's why I said she has gone a little mad. She would never talk like that otherwise.'

I looked at my sister. How could she be so touched by the spirit world and yet still be unable to see things she was afraid of? There was nothing *wrong* with our mother. I knew that as certainly as I knew that Jayaike was missing, like a cold knife had carved the knowledge into my stomach. Nkadi didn't understand. She wasn't a normal child, she never had been, but Mama had never looked at her the way she looked at my twin and me. Mama had never called her an abomination. There were *names* for what Nkadi was. There was no name for us, no language to make us make sense.

'Is it that she thinks he will come back on his own?' I asked, trying to cling to a reason that would hold up against the light.

Nkadi shook her head. 'She . . . she said she doesn't want him back.' Her voice shook, but only briefly, before she dragged it under control.

I flinched. As far as everyone else knew, Jayaike and I were still one person. 'But I'm here,' I said, and my voice sounded crushed and forlorn. 'How can she not want him back if I'm still here?'

The room had fallen silent again. I looked for an answer in Nkadi's face, but there was too much sorrow there for me to see anything clearly. I glanced over to Papa, and he finally moved, coming over to kneel on the floor beside me.

Don't hate me, he pleaded silently. *It's just until she gets better.*

My eyes filled with hot tears. 'You're sending me away?'

He cupped my face in his palm. *Your mother needs me,* he said. *And she is . . . not safe for you right now. Neither is this town. Zerenjọ and Nkadi will search for Jayaike. You will stay with Ahụdi and Ọlụchi. We all think it is for the best, Sọmadịna.*

I didn't know what to say. There had never been a betrayal that cut as deep as this. My own mother was throwing me away. She didn't care if Jayaike was alive or dead if she didn't want to look for him, if she didn't want him back. Which meant she didn't care if I lived or died, or maybe she wanted me dead. Maybe she wished we had never been born.

'Does she not love us anymore?' I asked, my voice thick with tears. I was fighting the urge to break. Jayaike needed me.

Zerenjọ put a hand on my shoulder. 'Ngọzị is haunted by old wounds that have nothing to do with you, Sọmadịna. Don't worry. We are always family, no matter where we scatter to.'

It didn't sound like enough. It sounded like a lie. No mother threw away their children like this. I was crying now, even though I didn't want to, hiccuping as my tears fell against Papa's hand.

'Is Jayaike dead?' I asked, even though they wouldn't have the answer. If the hunter were here, I would scratch out his eyes as I screamed the question. 'Is it because I killed Chidị? I didn't mean to do it—'

'Jayaike is not dead,' Nkadi insisted. 'The divinations were clear that he is not dead.'

'You mean he's not dead *yet,*' I countered. Papa pulled his hand away from me and choked back a sob. I wanted someone to disagree with me but nobody did.

'We will find him,' Zerenjọ said.

'How?' I didn't care if I was being disrespectful. 'You don't know who the hunter is, your divinations didn't even show him to you, and you said Jayaike is veiled, so how? How will you see him? How will you find him?'

'You have to give us time,' Nkadi answered. She didn't notice she was wringing her hands together. 'We have to do more divinations, more rituals.'

'He doesn't *have* time!' I shouted, knowing it to be true, deep in my bones. There was no description I could give them that would accurately convey the hunter's hunger. He was a creature who would not wait long for what he wanted, whatever it was. Our power, he had said. Would he break my brother apart to get it?

Papa backed away. 'I have to check on Ngọzị,' he said.

Nkadi's nostrils flared, just a fraction, but enough for me to sense her contempt. Ahụdi was the one who laid a hand on my father's arm. 'Go,' she said. 'We have this under control.'

Papa looked at me and his throat worked as he tried to find something to say. 'I'm just a farmer,' he managed eventually. 'These spirit things, Sọmadịna, they can handle it better than I can. Everything will be fine.'

I wanted to tell him that he was both a coward and a liar, but it hurt too much to see the father I loved choose Mama over us, so I said nothing. His gaze ducked away and he left the room. Nkadi spun away from me but I saw her dashing tears from her face anyway. Zerenjọ said her name softly and my sister turned back.

'I know, I know,' she muttered, then she lifted her reddened eyes to mine. 'I'm so sorry, Sọmadịna.'

I nodded stiffly. There were many things she could be apologizing for, but it didn't matter now. Everything was pressing against my skin, like there was no air or space around me. I wanted my twin back. I wanted my life back. I reached for the twin bond again as if I would find Jayaike through it, as if he would appear in the room and come back to me. The bond was still a gray haze, but then it tugged sharply on me, making me stumble.

Zerenjọ's eyes narrowed. 'What just happened?' he asked.

I opened my mouth to answer, but a wave of dizziness crashed over my head and I staggered again as the bond strained against me. It felt as if Jayaike had stretched it as far as it could go, and now it was pulling on me to compensate. The room blurred and I fell forward, the earth sliding to meet me.

Ahụdi gasped and caught me in her arms. 'Sọmadịna!'

She and Nkadi helped me lie down on the ground. Their faces were indistinct, their voices thick and warped. I should have been afraid, but instead I felt a deep relief. If the bond was active, then it meant Jayaike really was alive, somewhere on the other end of all that gray. I felt heat sweep through me as Ahụdi did a quick scan. Her face kept blurring before my eyes.

'Zerenjọ,' she said, asking my grandfather for help. 'I'm not sure what is happening.'

He knelt beside my body and I felt his scan pass through me, sharper than Ahụdi's, and slightly painful. I closed my eyes as he exhaled and placed his fingertips on my temples.

A voice came in from the doorway, tentative and worried. 'Is she all right?'

I turned my head toward the sound, and the room moved in uncertain slants as I did so. Ụwafụlamiro was standing at the threshold, a leather bag slung over his shoulder. His clothes were dusty. My heart kicked up a little at the sight of him.

'I traveled to see my cousins,' he said, his voice quick with anxiety. 'I came back and they're saying that something happened to the twins, but no one will tell me. So please, is she all right?' His cheeks were mottled red from the sun. I hadn't seen him since the kiss at the stream, and that felt like a completely different life. I was unrecognizable to myself now, spinning away.

Nkadi smiled at him kindly. 'You must be Ụwafụlamiro,'

she said, reaching her hands out to him. 'You are welcome, come inside. Jayaike is missing and Sọmadịna is unwell.'

He threw down his bag and hurried to us in a few long strides, taking Nkadi's hands and squeezing them in greeting, then crouching beside me while making sure he didn't get in Zerenjọ's way. My grandfather was continuing with the more thorough and painful scan. I was too dizzy to protest and it was difficult to keep my head straight. My neck felt so tired, and my vision kept going in and out. The twin bond was creating intense and painful pressure in my head, quickly mounting into agony exploding behind my eyes. Grandfather inhaled sharply and moved his hands, placing three fingers in the softness behind my chin and spanning his other hand over my forehead. Swift fire flared up in me and I cried out, but it slid away as fast as it had arrived and with it, the terrible pressure was gone. I felt him release my head and gently transfer me into Ụwafụlamiro's grip. My friend rested my head against his shoulder and put his chalk arm around me.

'I think she needs to come with me and Nkadi,' I heard Zerenjọ say to Ahụdi. 'Jayaike has moved too far away from her for their bond to be comfortable – it will cause her serious suffering if she doesn't have a dịbịa around to manage the pain.'

'So we need to find him quickly,' Ahụdi replied. 'Will this distance also be causing him the same pain?'

'I hope not. If he does not have a dịbịa nearby . . .' Zerenjọ paused and continued in a strained voice. 'May Ala protect him from this.'

'We should leave now,' said Nkadi. 'We can help them both better with our resources in the Sacred Forest.'

I felt Ụwafụlamiro tense up against me. 'I'm coming with you,' he announced.

Nkadi and Zerenjọ refused in unison. 'Mba.'

Ụwafụlamiro carefully moved me so I was leaning against the wall, and stood up, stepping toward my grandfather and kneeling to touch his feet. 'Dede,' he said respectfully. 'I may not understand everything that's going on, but I love Sọmadịna and Jayaike. I am fast and strong. I can hunt. I can be useful on this search. Allow me to join my hands in helping her and bringing him back.'

The corners of my vision were shading back into focus and I could see my grandfather give Ụwafụlamiro an evaluative look. It reminded me of Mama, and my stomach folded over in grief. Ụwafụlamiro was taking quick breaths from his kneeling position. I knew I didn't deserve his loyalty. He didn't even know what I'd done to Chidị. Still, I wanted him to stay close to me; I didn't want to lose anyone else because of what I'd become. I struggled to find my voice, then directed it at Zerenjọ.

'Let him come.' I meant it as a plea, but it came out sounding like an order. My grandfather didn't seem to take offense. He just looked at me with softened eyes, then shrugged.

'Small god,' he said. 'Let it be so, then.'

We left that same morning, before the sun hit its peak. Nkadi helped me pack my things while Ụwafụlamiro ran home to speak to his family. His parents had always taken him on their trading trips since he was a child, and he was confident they wouldn't mind him coming with us.

'Even with everything that's happening?' Ahụdi had asked him, her eyebrow raised. 'The twins aren't very popular right now, you know.'

Ụwafụlamiro had given her a grim smile. 'My parents know what Sọmadịna and Jayaike did for me when the blacksmith's family tried to convince the whole town that I was an unclean thing. I am their son, and we know who we're loyal to.'

'We're entering the Sacred Forest,' Nkadi reminded him.

He'd grinned. 'They'll be so jealous! This is the kind of adventure they dreamed of in their own travels.' I envied him in that moment, for having parents who would stand not only by him but also by his friends, parents who saw him as powerful and capable, not strange and wrong. My mother's rejection burned under my chest bones, an ember that wouldn't go out. I wore Jayaike's leather bag slung around my body, a reminder of where my focus had to be.

I didn't look back at the compound when we walked out and I didn't say goodbye to my parents. Ahụdi walked with us to the tallest palm tree, where we were waiting for

Ụwafụlamiro, and we stood there with her hand on my shoulder. Zerenjọ and Nkadi were speaking softly to each other. I looked up at my grandmother.

'Where is Da Ọlụchi?' I asked. I didn't want Ahụdi to be alone as she traveled home. Mama wouldn't be transporting anyone soon.

'She's coming,' Ahụdi replied. 'She was just a town over. Not far.'

Her face was composed, but I could see the sorrow bubbling in her eyes. I couldn't imagine how helpless she felt, when she had been the one guiding us all our lives, for this to have spun so far out of her hands. I held all my pieces together for her and tried to smile. 'I'll find him, Ahụdi. We are one person; he cannot get away from me just like that.'

She turned up a corner of her full mouth. 'I know. How else can it be but that you will find him?'

I nodded, tears bloating up my eyes. Ahụdi sighed and pulled me into a tight hug, resting her cheek against my temple.

'Listen to me, Sọmadịna. I know the world has shattered around you. This is one of the times I wish your grandfather Kesandụ was here to share his wisdom with us. These pieces are big and sharp and they are cutting your heart and there has been no time to sit with any of this. But you are *our granddaughter.* You are a bundle of power, and you belong to yourself first before you belong to Ala. Just remember that, you hear? You are not alone. We are all with you, your family here and Kesandụ in spirit. We will get Jayaike home. *None of this is your fault.*'

I broke down sobbing at her last words, remembering when my twin had tried to reassure me as well. 'I should have said something about the man in my dreams. Then he wouldn't have taken Jayaike.'

'How could you have known something like this was even possible?' Ahụdi chided. 'I have been alive for decades and even I have never heard of anyone using the spirit world like this, to kidnap someone's child. No, the only person at fault is that man. What did you call him, the hunter?' I nodded and wiped at my face. My grandmother helped me, her rough thumb swooping under my eye. 'We will hunt him back,' she said, her eyes intent on mine. 'You will hunt him back.'

'I will hunt him back,' I repeated, and a kernel of furious determination grew with those words. I *could* hunt him back. When the twin bond had pulled on me, it had pulled to the east, and that was the direction I had fallen in. I would follow my brother and I would find the man in blue, and he would think I was delivering myself to him like he wanted but I would be a surprise. I didn't know how, but I would be a surprise, a crocodile roaring out of the still water. If the deity had given me power enough to kill Chidị, then in the Sacred Forest, I would figure out a way to harness that for myself and my twin. The god owed me that much.

I bent to touch Ahụdi's feet gently, just as Ụwafụlamiro

ran up with his bag bumping against his body, a small bundle wrapped in an old skin under his arm. He touched her feet and then Zerenjọ's in a quick greeting. Nkadi nodded at him and we turned toward the southern path that led to the sacred river full of crocodiles and beyond that, to the Sacred Forest. It was different from the various paths we took to get to the streams or to the palm groves or the People's Forest. This path curved around and avoided all more traveled areas. Trees and bushes grew over and around it, creating a fractured tunnel. Ahụdi waved as she set off on one of the main roads, and the four of us stepped onto the cool green road that would take me to my brother.

CHAPTER TEN

WE WALKED AT A STEADY PACE, THE SUN HANGING HIGH AND HOT overhead as chattering birds wheeled against the sky. Nkadi led the way and Ụwafụlamiro kept close to my shoulder while my grandfather followed behind us. Once we crossed the river, the path began to take us out of sight of the village, curving into land I'd never been allowed to step on. The forest started to change around us and I stared up at the trees soaring higher than I thought possible, their canopies fracturing the sunlight. Thick creepers swung from branches and the air tasted like water. It was so different from the People's Forest that I turned my head to tell my twin, only for ash to rise in my mouth when I remembered he wasn't there.

'I can't believe we're in the Sacred Forest,' I whispered to Ụwafụlamiro instead.

Nkadi heard me and glanced over her shoulder. 'The People's

Forest you're used to is shallow, thinned out by humans,' she said. 'Things are more pristine here. Ancient. You'll see.'

That was the right word – *ancient.* I could feel the weight of time in the trees around us, and I wondered how many hundreds of years they had lived, locked into the earth and growing into the sky, how many generations of creatures had lived and died in their branches and under their shadows. Everything in this part of the forest felt touched with reverence, yet untouched by people. We saw golden monkeys swinging curiously through the trees, their shiny black eyes glittering at us as they followed for a while. Gleaming parrots crossed our paths, rising in a rare flock and filling my eyes with wheels of color.

Sometimes, Nkadi instructed us to step over carefully laid lines of white sand and each time we did, everything got heavier. Sound slowed down to a muffled drone and the colors thickened. I felt like I was pushing through the air instead of walking easily. As soon as we crossed another line of white sand, everything would snap back and we could breathe easier. I wasn't sure I was allowed to ask what was going on – this was the Sacred Forest, after all, full of dịbịa secrets – but when it happened the second time, Ụwafụlamirọ's eyes narrowed.

'What magic do you have in the sand?' he asked bluntly.

Nkadi spun around, walking backward with a sly smile. 'You've noticed our shortcuts.'

Ụwafụlamiro and I gave her blank looks, and Zerenjọ chuckled. 'Think of them as sections of land that are folded together,' he explained. 'It would take us maybe a day to cross them if they were laid out properly, but the shortcuts press the land together so we can cross in less than forty steps.'

I thought for a moment. 'What happens if someone breaks the line of sand?'

'A good question.' My grandfather gave me an approving look. 'It's dangerous to do that. If a line is broken while someone is still inside the shortcut, it unravels quickly. The person inside could be severely injured, or even killed.'

'But you still leave the lines lying around like that?' Ụwafụlamiro sounded shocked.

Nkadi laughed. 'No one enters this deep into the Sacred Forest without a dịbịa,' she pointed out. 'We're the only ones here, so the lines are safe.'

Sunlight fell over the chalked side of her face and my heart twinged. Even though she was right in front of me, I still remembered what it had been like when Nkadi went away, the hurt and confusion that was left behind. Being here made it clear that Nkadi truly had a new home now, another life, one that was full of secrets. She looked so comfortable in this strange forest. The tightness in my chest was a reminder that *both* my siblings had been taken away from me. As if he could sense my feelings, Ụwafụlamiro slid his hand around mine and squeezed it gently. I glanced at him, but he wasn't even looking at me. His eyes were fixed ahead of us, his pupils dilating. 'Am I seeing what I think I'm seeing?' he asked.

I followed his stare and hissed in a quick breath as he pointed with his free arm to a cocoyam plant a few paces ahead of us. It was throbbing with pulses of color, waves of bright and dark green rippling from the stem to the tip of each leaf. I inhaled sharply and the air smelled like iron, like it had that first night back home – a smell I was beginning to associate with power and terror and a life ripped from my recognition.

Nkadi put her hand on my shoulder. 'You can touch it if you want,' she said. 'It won't hurt you.'

I stepped carefully toward the plant and laid a few fingers on one of its broad leaves. It was warm to the touch, and to my surprise, there was a light rhythm thrumming through it. I drew back my fingers with a gasp, then touched it again to feel the rhythm, a steady drum more alive than I thought possible. Once I focused, I could feel the rhythm reverberate through my body, down through my flesh and bones, until the soles of my feet could feel it humming in the soil.

'Come and see,' I said to Ụwafụlamiro. He stepped forward and laid his entire palm on the leaf, his mouth breaking into an open smile when he felt the rhythm. I stared at the delight in his face, and for a moment, he looked like a stranger. Not in a bad way, but just far away from the boy I'd grown up with. The bones of his face were reshaping along with his body and even his skin smelled different. It felt like so long ago that he'd kissed me at the stream. I felt like I was someone much worse than whoever I'd been back then, and I wondered if I had become a stranger to him too.

'What are we feeling?' Ụwafụlamiro asked my grandfather.

Zerenjọ leaned on his staff, smiling. 'It is the beat of magic and life, child. It's what the Sacred Forest dances to.'

'Like a pulse?'

Zerenjọ pointed the tip of his staff toward Ụwafụlamiro in approval. 'Like a pulse,' he affirmed.

'But these colors,' I said. 'I've never seen anything like this before.'

'Magic,' Nkadi explained with a shrug. 'It's everywhere, you know? It runs in the sap of the plants and in the water under the soil. It settles heavily around the home of every dịbịa, so it's especially reflected in the life that grows around us.'

True to her word, every step we took revealed more plants illuminated from their cores, their colors pulsing and shifting according to the Forest's beat. I wondered briefly about the ritualists who had been killed and dumped there – if the Forest leached the magic back from their bodies until their bones decayed into these drumming colors. Butterflies dove in flocks around us, sparkling like raindrops in the sun, and I even glimpsed a white leopard streaking through the undergrowth, illuminating the ground under it. Ụwafụlamiro refused to believe that I'd actually seen the leopard, and we were arguing about that when we arrived at Zerenjọ's house.

'We're here,' Nkadi said, and Ụwafụlamiro and I fell silent as we gazed into the clearing of my grandfather's exile. There was an enormous mahogany tree twisting up into the sky, and a house wrapped around it, made of wood and clay and even some woven creepers. It rose several stories high and pulsated with a faint glow. In the silence of our awe, I could almost swear I heard the Sacred Forest's rhythm chiming lightly from it.

'It's so beautiful,' I whispered. Jayaike would have loved to see this, and it hurt that we were not standing there together. Zerenjọ's home was nothing like I'd imagined for my grandfather. Ever since he'd come to collect Nkadi, I'd always imagined that he lived in a cave deep in the Forest, somewhere dark and foreboding. Somewhere people would be afraid to come to, somewhere that could explain the painful depths of the space between him and Mama, but this house was soaring, light, and welcoming.

Zerenjọ sighed gently. 'It is a good home,' he said. There was a faint note of sadness in his voice, but he walked away even as I looked up at him.

'Let me show you where you'll be sleeping,' offered Nkadi. 'Will you be afraid if I put you off the ground?'

I drew myself together. 'Me that has been climbing trees since before I could walk? Put me on your highest floor.'

'Ha! I've slept in tree branches while hunting,' Ụwafụlamiro shot back. 'You that always just climbs back down.' I shoved him and we jostled at each other as Nkadi shook her head and took us to the second floor, but she was smiling, which was what I wanted.

The interior walls of Zerenjọ's house were covered with painted symbols and animal skins, indigo and ocher and preserved hides. We climbed a carved ladder to get to the large room where Nkadi said we would be sleeping. There were a few beds arranged against one wall, an eating area, and some benches scattered around. The floor was made of wood fastened together with thick fibers, and it creaked as we stepped on it. I was a little nervous, since it was my first time being suspended above the ground like this, but I didn't want to show Ụwafụlamiro that it was affecting me at all, so I kept my face controlled even though it felt odd to not have earth under my soles. I was grateful when we headed downstairs after dropping our loads, and Nkadi showed us the bathing area. It was located in a clearing south of the house, with pale green pools of water patching the grass together. Ụwafụlamiro knelt down to touch the water and splashed some on me before I could dodge it. The droplets were cool against the heavy heat of the Forest, and the pools shone with that same humming magic.

'I'll leave you to clean up,' said Nkadi, 'and there will be food in your room when you're done. Go to sleep afterwards. Grandfather and I will see you in the morning.'

'What about you?' I asked.

'I'm always in training, Sọmadịna. I have work to do.' She smiled at us. 'Take your time, you did well on the journey today.'

We watched her leave, with that smooth, slinky walk she did so well.

'Your sister is very beautiful,' Ụwafụlamiro said. A quick curl of hot jealousy wrapped itself around me, but when I looked at him, he was watching me with a mischievous grin on his face. Refusing to rise to the bait, I lifted and dropped one shoulder.

'Of course. She's related to me.'

He made a mock serious face and nodded. 'Of course, of course.'

I moved quickly and shoved him into the pool he was kneeling by, but his reflexes were faster than I'd expected, and he pulled me in with him. I screamed as we both splashed into the pool, then we broke out laughing, and for one traitorous moment, far worse than when I'd taken Ụwafụlamiro's hand on our way back from the stream, I forgot about my brother. It lasted barely a few seconds, and guilt rushed into me as soon as I realized what I'd done. I pulled away from my best friend and climbed out of the pool, my shoulders tight. Even as I walked away, I could feel Ụwafụlamiro watching me leave, his eyes sad and understanding.

The next morning, Nkadi was waiting for us when we came downstairs. Her head was oiled, clear of chalk, and she wore thick slivers of ivory through her ears with elephant whiskers knotted on her upper arms. The ivory was carved with delicate designs that reminded me of the necklaces our mother kept in her jewelry collection. We'd never been allowed to touch them because of how rare the ivory was – all the elephants had been killed in the war. Ahụdi had described them to us, but they were just another old thing dead in an old story. The thought of Mama sent a familiar shot of pain through my stomach, and I took a deep breath so it could dissipate.

'You look good,' I told Nkadi, running my fingers against the elephant whiskers. 'Why don't you wear this when you come to town?'

She shrugged. 'People don't need to see everything,' she said. 'Did you find the morning food in your room?'

Ụwafụlamiro nodded. 'We ate already, thank you.'

'Good. Follow me.' She started walking and we fell behind her. 'Grandfather is working on a medicine that will allow you to use your twin bond more clearly so you can track Jayaike.'

I exhaled in relief. 'I'm so glad to hear that.' I needed that direction. Being without Jayaike felt like walking in a world that had slid out of order, like something somewhere was always so terribly *wrong*.

Ụwafụlamiro squeezed my shoulder but didn't say anything. He walked by my side easily, as if we were a unit. Maybe that's what we had become, I thought, a new unit looking for the missing half of the unit I used to be. Maybe that would help me feel like less of a traitor.

Nkadi was still talking. 'Grandfather is also working on another medicine, an antidote for that pain. So that even if Jayaike goes out of range, it won't hurt you as badly.'

I stopped in my tracks. 'No. I don't want that one.'

My sister paused to stare at me. 'What?'

'I don't want more distance to grow between us! That antidote just sounds like it'll allow Jayaike to be taken farther and farther away, and I wouldn't even notice because the pain would be gone.' I shook my head stubbornly. 'The pain is good. The pain tells me he hasn't gotten too far from me.'

Nkadi narrowed her eyes. 'Are you feeling it now, Sọmadịna?'

I thought about lying, but the crushing in my head *had* been slowly creeping back in. 'It's starting again, but it's not as painful as it was before,' I admitted.

'Let me try this.' Nkadi faced me and slid three fingers under my chin, placing her palm on my forehead, just like Zerenjọ had the day before. Her eyes closed in concentration, and I felt her power jolt through my head. It tingled with a cold and high sharpness that was different from the burn of Zerenjọ's touch. I wondered if everyone's gift had a flavor that way, a signature. The pressure in my head receded and Nkadi opened her eyes, a satisfied look on her face.

‘I did it,’ she said, her voice tinged with pride. ‘We’ll continue this whenever the pressure returns, but, Sọmadịna, I beg you to consider the antidote. It’s basically the same thing I just did, and we might not be able to move fast enough to keep the distance between you and Jayaike consistent.’

I knew she was making sense, but I couldn’t become complacent. ‘Then we should be moving faster,’ I snapped. ‘When will Grandfather finish the first medicine, the one to clear the bond?’

Nkadi sighed and exchanged a look with Ụwafụlamiro that I didn’t appreciate. I wasn’t being unreasonable. My brother had been *abducted* through the *spirit world*. Why was everyone else being so *calm* about it? I opened my mouth to yell at them, but Ụwafụlamiro put his hand on my arm.

‘We move slow now so that we are prepared to move fast later,’ he told me. ‘That is how we get Jayaike back. I know it’s hard, Sọmadịna, but give your grandfather some time, ehn?’

Nkadi seemed impressed by his response. ‘Grandfather will let us know when he’s done,’ she said. ‘You cannot rush medicine. In the meantime, I have something else to help you prepare.’

She led Ụwafụlamiro and me to another clearing, a tight circle of packed and flattened red sand. The grass had been cleared from the ground, and a long carved box sat under a thatched shelter off to the side.

‘What’s this?’ Ụwafụlamiro asked. I wasn’t sure I wanted to know the answer to that question. The red sand was too organized, too intentional. It was waiting for something, as if it wanted to become even more red, soaked through with blood.

'This is the training circle.' Nkadi had a smirk on her face that made me even more suspicious.

'Training for who?' I asked.

My sister dropped to one knee and plunged her arm into the sand up to her elbow, the ground swallowing her with ease. When she pulled it out and stood up, there was a deep red flame encasing her forearm and hand. Nkadi examined it with detached eyes, rotating her hand before pointing the flame at us. 'For you.'

Ụwafụlamiro took a step back, shaking his head. 'Mba.' He poked my back in short jabs. 'Tell your sister to stop pointing that fire at me.'

I was fascinated by the flame, and against most of my instincts, I went a little closer to it, watching how it seemed to hover just above her skin. 'Why do we need training? Aren't you coming with us?'

Nkadi shrugged, keeping her arm still so that I could look at it. 'Yes, but Zerenjọ isn't.'

'What?' Ụwafụlamiro's voice pitched high and outraged. 'He's not coming? It's just going to be the three of us?'

Nkadi narrowed her eyes. 'It's going to be the two of you and a dịbịa,' she corrected.

I prayed that Ụwafụlamiro wouldn't say anything stupid about her still being in training. 'Why can't Grandfather come?' I asked instead.

Nkadi's eyes remained smooth, although I could swear I saw a flicker of something pass over her face. Uncertainty? Fear?

'He has to attend to other matters,' she said. 'I am sufficient.'

In any other circumstance, I wouldn't have tried to argue with her, not because she was my big sister, but because she was a dịbịa. She had access to worlds I couldn't even imagine, powers I would never guess at if she decided not to reveal them. Unfortunately, this circumstance was that my twin was missing, so her vague dịbịa evasions simply weren't good enough. I pushed my face right in hers.

'Why is Grandfather not coming?' I asked again. 'And give me a proper answer this time.'

Her eyes flashed. Nkadi never liked being cornered; no leopard does. 'I don't have to explain dịbịa things to you,' she growled.

Rage was always one breath away for me these days. Power was even closer, but I had been pressing it back because it had caused me enough trouble already. This time, I let it surge up in me, and it felt like thick muscle flexing under scaled skin, a jaw heavier than a world. Like I said, if I belonged to the god, then she belonged to me too. I didn't touch my sister. I just looked at her with all the weight I had in me, down to the silt at the bottom of the river, dark and cloudy and holding a waiting fury.

'You will explain,' I said softly. I heard Ụwafụlamiro hiss in a breath, but I didn't take my eyes off Nkadi. A leopard is a leopard, true, but it cannot fight its way out of a crocodile's

bite. My sister stared back at me, then exhaled, her shoulders deflating.

'He did divination,' she said simply.

'What does that *mean*?'

Nkadi's mouth twisted at one corner. 'It means he asked the deity, Sọmadịna. And Ala said no.'

I took a step back, rocked with surprise. 'What?'

My sister didn't break our gaze, and I saw a glimpse of pity as she looked at me. 'Ala forbade Grandfather from accompanying us.'

'Why would she do that?' Ụwafụlamiro asked. 'I don't understand. Isn't Jayaike hers?'

I nearly laughed out loud, bitterness full in my mouth. 'All my mothers are the same, it seems. Willing to throw me and my brother away.'

Nkadi looked aghast. 'Sọmadịna, no! It's not like that.' She grabbed my hands and tugged at them. Her arm was still cloaked in flame, but it didn't burn my skin, it only brushed me with warmth. 'Listen to me. The deity knows what she's doing, even when it is veiled to us.'

'Veiled . . .' I tried to pull my hands away, but she wouldn't let them go. 'That's what you and Grandfather said about Jayaike. That he was *veiled* when you tried to divine for him.'

'Yes, that's correct.'

'Is it her, then? Is Ala veiling him so we can't find him?' I was nearly shouting now. If the deity betrayed me, I didn't know what I would do. She could take my entire body and make me something else.

'No, no.' Nkadi let go of my hands so she could hold my face and force my eyes to her. The flame caressed my cheek. 'Zerenjọ thinks it's the hunter who has him veiled, and that's also what's obscuring your twin bond. But your bond is so strong, Sọmadịna, the medicine will be able to clear some of that veil, that fog. Just trust us, please. Trust Ala. All will be well.'

I could feel Ụwafụlamiro's hand on my back, rubbing in calm circles. I took a breath and nodded. 'What do we do while we wait for the medicine?'

Nkadi smiled in approval and stepped back. 'Grandfather wants me to see if you have other dormant gifts we can uncover. Whatever we find will be useful. Ụwafụlamiro, we need to test the extent of your disappearing and teach you a few other things. Beyond the Sacred Forest is a world you two have never seen before. You have to be prepared.'

My sister waved her arm and the flame died, a fine mist of ash wafting from her skin. Ụwafụlamiro sighed in relief, his eyes tracking her as she went to the carved box and opened it, taking out a thin bone carved with tiny etchings. She threw it over her shoulder without looking and Ụwafụlamiro caught it.

'What's this?' he asked, turning the narrow piece of bone over in his hands. 'It feels . . . old.'

'It's a wind whip,' Nkadi replied, pulling a spear out of the box, which she then handed to me. I took it cautiously and weighed it in my hands. It wasn't as light as it looked, but it wasn't as heavy as I'd feared.

'How does a wind whip work?' Ụwafụlamiro was tentatively making sweeping motions with the bone.

'How does a whip work?' retorted Nkadi. 'Just try it.'

He took a deep breath and raised the bone over his shoulder, then brought it forward sharply. There was a crack, and the whip sprang out from the handle, curling into the air. It was almost invisible, but you could tell it from the air around it because it was shimmering like rising heat and humming in a thin column of restrained wind. Ụwafụlamiro's mouth fell open in shock, but I made a face.

'He gets a magic whip and I just get a spear?' I complained. I knew I sounded whiny but it didn't feel like enough. I wanted to go to war against the hunter. *Nothing* felt like it would be enough to force the world to give my brother back to me.

'This is amazing!' Ụwafụlamiro yelled as he whipped the loop around his head.

Nkadi cuffed me lightly behind my head. 'You don't need a magic weapon. You *are* a weapon.'

She clapped her hands, then stood with her legs apart in the center of the circle, angling her dark gold face toward us, her voice slicing.

'Let's begin!'

CHAPTER ELEVEN

TO MY SURPRISE, I LOVED SPENDING THE DAY TRAINING WITH NKADI. It was the most time I had spent with my sister since Zerenjọ took her away and broke something in Mama, but it also gave me purpose, something challenging that took up all the wailing spaces in my head. If I could become more powerful – maybe as powerful as Zerenjọ, maybe more so – then no elders could ever point at me again and order my death. I wouldn't be afraid of roaring blacksmiths – I wouldn't be afraid of *anyone.* Nothing would keep me apart from my twin, and maybe I would even be strong enough to tell a god to leave me alone when she reached inside my body. I wouldn't be a pawn or a tool or an abomination. I was something feared but I could become someone respected.

Nkadi used the lines of sand to fold her way into the Sacred Forest, challenging me to reach out with my mind to communicate with her, so she could see how far my range went.

We pushed it more and more, but it was never long enough for me to connect with Jayaike. That veil of fog was always there, reminding me of the man with the corrupted eyes who had whispered threats and touched my brother's head. I hated him so much that my blood hummed with it. I tried to use that hate to pull out whatever dormant gifts Zerenjọ thought I had, but nothing came forth.

'Grandfather's concerned,' Nkadi admitted while we took a break and drank cold water out of a clay pitcher. 'It's as if you're carrying weapons but none of us know what they are, or how strong they are, or when they will come out of you.'

She didn't need to tell me any of that. I was already terrified of what I could become. I could see Chidị dropping like a felled tree under my will, and my fears danced around like pictures in my head – me being possessed again, but this time striking Mama down, watching the light blink out from her eyes like a dead ember. I missed my twin more than my heart could bear – it was as if everything important in me was already dead without Jayaike by my side.

By the time the sun was at its highest point, Ụwafụlamiro had taken to the wind whip as if he was born with that bone welded to his palm, the shimmering coil of air dancing around his body. With Nkadi's guidance, he practiced holding his gift while wielding the whip, and both of them turned invisible. Ụwafụlamiro became a displacement in the air, a silent whistle lashing about, and Nkadi glowed with pride.

'Now try it with Sọmadịna,' she said, and he grinned as he offered his hand to me.

'Don't be afraid,' he said.

'I'm not,' I shot back as I slid my palm against his. Ụwafụlamiro just smiled and vanished. The disappearing crawled over my skin like cool water, reducing me to a glimmer somewhere in the wind as I gasped in shock. I couldn't see Ụwafụlamiro but I could *sense* him beyond our hands, in a way that almost reminded me of my twin bond with Jayaike. It made me feel both comforted and horribly lonely at the same time.

For my training, Nkadi told me to wield my spear as if I had no gifts, as if it was and would be my only defense. I found my balance in it quickly, and I enjoyed learning how to flow with what I had thought would be a clumsy and inconvenient weapon. The smoothness of the spear gliding through my palm to become a natural extension of my arm was deeply satisfying. My sister watched as I practiced my techniques, correcting and giving me pointers, showing me how it could be thrown across great distances or through the water for fishing.

'You must practice every day, as often as you can,' she advised. 'A few hours is not enough time to master the spear, not even for someone like you. Think of it as part of your body, even when it is flying away from you. Its destination should be as accurate as if you were pointing out something close to you with a finger.'

I was determined to learn how to become as dangerous with

a spear as I could be, but then Nkadi interrupted that training and asked me to sit outside the circle.

'This is how you try to connect with your dormant gifts,' she said. 'By being with yourself. A dịbịa cannot reach into you and pull your gifts out. Only you can reach you.'

I grumbled but obeyed, sitting cross-legged on a patch of grass and closing my eyes. I didn't like the idea of slipping inside myself, because I could still remember Jayaike and me staring into the chasm that started all of this, but I did it anyway. As expected, I was full of grief and rage, but when I reached beneath that, there was simply nothing. I was bereft, empty. I considered coming back up, but a wave of exhaustion swept through my spirit. Jayaike was just a face lost in a surging darkness and I was a child with no brother, running and running. I was thick with absence, empty and terrible, and I let it extend through me like it wanted to, the nothingness trembling through my veins, pouring over my skin. My mother didn't want me. My father had chosen her over his children. My people had sentenced me to death, but I was already dead. The sounds of the Sacred Forest faded away, the grass I was sitting on dissolved, and the warmth of the sun on my face cooled into a blank space. I exhaled and it felt like the last of me floated away.

Time stopped.

I don't know where I went, but I knew when I started to come back because someone was shouting my name with the weight of a dịbịa's magic behind it. My eyes snapped open and my body rocked from the force of my return. Nkadi was on the far side of the training circle, one arm stretched out to shield Ụwafụlamiro, who was standing behind her with confused eyes.

'Sọmadịna? Are you with us?' My older sister's voice was still heavy with magic, rattling iron in the air.

I blinked and placed my hands on the ground to steady myself. Instead of the lush soft grass I was expecting, my palms pressed down on something dry and crackling. I looked down and my breath caught in my chest. All the grass beneath me was dead, a crushed circle spreading like a stain around me. The earth was now arid sand, something nothing could grow in, as if life had just . . . stopped in my presence. A cold, terrible feeling crawled down my spine, and I jumped up, scrambling away from the patch. Nkadi ran across the circle and caught my elbow just as I started to gasp for air, panic wrapping itself between my ribs.

'Breathe,' she ordered, but I couldn't. All I could see was Chidị's body thudding to the ground, that same feeling of nothing washing through me.

'What did I do?' I choked out.

Ụwafụlamiro knelt down to touch the circle I had killed into the ground. 'We could feel it from where we were,' he said, but his tone was curious, not afraid. 'It felt like the air was missing, like something was pulling everything to you.'

'A vacuum,' Nkadi said. 'Sọmadịna, I think it's a gift.'

'I don't want it!' My voice came out shrill, but I didn't care. She didn't understand what it meant, what it really meant.

'Let's ask Grandfather,' she said, patting my arm. 'Maybe he's finishing with the medicine by now.'

Ụwafụlamiro came up to my other side and took my hand. I knew they were trying to placate me, but I was also grateful that although Ụwafụlamiro had seen me kill the earth, he still held my hand without fear. He wasn't like the others back home, the ones who were afraid of me. Like Mama.

We headed back to Zerenjọ's house with a new silence wrapped around us.

My grandfather stepped away from the medicine he was working on to listen to Nkadi, then he took me to the back of the house, just the two of us. Vines hung from trees around us and branches canopied above our heads.

'Try it again,' he said, keeping his voice gentle.

I shook my head in refusal. It was too terrifying, whatever was inside me. This wasn't the crocodile's power; this wasn't even the entity looking down at the anthill – this was *nothing*.

Zerenjọ bent to look into my eyes. 'This is important for Jayaike. We need every bit of our power, Sọmadịna. People like us cannot be afraid of our gifts. Do you understand?'

I bit my lip. He was right to bring my twin into this. There were many things I would not do for myself, would not face for myself, because I was not brave, but I would willingly walk into a whirlwind of fire for Jayaike. That wasn't bravery. It was just love. I took a deep breath and slipped inside myself again. The emptiness was there, waiting. I touched it a little, then shuddered and slipped back, running away from it. I opened my eyes to see my grandfather staring at me with a strange look in his eyes.

'Small god,' he murmured. 'You are not ready to hear some things.'

I didn't know what he meant, but I wasn't going to argue with him or ask him why he had started calling me that. Because I belonged to the god? There were dịbịa secrets I was happy to leave alone.

Besides, I had my own problems. With just that brief touch of the emptiness, the grass I was standing on had died again, some of the vines near me had wilted, and even Zerenjọ had taken a little step backward.

'Come with me,' he said, and I followed as we walked away from the house into the Sacred Forest. He asked me to test my power again and again. We discovered that whenever I held that emptiness, that absence, I could wilt and kill plants, yes, but I could also stop the flowing water of a stream, put out fires, and halt wind.

'Is this not death?' I asked my grandfather, with Chidị's face burned into my memory. It felt like destruction, like rot.

Zerenjọ shook his head at me. 'Think of it as a stopping force,' he explained. 'Think of it as a void.'

I didn't want to. A void was that hole that had opened between me and my twin in our bedroom, the pit that broke our joined gaze into two pieces, which broke our family. It smelled of Ala, and I didn't want anything to do with the gods, no matter what Mama had or had not done in exchange for us. Zerenjọ and I walked back to the house with new knowledge dripping off us. I knew there was more to this than he was telling me, but it was also hard to care. I felt like I was floating away, I had touched the emptiness so many times. I barely listened as he told Nkadi and Ụwafụlamiro what we had discovered, not until my sister looked at me with bright eyes.

'Have you tried it on a living creature?' she asked.

I blinked as I dragged myself back. 'What?'

'This your new gift. Have you tried it on animals?'

I flinched in disgust. 'Of course not! Why would I?' I looked to our grandfather, but his face was impassive.

'To find out what happens,' she replied, as if it was obvious. 'Sọmadịna, this could be a weapon you use against the man who took Jayaike. Don't you want to know how it works?'

I should have wanted to know. I thought I was willing to do anything to get my brother back, but all I could see was

Chidị's body toppling in my head over and over, and maggots crawling out of gold eyes.

'I won't do it,' I said.

Nkadi frowned. 'Sọmadịna.'

'I said no!' I was surging to my feet before I knew it, leaving the room and climbing to my sleeping quarters, where I curled up tight on my side. After a few minutes, my grandfather came up and joined me, sitting next to where I lay.

'You don't have to use it,' he said. 'Not until you're ready.'

'So you admit it's death, then,' I replied, daring him to lie to me again.

My grandfather, the greatest dịbịa in the land, dropped his gaze. 'There is much you do not know yet, small god. This is a heavy gift to carry.'

When I didn't move or reply, he sighed and brushed his hand over my head before he stood up to go. I watched him as he left. I didn't want to ask any more questions or get any more answers. They could all keep their secrets as far as I was concerned. I wished I had never wished to know more, to have more. I wished I had been content with my boredom. I would give anything for the gifts to have never arrived, because then Jayaike would be where he was supposed to be, right next to me. I said as much to Nkadi when she came up to check on me. She didn't like hearing it.

'What were you two going to do if your gifts hadn't come?'

she asked. 'Continue living like that in the village while everyone pointed and wondered?'

'They point and wonder even worse now, Nkadi. They wanted to kill me.'

'But we know who you are, *what* you are,' she replied, her voice low and intent. 'Knowledge is worth *everything*.'

I wanted to speak harsh words that would cut at her heart, tell her she was truly becoming more of a dịbịa than a sister, but I held my tongue. What would have happened to me if she and my grandfather *weren't* dịbịas? Would our people really have executed me, tossed my body out for the Sacred Forest to eat in its own time?

Nkadi watched my face as I chose a mutinous silence, then shook her head. 'I'm sorry, Sọmadịna. You're right. It's been a lot.'

I didn't reply. What was there to say?

She leaned over and nudged my shoulder. 'Ah-ahn, so now you're not talking to me? Don't be angry, little sister. I've been in the Sacred Forest so much, me, I forget how to talk to people. You know I love you.' Her voice lilted as she teased me and I softened unwillingly, letting myself lean toward her in return. I had missed these silly sister moments when we irritated each other and then made up.

'What if I tell you the medicine is ready?' she whispered, her eyes gleaming.

I gasped and smacked her arm. 'Nkadi! Why wouldn't you start with that?'

She laughed and jumped up. 'Grandfather said to give it a few minutes before I told you. He was just finishing.'

I scrambled down the ladder and barreled into the main room. Zerenjọ and Ụwafụlamiro were standing there, both looking at a stone bottle Zerenjọ held in his hand. It seemed so unassuming, but my heart was caught in my chest because it held hope – the possibility that I could sense my twin again through our disrupted bond, that I'd finally be able to track him.

'Can I try it now?'

My voice filled the space, loud and eager, and my grandfather looked up. 'Sọmadịna.' He held the bottle out to me and let it drop into my hands. It was cold and heavy. 'You can try it after you eat,' he said.

I began to pout but Zerenjọ quelled it with a firm shake of his head. 'No arguments. You can't take this on an empty stomach.'

Nkadi was placing bowls of food on raffia mats on the floor, and so we all sat down. I placed the bottle next to me and ran my thumb over its wooden stopper. Zerenjọ reached into his cloths and passed me a small bag made out of crocodile leather. I hesitated to take it – crocodile leather was forbidden to anyone who wasn't a dịbịa, and even they only harvested it with great care when a crocodile died, which happened maybe once every two or three generations.

'Which one is this?' I asked, finally letting the weight of the bag sink into my palm.

'That's the antidote for the pain that crushes your head,' my grandfather replied.

I opened the bag and looked inside. It was filled with a dark powder that smelled like shadows, vague blood, and salt. I didn't ask what it was made from; I didn't want to know.

'How much do I need to take when it happens?' I already planned to take as little as possible.

'A pinch under your tongue,' Zerenjọ instructed. 'The *moment* you start feeling the pain, Sọmadịna. Don't wait for it to get bad.'

Nkadi scoffed as she ladled out portions of okro soup into our bowls. 'That's exactly what Sọmadịna is going to do,' she said.

I glared at her and put the bag down next to the bottle. My grandfather gave me an evaluative look. 'You can do that if you want, Sọmadịna, but consider that each moment you incapacitate yourself with unnecessary pain is a moment wasted in the search for your twin.'

I looked away, chastened. 'I just want to make sure we're moving as fast as possible. We already lost today.' As if reminded, the pain began to creep back into my head. It had been hours since Nkadi helped drive it away. 'I mean – I know today was preparation and I thank you, Grandfather,' I added clumsily, not wanting to sound ungrateful. 'I'm just afraid of losing Jayaike.'

Ụwafụlamiro leaned toward me. 'Are you in pain, Sọmadịna?'

'What?' I turned my head too fast to look at him and winced when the pain stabbed a little sharper. How could he tell?

Zerenjọ snapped his fingers. 'Time to test the antidote.'

'Does she need food for it?' Nkadi asked. She was sitting on his right side, her whole spirit bending in his direction as she learned from him.

'No, the powder can be taken at any time.' My grandfather raised his eyebrows at me. 'Like right now, Sọmadịna.'

I opened the bag and took a deep breath, sending a silent apology to my twin as the distance between us widened. *I will catch up,* I promised. *I'll find you.* The powder was soft and fine between my fingers as I took a pinch and placed it under my tongue, closing my eyes. It tasted slightly sour and it melted away quickly, dissolving into the membranes of my mouth. A few seconds later, the pain paused and began to recede. I opened my eyes and nodded at my grandfather.

'It works,' I said, and he smiled.

'Of course it works,' he replied. 'I made it. Now eat so we can try the other one and see if it clears up your bond to Jayaike.'

Ụwafụlamiro bumped my shoulder with his. 'Thank Ala,' he said fervently. 'I hate seeing you in pain.'

I hid a smile and ignored the wink Nkadi threw in my

direction. The pounded yam was soft and steaming, and the soup was filled with gamey bushmeat. I ate quickly, impatient to get to the medicine in the stone bottle. After one bowl of soup and several finger scoops of yam, I looked up at Zerenjọ. 'Can I try it now?' I pleaded.

He laughed and shook his head. 'I think you should, before you choke on your food.' Nkadi giggled next to him and propped her chin in her hand.

'Make sure you drink the whole thing,' she said. 'I have a good feeling about this, Sọmadịna. You'll be able to feel Jayaike again. I just know it.' When I looked at her, her eyes were both pained and hopeful. It made my chest hurt. She had been so busy taking care of us as a dịbịa that I had forgotten Jayaike was her little brother, the one she used to carry on her shoulders because I was too scared to be up that high when we were small. I had many memories of both of them – Nkadi running through the compound, Jayaike shrieking with his arms waving above her head as she gripped his legs.

'We're going to find him, Nkadi,' I said. Did she let anyone comfort her? Or was that something only our grandfather could do? Even as I watched, she straightened her back and her feelings slid somewhere behind her eyes.

'Of course we will,' she replied. 'Drink up, little sister.'

CHAPTER TWELVE

THE MEDICINE TASTED LIKE FIRE. IT BURNED ON MY TONGUE, IT burned going down my throat, and it burned in my stomach. I gasped for air, coughing as tears dripped from my eyes. Ụwafụlamiro patted my back and glanced at Zerenjọ.

'Should this be happening?' he asked, worried.

My grandfather nodded and passed me a cup of water. 'The medicine needs to be hot enough to burn away the fog.'

'It feels like you're trying to kill me!' I drank the water down in one gulp, and the heat in my belly lowered but continued to burn. Nkadi hid a smile.

'You'd never survive dịbịa training,' she said. 'Grandfather has made me drink much worse things than that.'

I shook my head. 'At least tell me I don't have to take more doses of this.'

'Well, let's see.' Zerenjọ tapped his fingers against the side of his cup. 'Reach for the bond and tell me what you find.'

Obediently, I closed my eyes and felt for my twin. Our bond snapped into focus, pale and twisting into darkness. Relief poured over me. 'The fog has cleared,' I said out loud. 'I can see more of the bond now.'

'Good, that's good.' Zerenjọ sounded like he had expected nothing less. 'Can you connect to your twin?'

I stared at the emptiness that the bond disappeared into. 'It's not hazy anymore, but the bond cuts off into . . . nothing. Just darkness.'

'Darkness isn't the same as nothing,' my grandfather replied. 'Can you *feel* Jayaike?'

I reached for my brother. *Jayaike? Are you there?*

'Don't be tentative,' Zerenjọ told me. 'Use your force.'

I took a deep breath and then I shouted down the bond, *JAYAIKE! Answer me!*

My demand barreled down the bond, collided with the darkness, and then a blast of power ricocheted right back at me, knocking me off balance. I fell back on the raffia mats as if someone had kicked me in the chest, grunting with pain. Ụwafụlamiro sprang to my side.

'Sọmadịna! Are you all right?'

Nkadi hurried over and helped me sit back up. 'What happened?' she asked. 'Can you breathe?'

'I'm fine.' I felt a little short of breath, but it was nothing. 'The darkness threw me back when I tried to reach through it.'

My sister frowned and looked to our grandfather. 'Should she try and connect with the darkness itself? Instead of going through it?'

Zerenjọ shook his head. 'No. I believe the darkness is the hunter. It could be dangerous to try and connect with him. We've cleared the fog, but he's still a cloak around Jayaike.'

'What do we do?' I asked, rubbing my chest. The bones there ached. I wanted to rip through that darkness, reach in, and drag my brother out.

'You'll still be able to track your brother,' Zerenjọ said. 'We might just need to time it for right *before* you take the antidote.'

I couldn't resist a smirk. 'So I was right – the pain *is* good.'

Nkadi rolled her eyes. 'No one said that. It's somewhat useful at best.'

I didn't care. It would help me find my brother. Except –

'Even if I can track Jayaike, how do we catch up to wherever he is?' I asked, my heart dropping. 'The hunter isn't tied to this world. He could be taking spirit shortcuts this whole time.'

Zerenjọ didn't seem concerned. 'It would take an unthinkable amount of power to keep moving Jayaike in and out of the spirit world, shortcuts or not. This isn't like your mother's traveling – taking a human body into ala mmụọ and bringing it out again is difficult. He'll have to move on this side if he doesn't want to burn out and kill both himself and your brother.'

'We still need to catch up, though,' Ụwafụlamiro pointed out.

My grandfather molded a ball of pounded yam with his fingers and dipped it into the okro soup. 'You do,' he agreed, swallowing in a rippling contraction of his throat. 'That's why I've decided to let Nkadi fold the land.'

Nkadi looked at him in surprise. 'Grandfather? You said that was too dangerous for me to try.'

He raised his hand. 'That was months ago. You've made good progress, Nkadi. I believe you're ready now. Unless you're afraid?' He looked like he was hiding a smile.

Nkadi flushed and her jaw set, bone jutting out against her skin. 'I can handle it. Even with two of them.'

'How do you fold the land?' I asked.

Zerenjọ nodded at my sister to explain, and she dipped her fingers in a bowl of water, giving him a glare before turning to me.

'It's the same as when we were traveling in the Forest,' she said. 'Remember the lines of sand?'

I did, along with the feeling of walking inside them, that thick and slow crawl.

'A dịbịa – a strong dịbịa – can fold the land without the

lines. We'll be able to cross great distances in a much shorter amount of time.'

'It is not without risk,' my grandfather warned. 'You must find a village or town as your destination each time Nkadi folds the land. As soon as you arrive, find food and eat. Eat as much food as possible, then eat some more. Eat for as long as you can. Folding without lines will burn up much of your body and you have a small window of time to feed yourself before it burns you to death.'

Ụwafụlamiro and I exchanged worried glances. I braced myself and looked back at Grandfather. 'As long as it gets me closer to Jayaike.'

'Brave girl. You all can leave at first light.'

I helped Nkadi clear the bowls and Ụwafụlamiro offered to do the washing up. In the back of my head, I wondered if the hunter had his own tricks to speed up his travel, if I would end up chasing my brother endlessly, never catching up until it was too late. That night, I slept poorly, afraid to dip too deep in case the hunter knew I was coming after him, in case he was waiting for me in my dreams with his black-and-yellow nightmare eyes.

In the morning, we ate heavily, until our stomachs felt tight and uncomfortable, preparing ourselves for the drain that the folding would take on our bodies. After the meal, we went to the bathing area to wash ourselves before the trip. I was quiet as I splashed the cool water over my head and body, and Ụwafụlamiro was solemn beside me, still as beautiful as he always was. Watching the translucent drops roll off his chest made me miss when we were home and doing this in familiar water. I never even got to tell Chiotu about the kiss, and she wouldn't care now. Now I was just the monster who killed Chidị, walking around when the town wanted me dead.

'I don't think I can go back,' I said, the words spilling straight from my thoughts out of my mouth. Ụwafụlamiro wiped his face and frowned.

'What do you mean, you don't think you can go back?'

'I mean after we find Jayaike. I don't think I can go back home.' To be honest, I didn't think my brother would be able to go back either. His heart would break when he found out what Mama had said – there was no way I could keep it from him, even if she changed her mind. I would never keep a secret from my twin again. The one I kept had already cost him his freedom.

'Of course you'll go home, Sọmadịna.' Ụwafụlamiro seemed so sure. I'd told him what happened with my parents and the trial with the elders, but I didn't think he understood how bad things had gotten while he was away. He hadn't seen their faces or heard the whispers. He hadn't smelled Papa's guilt or Mama's hatred, and I couldn't share the emotions with him the way I could with my twin. Jayaike was the only one who would actually understand.

So I just shook my head. 'Jayaike and I will go and stay with Ahụdi.'

'But that's two towns away!' Ụwafụlamiro looked distraught, red blotches forming on his cheeks.

'You can visit us,' I offered. 'You're used to traveling.'

For the first time in a long time, Ụwafụlamiro actually looked angry. He took a deep breath and waded closer to me. 'Sọmadịna. I've been keeping quiet because I know I missed a lot of things while I was with my parents.' Regret and pain cracked through the anger. 'I should have been there for you and Jayaike. I shouldn't have run.'

'You didn't—'

'No, Sọmadịna, I ran. I got my gift, I kissed you, I held your hand, and I was afraid, so I ran.'

My mouth hung open. He *had* been avoiding me. The hurt had me taking a step back in the pool, water lapping around my thighs. Ụwafụlamiro reached out and grabbed my hand to stop me from pulling away further.

'Don't be angry,' he pleaded. He was a mess of emotions – anger, guilt, shame – but then again, so was I.

'You didn't even tell me you were going.' I threw the words at him like small stones, and he flinched.

'I wanted to. But I saw Jayaike first and I didn't know if I should have told him about the kiss or if we were keeping it private, but you and Jayaike never keep secrets, but then should I have been the one to tell him or should he have heard it from you? I didn't know what to *do,* Sọmadịna. And my parents had offered to take me on the trip and they were so excited about my gift, I thought it would be easier to just go with them and take some time to figure things out.' His fingers tightened on mine. 'If I had known everything that was about to happen, Sọmadịna, I would *never* have left. I would never have left you.'

Something that had been tight and knotted in my heart slowly unfastened. 'Truly?' I asked.

Ụwafụlamiro tugged me closer and cupped my face in his hands. 'I would never have left you, Sọmadịna. Why do you think I'm here with you right now? I couldn't let you out of my sight, not again.' His thumbs stroked my cheeks. 'Say you forgive me for not being there.'

I shook my head within the warm grasp of his palms. 'You don't need my forgiveness.'

Ụwafụlamiro scoffed. 'Yes, I do. I know you've been angry at me, somewhere deep down where you like to bury things. Say you forgive me.'

I stared into his face, at the ghost of the boy I had yelled at when we first met, still in there despite the ways his bones had matured, the new shadowed jaw. He still had the same pale eyelashes, the same silver eyes, the same thick eyebrows that were pulled together as he waited for my response. He still had the same mouth, and before I could think too hard about it, I stood on my tiptoes, my feet pushing against the floor of the pool, and I kissed my best friend for the second time in our lives. Ụwafụlamiro made a small, surprised sound that melted against my lips as he slid an arm around my waist and kissed me back, pressing me against his chest. This time, there was no one watching, and I let myself fall into the clean, clear taste of his mouth.

When we finally broke apart, his face was flushed and I was sure mine was too.

'Have you kissed other people?' I blurted out.

Ụwafụlamiro ducked his head. 'No, only you. Was I bad at it?'

'No!' I lifted his chin and made him look at me. 'You're just . . . suspiciously good.'

He barked out a laugh and pulled me into a hug. 'I'm glad to hear that.'

I pushed against his chest, embarrassed. 'I shouldn't have told you that. You let compliments swell your head.'

'I mean, you just said I'm the best kiss you've ever had.'

I splashed water at him. 'You're the only kiss I've ever had!'

'I know.' Ụwafụlamiro leaned in and kissed me again, quick and firm. 'It's just you and me.'

I stiffened as soon as he said it and I think he realized it too, the moment the words left his mouth. He immediately let go of me and took a step back in the pool, horror in his eyes, because he knew me, he knew me so well.

'I didn't mean it like that, Sọmadịna.'

I couldn't speak. It was always me and my twin. It had always been me and my twin until I started *lying* to him and he was *stolen* and I was here kissing *our* best friend as if Jayaike wasn't in danger. I was shaking my head and climbing out of the pool before my brain even registered what I was doing.

'Sọmadịna!'

'No, *no.* I can't do this. I can't do this to Jayaike.'

Ụwafụlamiro climbed out of the pool behind me and tried to grab my arm, but we were both slick as fish from the water and I slid out of his grasp easily. 'No! I don't—I don't deserve this.' My voice cracked and I dashed water out of my eyes. 'Not until I get him back.'

Ụwafụlamiro stepped around to block me from leaving, but he didn't try to touch me. 'That's foolish, Sọmadịna. You don't deserve what? Care? Touch? Affection?'

'I let that man take him!' I screamed, my grief roaring. 'I killed Chidị! Everyone back home wants nothing to do with me, don't you understand? Why can't you see that? What can you think I deserve?' I tried to slip past him, but he took a calm step and blocked me again.

'It wasn't your fault,' he replied, and a guttural growl ripped out of me.

'I need people to *stop saying that.* It's not true!'

'Sọmadịna. It wasn't your fault.'

I was becoming an animal, trapped in a corner, trying to run from his eyes. 'You don't know me. That god – she *took* me and she *changed* me and I am not the Sọmadịna you left behind anymore! Let me go, Ụwafụlamiro. Just let me go.'

'Never.'

I paused in shock, first at the iron in his voice, then at the silvery tears in his eyes.

'What?'

Ụwafụlamiro rolled his shoulders and tilted his head back to will away the tears. When his gaze lowered back to mine, he was resolute. Gentle, but resolute. 'I love you. I love Jayaike. You are my best friends. I can't give up on you and let you start hating yourself like this, Sọmadịna, because *he* wouldn't do it and he's not here. He's not here, so I have to be the one to do it. You understand? I won't allow you.'

I blinked a few times, unable to find words. My waistbeads were dripping water to the ground and both of our short wrappers were clinging to our legs. My anger had evaporated, clouding up into the sky, and I felt wrung out.

'I understand,' I said.

Ụwafụlamiro raised an eyebrow and held out his arms. 'Can I hold you? Or will you bite my hand off?'

I grumbled, but I walked into his embrace and let him enfold me against his damp chest. 'Don't get used to this,' I muttered.

'I wouldn't dare,' he answered, soft humor in his voice. We stood like that for a few moments, then he spoke again. 'I know you're different, Sọmadịna. I know it's terrifying and Ala is doing harsh things with you. I can't understand most of it, but I'm here with you. I'm changing too. We were always going to change. But the love doesn't change, you hear?'

I thought about what he was saying and remembered other things he had said. 'You said you love me and you love Jayaike. Is it—is it in the same way?' My face was tucked under his chin so he couldn't see my expression and I couldn't see his. Ụwafụlamiro didn't answer for a little bit.

'No,' he finally said. 'No, it's not the same.'

We returned to our room, where Nkadi was already waiting for us. She didn't ask questions, even though it was obvious that both of us had been crying, and I was endlessly grateful for that. Instead, she helped us pack our bags and wrap our weapons. She braided my hair into thin black rows along my skull and bound coral into the ends while Ụwafụlamiro sat at the window and wound his ivory curls around his fingers, watching us lazily. Once we were ready, all three of us collected our things and went downstairs to stand in front of Zerenjọ as he stirred camwood pigment in a coconut shell. Using the tip of an eagle's feather, he carefully painted lines and whorls on our bare chests. When my turn came, I tried not to breathe too fast as the wet color slowly marked my skin. My spear was clutched in my hand tightly and I let the warm heft of it calm me. I was as ready as I could be for what was to come. Zerenjọ put down the shell and feather when he was done, then folded his arms as he looked us over.

'Are you ready?' he asked Nkadi.

My sister's mouth was tight and tense, but she reached out and grabbed hold of my hand, then Ụwafụlamiro's, her fingers digging into our skin. 'Yes,' she replied, tilting her head high. Her symbols were by far the most complicated – they danced over her skin and almost seemed to move on their own.

A flash of pride shot through our grandfather's eyes. 'Good,' he answered. 'Sọmadịna, do you feel the pain approaching?'

I didn't know how he had figured out the timing, but he was right. It was mild enough that I had been ignoring it, but it was there. I gave a small nod.

'Now, focus on the bond,' Zerenjọ said. 'Disregard the pain and look for the pull.'

I closed my eyes and obeyed. The pain kicked up a notch, but I could see the old bone bond. It was now stretched past its capacity and pulsing weakly before it dipped into that darkness. 'I don't feel a pull yet.'

'Wait for it. Have your powder ready.'

I fumbled for the crocodile leather bag at my waist and took a pinch of the powder into my free hand. The pain swirled in my head like a whip made of thorns. Maybe this was useless. Maybe I wouldn't be able to track him.

Zerenjọ's voice cut into my thoughts sharply. 'Look for the pull, Sọmadịna!'

I had to try. Clearing my head, I focused back on the bond and I breathed into the pain. The pain was useful. The pain would show me where my brother was. The pain was a mark of what shouldn't exist – the distance between me and Jayaike. It was a tool. I just needed a direction. Closing my eyes, I lifted my arm and let the pain guide me along the bond, the wavering stretch of it.

I pointed with a closed fist, the powder warming in my palm. 'There,' I said. 'That's where it goes.'

'Well done,' my grandfather said softly. 'Hold on to the bond but relax – staying tense will worsen the pain. Trust in the connection. It's hard this first time—that's why I painted the camwood to help. Next time, it will be easier.'

I trembled as I took a deep breath and released the tension from my muscles. The bond stayed where it was.

'That is your direction,' he continued. 'Nkadi, can you tap into your sister?'

I gasped as I felt her presence shimmer into my mind, bright and green like a forest. My hand tightened even more against hers. I didn't know she could do that.

'I'm here,' she said out loud.

'It's time.' Zerenjọ's voice was strong and sure, like he knew that's what we needed to send us off. Not a scrap of doubt, even as uncertainty was swelling in my chest. 'Your powder now, Sọmadịna.'

I threw it under my tongue, grateful for the antidote I had tried to reject at first. I could already tell that, untreated, this pain would eventually break my mind into pieces, or just kill me.

Zerenjọ was still talking. 'Remember you must refuel as soon as you stop. Continue until Nkadi slows the fold down. That's when you can start looking for where there will be people and food. There is a coil of copper in your bag so you can buy things, and some small food you can eat while inside the fold. Do not rely on this food. It will not be enough. You hear me?'

I nodded and glanced at Ụwafụlamiro, who swallowed hard but nodded as well. Nkadi squeezed our hands. Zerenjọ touched three fingers to our chests, right on the drying camwood stains, and a shock shuddered through me. I heard Nkadi hiss in a sharp breath.

'Are you ready?' she asked us in a rough whisper.

'Yes.' Ụwafụlamiro's voice shook a little.

'Yes,' I repeated, then opened my eyes to see the air funneling into a channel before me. Terror stung inside my heart but I swallowed it down. For Jayaike, I would do anything. I had my sister. I had my best friend. Everything was going to be fine.

'May Ala protect you,' murmured my grandfather as he stepped back. 'Go.'

Nkadi took a step forward, tugging us gently along with her. The fold wrapped us in that thick air, warping sound.

'Don't look back,' Zerenjọ added, his voice already muffling behind us.

It was madness to be doing this without him. I had already lost so much of my family. 'Grandfather?' I shouted. 'Grandfather!'

His voice came calmly from behind us. 'Hold on to each other, children. Go now.'

Nkạdi pulled at my hand and we stumbled into the channel. It swept us up, bending grass beneath it as trees started to whir past, blending into a green blur. I slowed down by a tiny fraction, frightened, but then I heard Zerenjọ's voice spinning toward me.

'Go!' he commanded. My twin bond pulled on my spirit and my sister pulled on my flesh.

We went.

CHAPTER THIRTEEN

THE FOLDING WAS TERRIFYING. EVERYTHING WAS DISTORTED, AND the air was so heavy it felt like I was choking on it. Nkadi strode one step ahead of us, her body bent forward as if she was fighting a great wind. I turned my head with difficulty to look for Ụwafụlamiro. He was pushing forward with one arm raised in front of his face, as if to shield his eyes from the blurred world we were making our way through. Pressure dug into my ears.

'What's happening?' I asked, trying not to panic.

Nkadi looked back at me. 'Don't worry,' she said. Her voice was deeper and a little slow, but I could still understand her easily. 'The world is thick around us when it's folded like this. Stay focused on the direction of your bond with Jayaike and pull on my hand if I start moving off course.'

I nodded in agreement and took a closer look at the world we were walking through. It had colors and smells, brighter and more intense than I was used to, flickering past us swiftly. There was a fallen tree, gone in a blink. There was a river, and we crossed it in a single stride. The undergrowth of bushes and plants brushed against my knees and then was gone just as quickly. The thick green of the Sacred Forest vanished and we fell upon a stretch of water wider than I had ever seen in my life. It was my first time leaving our island, and I couldn't help looking over at Ụwafụlamiro. He smiled and I knew he understood – he'd traveled to other islands with his parents; he knew how momentous it was to leave the borders of everything we'd learned about. I didn't know if the water beneath us was an enormous river or if I was looking at the bits of sea that separated us from other islands created in the Split, but foam brushed against the soles of our feet anyway.

We passed it all too quickly, like a storm, over a beach and then through stretches of farmland, rows and rows of staked yam arranged in ridges. I thought of Ahụdi's stories of when the magic rippled out from the dịbịas breaking the earth to end the Starvation War. From the sun's place in the sky and the painful tug of the bond, I could tell we were heading north. We were far away from the Split and I hoped we found Jayaike before we drew too close to it, but all the history of our land pointed in the same direction. Were we retracing the path the magic had taken when it washed over the world and culled the people? I tried to imagine what it would have looked like – thundering ground as the islands were formed, churning water rising up in the cracks. There would have been screaming as the gifts tore through people.

Everything we passed looked normal now – settlements like our town, other forests, farms and such. People had enough food. The war was over and I had been born into this new world. How I wished my twin was here to witness it with me as we passed through lands my feet had never touched.

'Can anyone see us?' Ụwafụlamiro asked.

'No,' Nkadi replied. 'From the outside, we're just a whisper of wind, a fragment of sound passing by.'

Good, I thought. Being unnoticed was a relief – I wondered if that's how Ụwafụlamiro felt every time he disappeared. With each folded step we took, it became easier for me to follow the twin bond. It didn't feel like we had been in the fold long when Nkadi shouted for us to look out for a town. 'I'm going to start slowing us down.'

'No! We have to catch up with them – can't we go longer?'

My sister shook her head. 'We have to take breaks, Sọmadịna. Grandfather warned us.' She handed me some akara and a piece of honeycomb. 'Here, eat before we arrive, so we can have some time to find food. I see something over to the left.'

'I think it's a village,' Ụwafụlamiro agreed, squinting. We ate hurriedly as Nkadi redirected the folding toward the town. Her face was strained with effort, and I regretted my outburst. She looked like she had pushed herself even further than she should have.

'Take it easy,' I whispered to her. 'You can handle this.'

Nkadi bit down on her lip and didn't answer. The thick air of the folding was thinning out as we slowed, and a beat later, we were inside the village and its small houses were becoming unblurred in my vision. Nkadi directed us toward the main square, then she grunted and staggered, and we found our bodies abruptly stopping, suspended mere inches over the ground. It was like hitting a wall, and we all dropped down in painful heaps. My spear clattered to the ground and the village people walking about stopped in their tracks, gasping as they stared at us in shock.

Almost immediately, I could feel the aftereffects of the folding start – a terrible hunger twisting everything inside me and cramping my muscles. I groaned and clutched my stomach, swamped with pain. Strangers were looking at us with both curiosity and suspicion, gathering into small groups to whisper to each other.

'Help us,' Ụwafụlamiro choked out. 'Please . . .'

The flesh was beginning to thin off his face as he spoke, shading gray caves into his cheeks. No one moved and a few people pointed to him, clearly intrigued by his ghostly coloring. They kept watching and did nothing, his pleas going ignored.

'May-maybe they d-don't speak our language,' I whispered, my voice cracking with pain as muscles wasted away under my skin. But I could also see discomfort on some of their faces, transparent guilt, even as they continued to stand there without helping us. That was when I became afraid, when I realized they were going to just . . . leave us there. Nkadi was lying on the ground unconscious, my hand still wrapped in hers. I tried to crawl closer to her, but my body could not move.

We're going to die, I thought. *We're going to waste away here in front of all these strangers, get sucked into ourselves and become skeletons wrapped in leathery skin, lying in a sandy square.* How foolish I had been to think we could do this on our own, without Zerenjọ. The three of us were just children. We didn't stand a chance. The pain tangled up with fear inside me, and it got so loud that I just closed my eyes and let the ache envelop me in a dark redness. Everything could just fade away. It would be fine. Jayaike would find me one day. Maybe if the bond broke with my death, he would come looking for me instead.

I was pulled from that warm, painful place by a touch of metal being pushed between my lips as someone spooned heavily sweetened pap into my mouth. It took me a few moments to swallow it down, but then my body caught on and I was eating ravenously. A large bowl was lifted to my mouth and I drank down the warm food, my flesh gasping in relief. It felt like endless minutes passed until the edge of that ferocious hunger was taken off, and only then did I look up at the person who was feeding me. A young face smiled down at me with dark skin and large black eyes, their lips stained like ixora flowers and a delicate gap between their top front teeth.

‘More food is coming,’ they said. ‘Eat, eat.’

Behind them, Nkadi was sitting up, drinking just as hungrily from another bowl. My heart beat easier seeing her awake. Ụwafụlamiro had dropped his bowl and was drinking palm wine from a calabash, white rivulets spilling from the junction of his lips. I’d never seen him touch the liquor before. The young stranger caught the look on my face and patted my arm reassuringly. ‘It is rich, the body will use the sugar from the alcohol to build his flesh back.’

‘How do you know?’ I croaked. They smiled again, laugh lines forming in their burnt-sugar skin.

‘I have seen people like you before,’ they answered. ‘In another place far away. They always collapse when their magic runs out. There was a man, he didn’t get help in time and his body ate him up. We found him behind my uncle’s barn. We buried him.’ They handed me a calabash, and the scent of honeyed palm wine drifted up from it. ‘Drink.’

I obeyed, letting the fermented drink sting its way through my body. Maybe it would’ve made me tipsy under other circumstances, but my body was too ravenous to even process it like that. When I managed to sit up, dust from the ground clung to my skin and clothes. A little boy with a shaved head ran up holding a big earthen bowl, which he placed down with exaggerated care. The bystanders were still hanging around, gossiping heartily and making not a single move to help us. I felt a raw anger unfurl inside me, but the hunger pushed it aside and had me reaching for the bowl, which was full of cassava fufu. Ụwafụlamiro reached out for my other hand and squeezed it tightly, then he pulled Nkadi closer to us. We all scooped up handfuls of fufu, eating it as quickly as we could. The boy left and returned with another bowl, this one containing egusi soup, thick with fish and vegetables. The stranger with me sat down cross-legged, arranging their feet on top of their thighs as they watched us eat. The boy kept trotting away and returning with more items: a calabash filled with honey, a basket of roasted maize, and some dried meat.

We ate for a long time, right there in the middle of the square, ignoring everything around us. Occasionally, I would steal a look at the stranger in between hurried mouthfuls. They had bushy eyebrows and darkened eyelids, and a petaled mouth that seemed to always be curving in a little half smile. Their hair was threaded in an intricate sculpture and there was something fundamentally still about them, a calmness that seemed to pulse out from their bones. The little boy came to lean against their side after carrying out the food. He started playing with a wooden puzzle, barely sparing us a glance.

'What's your name?' asked Ụwafụlamiro, his mouth full.

'Obi,' the stranger replied. 'And this is my small brother, Uju.'

'I'm Sọmadịna,' I said. 'This is Ụwafụlamiro, and that's my big sister, Nkadi.' I cast a worried glance at her. Nkadi hadn't said a word since we arrived, and there was a hollow look in her eyes. Her skin seemed as thin as a spiderweb.

'You have beautiful names,' Obi said. 'Sweet to the ear.'

I smiled politely, then covered my mouth, embarrassed. Now that we'd met the worst of our hunger, I was painfully aware of how terrible we looked, with food smeared over our faces and spilled over our bodies.

Obi showed the gap in their teeth again. 'Don't disturb yourself about that. There is no shame in healing your body.'

They whispered to the boy and he fetched us a bowl of water to clean up with and a soft cloth to dry our faces. We kept thanking Obi profusely, which they waved off. Ụwafụlamiro brought out the copper coil and offered to pay for the food, but Obi jumped up and pushed it out of sight.

'Don't show that in front of this many people!' they whispered roughly. 'And don't offer to pay me again.' Obi looked around the village square and made a face. 'In fact, let's go to my family house, now that you can walk. All these vultures are getting too much entertainment from watching us.'

Next to me, Nkadi flicked her gaze up to the crowd that had gathered a short distance away, and something dark flared in her eyes, dark enough that it made me pause. 'They would have let us die,' she spat, as if she finally had enough energy to be furious. 'They would have let us die like *animals.*'

Ụwafụlamiro caught her expression in the same moment

that I did, and we exchanged a worried look. 'We have to go,' he said to me, his voice low. I was still angry, but Ụwafụlamiro shook his head and put an arm around me. 'That's between them and their gods. Hapụ ya,' he said. 'Leave it alone.'

He was right. Nkadi had too much power to be in this situation and be this angry. We had to get her away from the crowd. Obi got to their feet and we scrambled up behind them. I picked up my spear and took Nkadi's hand firmly in mine. She let me pull her along and I felt like I was a leash holding a storm in check. Ụwafụlamiro adjusted the straps of his bag before we followed Obi through the town and to their family house. Uju brought up the rear with his arms full of empty bowls.

Obi's house was built lower than we were used to in our village and with a different system of thatching. We had to bend our heads to enter the doorway, but once inside, the house was cool and airy, with dyed raffia mats strewn around the floor. Ụwafụlamiro helped Uju put away the bowls and then we all sat on the raffia mats, drinking water out of clay cups. Nkadi was now disturbingly silent, but I couldn't ask her about it in front of these strangers, no matter how kind they were.

'What brings you here?' asked Obi as Uju stood behind them, playing with the threaded branches of their hair. It was easy to see their family resemblance with their faces next to each other, and it made me think of my twin. Alarm shot through me as I remembered to check the bond that still linked me to Jayaike. To my relief, the bond was still there, and so was its direction. I hadn't lost him, not yet.

'We're looking for her twin brother,' Ụwafụlamiro said to Obi.

Uju flickered his eyes toward us and muttered something under his breath.

'Ehn? Say that again.' Obi angled their head back, exposing a smooth throat, and Uju repeated what he said a little louder. His voice was soft and light, like a breeze passing through a ray of sunlight.

'Sand.'

Ụwafụlamiro frowned. 'Sand?'

Obi tapped their fingers against their chin and gazed at us. 'Ohhhh, I see it now.'

'See what?' I asked.

'You're the other boy's sister,' they said slowly. 'Uju said he looked like red sand.'

Nkadi snapped her head around and my stomach jumped up. 'You saw Jayaike?' she asked, her voice sharp and slicing.

'That's his name?' Obi moved their shoulders eloquently, and their collarbone angled under their skin. 'He barely spoke to us. It's his uncle we spoke to. They only stayed one night. You two really look alike, you know.'

Cold fear made all the food in my stomach heavy, and my tongue felt too thick for my mouth.

'His uncle,' Nkadi said, her eyes narrowing.

'Blue!' Uju sang out. Obi laughed at him fondly.

'Yes, blue! Good job remembering. He wore blue cloths. A beautiful color. We don't see it often, that dye.'

'What was his name?' Nkadi asked. She looked like the golden leopard she was – I had forgotten how intense that energy could be, the clawed focus.

Obi took a moment to think. 'Ejike,' they finally said. 'His name was Ejike.'

The room fell away.

I was dropping through mists, the spray from a floating river hitting me in the face, then I landed on sand, wet and compact. My cheek smacked against the floor on impact, rattling my teeth. I lay there, winded, and a man's bare feet walked slowly over to me. I heard him sigh as he crouched next to me, and I wanted to kill him because I knew exactly who he was.

I spat sand and blood out of my mouth. 'Ejike,' I growled, and pushed myself up till I was sitting. We were surrounded by nothing but clouds and water, stranded on a patch of land. The man in blue shook his head as he met my eyes. His irises still swam in that evil yellow.

'Your new friend shouldn't have told you my name,' he said, clicking his tongue disapprovingly. 'I might have to kill them for that.'

'You won't live long enough to do that,' I snapped out.

He just laughed. 'What are you going to do, small god?

Even if you could kill me now – a child's thought, by the way – you have no idea where your pretty, pretty brother is.'

'I'll find him.'

Ejike widened his eyes comically. 'I should *hope* you find him, considering that was my plan from the beginning.'

'Why did you take him?' Maybe I could get some answers, understand what kind of creature this was so that I could tell Nkadi and we could figure out how to kill him.

'Because I'm going to eat his power. And then I'm going to eat yours, godtouched or not. And then I might eat your sister's power as well, just for a treat.' He shrugged as if none of it mattered. 'I have nothing to hide, small god. Knowing what I want won't help you stop me.'

His indifference was more terrifying than any other emotion I could think of. I struggled to keep my calm, even though my fingers dug into the sand beneath them. 'You know we belong to a god, and you stole Jayaike anyway?'

Ejike hissed in a breath, nearly moaning. I thought it might be in fear of my mentioning the god, but to my horror, I realized it was a sound of pleasure.

'Jayaike,' he crooned. 'Why, thank you for his name, little girl. He wouldn't give it to me, you know, and I need a person's name before I can eat their gift.'

I bit back a scream of rage at my own carelessness. 'Ala will strike you down,' I growled. 'I will hold your life in my hand and I will watch you *die*.'

Ejike stood up and laughed. 'Where was your god when I took your brother from the bed you sleep in?' he asked. 'You are a fool if you think your little crocodile deity cares about you, and an even bigger fool if you think you can summon her. She uses *you,* small god, not the other way around.'

I pushed myself up to my feet as well. My knees were skinned. 'What do you *want*?'

He glanced at me in mild surprise. 'I want to eat your god's power, of course. Couldn't you see where this was going? When I eat your power, I will eat part of her too. I can't wait to find out what she tastes like.'

He wanted to eat a god's power? 'That's impossible.'

Ejike threw his head back and laughed and laughed. The inside of his mouth was deep scarlet and his teeth were sharp. 'Oh, little girl.' He leaned down toward me and grinned into my face. 'How do you think I got here?'

He reached out and poked me in the chest, and the world was lost to me once again.

I woke up on an unfamiliar sleeping mat that smelled faintly of dried fish. A soft conversation was happening around me.

'What about your family?' Ụwafụlamiro was asking. 'Is it just the two of you?'

Obi's voice answered, 'Our parents are traders. It's hard

when they're gone, but then they bring us back amazing things from all kinds of places, and it makes up for it.'

'I know what you mean.' I could hear Ụwafụlamiro smiling. 'Mine are traders too.'

I blinked my eyes halfway open, pretending to still be out of it so they wouldn't notice me yet. I was in a small room that held the sleeping mat and a low bench. Obi was lounging on the bench, their strong thighs and calves outlined under their long wrapper. Brass rings were stacked on their ankles, clattering each time they moved. I hadn't noticed those before. Ụwafụlamiro was sitting on the floor next to the sleeping mat I was on. He was leaning against the wall, his head turned toward Obi as they talked. I could see the taut curve of his neck, and suddenly I didn't want them whispering together anymore.

'Where's Nkadi?' I asked. My voice sounded hoarse and scratchy. Ụwafụlamiro whipped his head around, back to me, and reached over to stroke my head.

'Sọmadịna? You're awake.'

'Let me fetch the dịbịa.' Obi rose smoothly from the bench and left the room.

I felt dizzy, like my head was too heavy to lift up from the mat. Ụwafụlamiro murmured a comforting stream of words to me until Nkadi came into the room and knelt by my side.

'Where did you go?' she asked me immediately.

'I was dreaming,' I mumbled back, and my sister exchanged a look with Ụwafụlamiro. He turned to Obi.

'Can we be alone for a moment, please?' It was blunt, but they didn't seem to mind. They just smiled and nodded, shutting the wooden door behind them as they left. Still, Nkadi spoke in lowered tones.

'Did you see him?'

I didn't know if she meant Jayaike. 'I saw the hunter,' I whispered back. 'Don't use his name. It draws his attention.'

Nkadi nodded. 'You don't look well, Sọmadịna. I think you need to sleep some more.'

I shook my head. 'What if he comes back?'

'Don't worry. I have medicine for that.' She was untying one of the bags at her waist, which I always thought were full of charms. 'I wish you'd told me you were worried about your dreams. This will protect you in them.' Nkadi took out a small bundle of dried leaves and fragrant wood, then struck a flint and lit it aflame, leaning it against a stone so that the smoke blew in my direction. 'Sleep now,' she ordered.

'We'll find Jayaike tomorrow,' Ụwafụlamiro added.

His words set a hungry hope unfurling in my chest, and I fell asleep with a prayer tucked into my cheek that he was right.

CHAPTER FOURTEEN

IT WAS STILL DARK WHEN I OPENED MY EYES AGAIN, AND THE AIR tugged with a feeling that set my nerves on edge. I sat up and looked around. Ụwafụlamiro lay fast asleep on another mat next to me, but Nkadi wasn't in the room. Panic rang through my chest and I shot out of the bed, glancing around wildly. People could be taken at night, and Ejike could walk through the spirit world. Ụwafụlamiro snuffled and turned over in his sleep, his face slack and his mouth soft as moonlight drifted in through the window, lazily draping itself over his lower lip. I went to the small arched window and exhaled shakily as I saw Nkadi standing outside in the compound, looking up at the sky. Making sure not to disturb Ụwafụlamiro, I let myself out and walked over to join my sister.

Crickets were singing in the night air and Nkadi's skin was luminous under the moon. She looked over at me with dark and solemn eyes, and I wondered if I was standing with Nkadi my sister or Nkadi the dịbịa. Maybe we were all becoming a family of strangers.

'You couldn't sleep?' I asked.

Nkadi shook her head and looked back up at the moon but said nothing.

I frowned. She should have been resting and my sister was always the practical one, so I knew something was wrong. I nudged her with my shoulder and her body rippled away, then back toward me.

'I failed,' she said finally, letting her body lean slightly against me. 'One day in, and I already failed.'

'What are you talking about? You got us here.' I couldn't have imagined how powerful my sister would become when they first took her, but watching her fold the land yesterday had imprinted it deeply in me. That was strong magic, strong medicine. 'You've done so well, Nkadi. Grandfather would be proud.'

She shook her head. 'I folded for too long. I should have stopped earlier, and we wouldn't have burned up so much.'

I slid my hand into hers and squeezed it tightly, finally understanding why she had been so quiet when we first arrived. 'Isn't this your first time doing this by yourself? Without Grandfather?'

Nkadi nodded. 'It is.'

'And do dịbịas usually do this kind of work at your age?' I was just guessing, but it felt like a safe bet.

'No,' Nkadi replied softly. 'I'm still an apprentice. It takes years before we're allowed to fold alone.'

The skin of her palm was cool and I squeezed her hand again, trying to warm her up. 'You see?' I said. 'You're already doing something spectacular. Even if it's not perfect, you can't compare yourself to Grandfather. I already know he would be pleased with what you've done so far.'

Some of the tension seeped out of Nkadi's shoulders and she squeezed my hand back. 'Thank you,' she said. 'How are you managing?'

Her question was gentle, and a surprising wave of emotion rose through me. So many things hurt in my spirit. Chidị was dead. A god had used me and spat me out to a community that hated me for it, that would have put me to death. Jayaike was still missing, my other half, my soul's reflection. I still blamed myself for it, for not warning him about the hunter, for not telling Ahụdi or Nkadi or someone who could have *protected* my brother. Mama had turned her back on us and Papa had chosen his wife over his children. It felt like a litany of grief that wouldn't stop, that just wanted to break more and more of my already shattered heart. Before I could stop them, tears filled my eyes, and I tried to dash them away quickly on the back of my hand.

'Oh, Sọmadịna!' Nkadi let go of my hand to wrap me in a tight hug, and I immediately burst into tears. I *missed* my brother. I missed him so much I could barely stand to think about it. I wanted him back. I wanted his calm surrounding me again, his eyes echoed in mine, his hand curled around mine. But right then, in my sister's arms, I realized I had also missed *her*. When Zerenjọ took her away, I'd had my twin. I'd always had my twin, and no matter what else happened, we were together. Maybe that's why I had been able to withstand Nkadi's absence, the gap she left in our house when she was gone. I couldn't imagine what it was like for Mama to lose her firstborn. But it was different with me and my twin. Mama lost Jayaike too, but she said she didn't want him back. As for me, she didn't even lose me.

She threw me away.

The grief slid to the side, making way for a resentment that burned through my veins like molten iron. Nkadi pulled away to look into my face. 'What is it?' she asked.

My mouth twisted. 'Mama,' I said.

Nkadi grimaced. 'I know.' She looped her arm around my shoulders and stood next to me. 'None of us thought she was going to behave like that.'

'I can't go home, Nkadi. Maybe Jayaike will be able to, but I—I just can't. Not when she doesn't want me there.'

There was so much more I didn't say out loud. What kind of mother threw her own children away? What kind of mother had a missing child and *wanted* him to stay missing?

I knew Mama was hurting deeper than anything I could understand. I could even tell that some of it involved Zerenjọ and the way she felt about dịbịas, but I couldn't forgive her. I also couldn't predict how my twin would react, not now that we'd been torn into two people – but I wouldn't forgive him either if he dared to forgive her.

'Don't think about any of that now,' Nkadi said. 'One thing at a time. We find Jayaike first, and then we will take care of the rest together. You, me, Grandfather, Ahụdi, and Da Ọlụchi.' Her mouth curved slightly. 'And like Ahụdi said, Kesandụ in spirit. Your people are around you, Sọmadịna.'

I nodded tearfully. When she put it like that, it didn't sound so bad. I noticed she hadn't mentioned Papa, but that made sense. He had chosen Mama over me and Jayaike, after all.

'Don't worry, little sister.' Nkadi looked at me and moonlight struck her eyes. 'You will always have a family.'

As the crickets sang around us, it felt like the truth, and I let it comfort me. She still didn't ask me about the waking dream I'd had, maybe because she was being my sister, not the dịbịa, and I had missed it enough that I didn't offer up the details either.

It could wait till morning.

When I woke up a second time, the sun was hammering on my eyelids, and this time it was Ụwafụlamiro who wasn't in his bed. Nkadi was already awake, organizing the things in her bag.

'Good, you're awake. We're leaving soon.'

I nodded and scrambled off the sleeping mat. 'I need to tell you something.'

Nkadi's head swiveled sharply in my direction. 'What is it?'

She was definitely the dịbịa again, a keen edge with wary eyes.

'The hunter I saw when I dreamed yesterday, he told me he wants to eat the deity's power.'

Nkadi straightened and frowned. 'That's not possible.'

'He said he's done it before.'

Her mouth pressed into a tense line. 'What else did he say?' She wasn't reprimanding me for not telling her this sooner, at least not outright, but I still felt the sting under her words. It was followed by a surge of shame when I remembered what else I had to confess.

'I made a mistake,' I mumbled, hanging my head so I didn't have to look at her face. Her footsteps sounded through the room as she walked up to me, then her hand clasped my chin gently as she lifted my head up.

'You cannot make a mistake,' Nkadi said softly. 'You are dealing with an impossible situation. Everything you do, you are doing your best, with no training in these kinds of matters. You understand?'

Tears filled my eyes anyway. 'I gave him Jayaike's *name.* I didn't mean to; it just slipped out and he was so happy, he was so *hungry,* and he said Jayaike had been refusing to give it but now he has it, because I *gave* it to him and he said he needed it to eat Jayaike's gift!'

Nkadi wiped the tears that had streaked down my cheeks as I was talking. 'He might try to do that,' she agreed, sounding far calmer than I thought she had any reason to. 'But, Ṣọmadịna, I need you to try and remember something.'

I sniffled. 'What?'

Nkadi gave me a ghost of a smile. 'First of all, take your powder, but only half a dose, we still need you to direct the fold.'

'I don't need it,' I said automatically, and she rolled her eyes.

'Your face is doing that thing again where you're in pain and you're pushing it away.'

I was always in pain. It made it hard for me to notice the vague beginnings of the distance pain from the twin bond. I took my half pinch of medicine obediently and waited for my sister to continue.

'You are not the only child of the deity involved in this.' She tightened a piece of coral in my hair that had come loose while I was sleeping. 'Things are happening to Jayaike as surely as they are happening to you. He will also be coming into his own power, so whether that man has his name or not, he does not know who he is dealing with.' I watched as she turned and looked around the room to make sure she had gathered all her things. 'Have faith in Ala,' she added. 'And consider that the deity has faith in both of you.'

If there were words to be said in response to that, I didn't have them yet.

Ụwafụlamiro's voice filtered through the window and I glanced outside to see him lounging against a palm tree. He was drinking from a fresh coconut and laughing with Obi, who was taking out the last of the thread in their hair. Once freed from the thread, Obi's hair stood around their face like a small black eclipse. I didn't like the way Ụwafụlamiro bent his head toward them as they talked together, but I told myself it shouldn't matter as I washed up by the earthen pot in the corner of the room. There was nothing to be afraid of. We were leaving and we would probably never see Obi again. I slung my bag across my flat body and went outside to meet them.

'I'll be there shortly,' Nkadi called after me.

Ụwafụlamiro and Obi greeted me with smiles, and Ụwafụlamiro offered his coconut to me. I accepted it and took a sip, the freshness bursting over my tongue.

'Obi is insisting they have something to show us before we go,' he said. 'I've been trying all my charm, but they won't tell me anything more.'

I pretended to be shocked. '*All* your charm? And it still didn't work?'

He shoved at me lightly and I bared my teeth in play. Obi

smiled as they watched us, then their eyes slid over as Nkadi came out of the house.

'Are we ready?' she asked.

Obi stepped forward. 'There is someone you have to see.'

My sister raised an eyebrow. 'Is that so?'

Obi grinned. 'Trust me. It will help you find your brother.'

Nkadi's eyes flattened at the mention of Jayaike. 'I don't like vague statements about even more vague people,' she said. 'Speak plainly.'

'Of course.' Obi's face sobered and they clasped their hands in front of them. 'We have an Oracle in our village, and this morning I received a message that she would like to see you.'

I was immediately intrigued. I had heard faint stories about Oracles, a specialized type of dịbịa who could see both into the future and into the shadows, into things that people wanted hidden, into the underside of your heart and the inside seams of your desires. Oracles were rare, though, enough for many people to think they were stories, not a true thing. Nkadi looked doubtful.

'I'm not sure we have enough time to make a detour,' she began, but Obi was already shaking their head before she finished speaking.

'We do not ignore a message from the Oracle.'

'We are not held to your customs,' Nkadi retorted.

Obi frowned. 'Let me say that another way. We *cannot* ignore a message from the Oracle.' They sounded more serious than I'd ever heard them, much older for a moment. 'I urge you to reconsider.'

Ụwafụlamiro nudged Nkadi. 'You can't say no to this,' he whispered.

I agreed. 'We have to do everything that could help find Jayaike.'

Nkadi looked at both of us, then set her jaw and nodded. 'Very well.' She turned back to Obi. 'Let's go, then.'

Obi laughed in a loud bark, shedding their seriousness like bean chaff blowing away in the wind. They fluffed their hair out with their fingers. 'This will be exciting! Follow me.'

We followed as they led us behind a row of houses and into a heavily fenced area. I could hear growls and roars coming from behind the reinforced walls, a wild chatter that was making me nervous. Nkadi's eyes were narrowed into slits and one of her medicine bags was resting easily in her palm.

'Where are we, Obi?' I asked.

'You'll see,' they answered, mischief all over their face as they pushed open a large bamboo door.

We found ourselves in front of a short, fat man holding a long cowhide whip by his side. He wore a faded red wrapper and was shouting at some boys who were running around carrying large bundles and pots. As the door opened, the man spun his head around to look at us and I saw the large, bulging scar that ran across half of his face, slicing across one eye. He seemed angry to see us, until his good eye fell on Obi.

'Oh, it's you,' he complained, but with a small smile.

'Ọgaranya,' they greeted him, using both hands to clasp one of his.

'I don't have time for you to play with the cats today,' he said, ill-tempered. 'Someone forgot to feed half the pen this morning and now all of them are in the foulest of moods.'

'It's no problem, Ọgaranya. I'm here on business anyway.'

He laughed shortly. 'Business with what? Unless you marry me, I can't sell you a cat.'

Obi shook their head, amused. 'We're here to see the Oracle. She asked us to come.'

The man folded his arms and whistled a long tune. 'Is that so?' he said with wonder. 'She hasn't seen anyone in a long time.' He looked over us, his eyes snagging on Nkadi, then he jerked his head to the side. 'Go ahead, then.'

Obi led us past him, down a corridor, and out into an open courtyard. It was full of spreading palms and gleaming stones, but it only took half a second before we noticed the enormous jungle cats everywhere, large enough to reach our shoulders. Some were stretched out, asleep in the sunlight, while others strolled among the plants, their eyes slitted and gleaming, their pelts shiny. They were black and dappled, spotted and marked, all with vicious teeth and long whiskers. I gasped and Ụwafụlamiro gave a small whimper next to me.

'Is that a wild leopard?' he whispered loudly, pointing to a beast that was yawning enough for us to see inside the wet cavern of its mouth.

'That's actually a *few* leopards,' Nkadi replied, looking around cautiously. Her body seemed coiled, ready to spring, or run, or attack – I wasn't sure which.

Obi patted my back. 'Don't worry, none of them will hurt you.' They pointed toward the center of the courtyard and we could hear the sound of running water. 'The Oracle will see you there.'

I glanced at them. 'You're not coming?'

They shrugged in response. 'I'm not the one who was summoned.'

Ụwafụlamiro grabbed my hand and Nkadi gave us a steady look. 'Let's go,' she said. 'We don't have time to waste.'

'I'll wait here for you.' Obi sank gracefully to the ground cross-legged and tilted their face up to the sun.

'Thank you,' Nkadi replied. 'We appreciate your help.'

Obi just smiled and waved us on, so Ụwafụlamiro and I followed Nkadi as she walked regally past the wild cats, who tracked us with those eerie eyes of theirs, membranes flickering across as they blinked. The center of the courtyard had a circle of carved benches laid out with a fountain in the middle. A woman was standing by the water, watching the way the light broke into patterns against it. She looked up and I had to hide my surprise. I'd expected the Oracle to be old, someone Ahụdi's age, but this woman was shockingly young. She looked barely a few years older than Nkadi, at least until I looked into her eyes, and then it was like being punched by centuries, a horrifying sense of time stretching in every direction. Her mouth pulled into an empty smile as she looked back at me.

'Daughter of Ala,' she said, and my skin crawled in discomfort. 'Girl who is not a girl.'

Nkadi sank into a deep bow, the skin around her mouth tight and pale. 'We greet you,' she said, and I was impressed that her voice didn't shake.

The Oracle shifted her gaze to my sister. 'Apprentice. You are welcome.'

Ụwafụlamiro copied the bow and I did too, although I was hesitant to lower my eyes and expose the back of my neck to her. As we straightened, the Oracle was watching us, and I noticed that her body was unnaturally still, like she wasn't even quite alive. Her black eyes swirled back to me.

'You have questions for me,' she said. 'You may ask them.'

A thousand possibilities shot through my mind – questions about my future, about what Jayaike would be like when we found him, did we have enough *time* to find him, how could we move faster, would Mama ever forgive my existence, would I ever forgive my parents, could the Oracle talk to the deity and ask her why she would do all this to me – endless turns of uncertainty that clamored in my head. In the end, I asked none of those questions because, for a moment, I wasn't the brokenhearted girl who had lost almost everything thanks to a god's claim. I was a hunter, and I wanted to know my enemy.

'Tell me about Ejike,' I said. I had no fear saying his name, not in front of this woman, not in this place. It felt different, secure.

The Oracle's eyes sharpened with interest. 'That is where your questions lie? With the hungry man and his deep blue?'

I nodded. I didn't ask *how* she knew those things. It was her job. 'I need to know what you know,' I told her.

She tilted her head. 'So you can kill him.'

My mouth tried to snarl and I pressed my lips together. 'Yes,' I bit out. 'Because I *will* kill him.' For taking my brother.

The Oracle glanced at Nkadi. 'Your dịbịa sister allows you to commit murder?'

'Is it really murder if he's so evil, though?' Ụwafụlamiro muttered the question, but the Oracle's crushing gaze moved over to him.

'Ghost boy,' she said. 'You should be practicing with your whip more.' A drop of water jumped out of the fountain and landed on her cheek, and she turned her head slightly to look into the water. Ụwafụlamiro was stricken at being addressed directly. I shot him a glare that told him to shut up and fall back. Nkadi's expression was strained but she remained quiet, as if recognizing that this was between me and the Oracle. For a few moments, the Oracle said nothing, and I wondered if she had simply forgotten we were there as she stared at the light fracturing in the water.

'Ejike?' I asked. 'What is he?'

The Oracle blinked and then looked lazily at me, her eyelids dropping. 'What,' she noted. 'Not who?'

I shrugged.

'Does that make it easier to imagine killing him? If he no longer becomes a person?' She seemed interested in my answer. I didn't want to tell her about the ants and the way a life could vanish in my hand because it was so, so small in the scale of things. The Oracle smiled and her mouth seemed to have too many teeth in it. 'I imagine the view is different,' she said.

I didn't answer and she sighed, dropping one hand to trail in the fountain's water.

'Do you remember the stories your grandmother told you about the Split?'

I rocked back, surprised. 'The Split? What does that have to do with anything?'

The Oracle clicked her tongue in the back of her throat. 'If you were listening, you would know it has *everything* to do with everything. Power. Magic. *Death.*' Her dark eyes locked on my face, and time pressed down against my skin. 'Where do you think you're headed, Sọmadịna?'

She shouldn't have known my name. *She shouldn't have known my name.* It was dangerous, I had already spilled my twin's name to someone else, these strangers who knew too much, and none of it felt safe. My fists clenched by my sides and I thought, briefly, of touching the emptiness inside me, letting it spread until the Oracle stopped smiling at me like she knew who I was. It was only the sound of my sister inhaling a sharp breath that stopped me, the reminder that people I cared about were here, too close for me to risk.

'So we're headed to the Split.' My lips felt numb as I said the words. We'd been going north, and yet I had hoped. Ahụdi would have never let us leave if she knew. 'That's where Ejike is taking him?'

The Oracle nodded. 'That's where Ejike lives. But what he is? That is something less known. He eats magic.'

'He said he ate a god's power.' This time, both Nkadi and Ụwafụlamiro made shocked sounds at the blasphemy. The Oracle's mouth tightened.

'There are many gods. It may be possible.'

'How?' Nkadi blurted out. '*How* could he steal a deity's power?' The Oracle simply stared back at her and Nkadi flushed with anger. 'You wouldn't tell me even if you knew.'

The Oracle shrugged. 'Ask your grandfather, little dịbịa. I am not your teacher.'

Nkadi growled at her. 'Then what is your *point*?'

'Nkadi.' I kept my voice level. 'She is helping us prepare to face a monster. Take it easy.' My sister bit her lip and turned her face away. I wasn't sure what it was about the Oracle that set her so on edge.

'You think he's a monster?' the Oracle asked me.

'With what he's done? What's the difference between him and a monster?'

'The difference?' A small smile curled at the corner of the Oracle's mouth. 'Well, Ejike is human.'

We waited, and then Nkadi prodded. 'And . . . ?'

The Oracle's smile widened. 'You can *kill* humans.'

I drew back, suddenly seeing broken waistbeads and dark soil on a farm, a boy gone stiff and a town gone bloodthirsty. The Oracle met my eyes and pulled back her lips even further, her smile warping. Her teeth were sharpened to points and a blinding white.

'Yes,' she crooned. 'Ala's daughter already knows that, doesn't she?'

Nkadi took a small step forward, drawing the Oracle's attention off me. 'Is that all you had to tell us? That we can kill the man we already planned to kill? We are heading to our brother anyway, no matter where he is. Even if we find him at the bottom of the Split, we will retrieve him from whoever we need to, at whatever the cost.'

The Oracle's gaze snapped over to her. 'Bold apprentice. Not afraid of being struck dead apprentice.'

Nkadi paled but didn't move, and the Oracle nodded in what seemed like approval.

'The human who took the boy can kill you all,' she said. 'Ala may let you die. It would return you to her, and death matters only to the alive, after all.' The woman sighed, almost wistfully.

Ụwafụlamiro swallowed hard. 'I personally would certainly prefer to live,' he muttered.

'You're toying with us,' Nkadi said.

The Oracle smiled again, a small and proper one this time. 'Yes,' she said. 'Games while we live. The pattern of thrown shells changes in the hands of a dịbịa, as you well know.'

I was now too irritated to be worried about our apparently imminent deaths. 'Do all Oracles talk like this? Round and round in circles?'

She raised an eyebrow. 'Truly I have never met a patient small god,' she replied with some bite in her voice, then leaned toward me. 'You seek a madman who seeks young and great power, but you know that already. The hunter has snares that even a small god does not see. Your eyes are too narrow and you need more of them. Every cutlass needs a handle. I would strongly suggest that you do not run from the leopard.'

She fell silent and all we could hear was the water.

'What?' I stared at her incredulously. 'You can't be serious.'

The fountain stopped moving, leaving the water suspended in the air, and the courtyard plunged into silence. 'Leave now,' ordered the Oracle.

'No!' I nearly stamped my foot on the stones. 'That told us

nothing! *What* is Ejike? Where did he come from? *How do I kill him?*'

'Erm, Sọmadịna. Maybe we should do what she says?' Ụwafụlamiro was staring at the unmoving water with naked fear in his eyes.

'You didn't say *anything* useful!'

The Oracle didn't look at me. 'I will not repeat my request,' she said, and there was something horrific and cold in her voice, like a child's bone in an adult's hand. Nkadi grabbed my hand and dragged me out of the courtyard. When I opened my mouth to complain, she shot me a look of pure white-hot anger.

'Be silent! You cannot disrespect an Oracle like that!'

'You've done *nothing* but disrespect her since we got here!' I shot back.

Blood heated my sister's face. '*I* am a dịbịa. *You* are not. Besides, that was before she gave us an actual prophecy.'

'A prophecy that made no sense,' Ụwafụlamiro pointed out.

Nkadi narrowed her eyes at him. 'It made no sense to *you.*'

I folded my arms stubbornly. 'Then explain it,' I challenged. 'Tell us exactly what she meant.'

My sister looked thoroughly annoyed with me. 'That's not how prophecies *work,*' she snapped. 'At least we know we'll end up at the Split eventually. That's something we need to prepare for.'

'Wait.' Ụwafụlamiro's pupils were still blown wide with

panic. 'I don't like how you said that. Is it that dangerous to go to the Split?'

Nkadi glanced at me and her gaze softened. 'I'm sorry,' she said. 'I wouldn't have brought you if I knew this is where we'd be headed. I would've made Grandfather come with us.'

Underneath my anger, fear blossomed in my stomach. Ahụdi's stories stopped when the magic came and the war ended and Kesandụ died. She never told us stories of people going to the Split afterwards. In fact, *no one* had ever told us stories about anyone going to the Split after the war. I had thought it was utterly abandoned because it wasn't safe, but Nkadi was talking like she knew something more about the Split. The only way the dịbịas would know how dangerous it was now is if they had tried going there already.

'How many?' I asked my sister, my voice unsteady.

'I think maybe we should stop,' Nkadi replied. 'Maybe we should turn around.'

I ignored her words. She was trying to protect me.

'How many dịbịas came back?' I asked her. 'In all these years, when you people go to check on the Split' – because of *course* they would have, now that I thought about it, it was their job to monitor the thing they had made – 'how many have come back?'

Nkadi hung her head. 'None,' she said. 'None of the dịbịas ever came back.'

CHAPTER FIFTEEN

WE ATE A QUICK BUT SUBSTANTIAL BREAKFAST WITH OBI AND UJU before saying goodbye, then the three of us left town quietly with the Oracle's words hanging over our heads, a looming destination. I was glad to turn my back on the town, despite Obi's kindness – it would be a long time before I forgot the feeling of being eaten alive by my own body while those people watched and whispered.

'Everyone there would have let us die,' I said out loud as we walked away, stamping the end of my spear into the ground. 'As if we were entertainment.'

Ụwafụlamiro shook his head sadly. 'Sometimes I think people in a group can do more wickedness than one person alone,' he replied. 'Everyone waits for someone else to do something, or they do nothing, or they do the wicked things together.'

'Sometimes doing nothing *is* the wicked thing,' Nkadi said, her voice sour.

Ụwafụlamiro's words had made me think of the trial back home and my heart grew even heavier as I remembered all the bad things that had happened *before* Jayaike was taken. I was running away from them, locking them in rooms inside my head, dodging and ducking so I didn't go mad. I said nothing, because there was nothing to say. No one could change anything that had happened; no one could turn a crocodile from its path. We fell into silence and walked until we were a good distance away from the town, too far for their eyes or ears.

Nkadi stopped and rolled her head around on her neck, the small bones cracking loudly. 'Are you ready for the fold?' she asked. 'Sọmadịna, how is your head? You have your powder?'

I nodded and tried to give her a reassuring smile. 'It's going to be fine. We trust you.'

She made a face but gave a small smile back. 'I'll do a shorter fold this time.'

I closed my eyes and breathed deeply into the pain, following the direction of the twin bond, stretching between me and my brother. It was already getting easier, both the pain and the navigating, and for a horrible moment, I wondered if Ejike was slowing down so that I could find him and Jayaike sooner, so I could prove him right, that I would come to him after all. He didn't have a real reason to run from us.

'There.' I pointed.

Ụwafụlamiro reached out and grabbed both my and Nkadi's hands. 'We're ready,' he told her.

The air got oppressively heavy. I forced myself to keep inhaling and exhaling as we set out, taking slow steps through the muddied world. Nkadi's jaw was set but her eyes were blazing with confidence. I wanted to smile and cry at the same time – Jayaike would have loved to be in this fold with us. He would've asked our sister questions I hadn't thought of, he would've turned and grinned at me and we would have known the unfettered joy of experiencing something new and magical together. These wonders were gifts from the deity, but she had allowed my brother to be abducted. She hadn't protected him, entered his body to give him enough power to overcome Ejike, the hungry thief. It would have made more sense if it had happened to me – all she had given me was death and terror, after all, so forsaking me might be the kindest thing she'd ever done – but that night in our room, Jayaike had spoken of her with life and wonder. What kind of god would crush his spirit like that?

We traveled for a length of time that meant nothing to me. I barely looked around, lost in the clamor inside my head. Landscapes blurred in greens and blues, and then Nkadi began to slow the world around us, allowing the fold to fall open. We staggered out of it and gasped full, deep breaths. The hunger was nowhere as bad as it had been the first time, and Nkadi was already unpacking parcels from her bag, wrapped with banana leaves and tied with string. 'Come and eat,' she said.

I took a minute to look around us. We were by the banks of a deep stream, clear water gushing over smooth stones while silver fish darted among the currents. The sun had moved across the sky into late afternoon and birdsong came from the trees around us. It was almost too beautiful and I didn't like how it felt, like someone had made a pretty picture and wanted to watch us inside it. My flesh gave me no time to worry about it, though, not as the hunger screamed for attention. I knelt down next to Ụwafụlamiro, who was already eating from the unwrapped parcels of food – large portions of dried meat, sooty chunks of roasted yam and plantain with fish and palm oil, fermented cassava – it was a small feast. I joined in and we all ate for several minutes in silence while our bodies caught up with us.

'Did Obi pack this for us?' I finally asked, sinking my teeth into a boiled cocoyam.

Nkadi nodded. 'They insisted, but they wouldn't accept payment. I owe them a debt, I suppose.'

I cut my eyes at my sister. '*We* owe them a debt.'

'Either way.' She shrugged but her face was pulled into a frown. 'I don't like debts. But I hadn't anticipated that anyone would reject the copper as payment.'

'We'll make it up to Obi somehow.' I ignored what Ejike had said, that he might have to kill Obi for telling his name. He was just trying to scare me. He'd lied to Obi, pretended to be Jayaike's uncle, and I didn't want to think about what he'd done to my brother to get him to play along. It was something all of us were stepping carefully around: not asking too many questions. Maybe that was a mistake. Maybe we should have interrogated Obi to get as much information as possible, but Ejike had pulled me into the dreaming world so fast, we had let it go.

I hoped we wouldn't regret letting it go.

Nkadi flicked a cautious glance in my direction, and I knew she was worried about me. Dreams colliding with the spirit world and a man walking in both who claimed to have eaten godpower before? I knew she was in over her head, but I wasn't going to point it out. She was doing her best. The deity was the one who had forbidden Zerenjọ from coming with us even though we clearly needed him. It wasn't fair. It wasn't *fair.*

'Did Obi mention what their gift was?' Ụwafụlamiro asked suddenly.

I thought for a moment, then shook my head. 'Not to me.'

'Not to me either,' Nkadi replied. 'But maybe it's just private, you know? Not every town runs the way yours does, with the registrations and the transparency.'

She had spoken easily, not even noticing how she pushed us away with her words. *Yours,* she'd said. Not *ours,* because she no longer belonged there. Because her town, her community, was magic and medicine in the pulsating Forest, not the maddened mother who still wanted her, not the bloodthirsty crowd that had called for my death. I felt a brief stab of anger and resentment. What would it feel like to be so special that our grandfather was able to dedicate himself to her, that our mother still longed for her instead of the abominations she'd gotten? Nkadi was powerful, yes, but Mama never held her being a dịbịa against her, and Mama *really* didn't like dịbịas. My sister was powerful, but not *too* powerful. What she was had a name. What she was didn't terrify our parents, didn't speak from a black room that smelled of iron with a warning hiss. She wasn't normal, not by any stretch, not after how many times she had died, but she wasn't a half-possessed murderer like I was. Nkadi was beautiful, and even with her head shaved and her dịbịa cloth, she was still a woman with a body that made sense.

I cast my eyes down to the food and swallowed back jealous tears. I couldn't talk to Nkadi about these feelings, or to Ụwafụlamiro. There was only one person who had ever understood, and he was lost in the darkness at the other end of our bone bond.

'Imagine if we didn't have to register,' Ụwafụlamiro was saying. 'Imagine if we kept our gifts secret. I wonder what our town would be like.'

'Imagine if the war didn't happen,' I cut in. 'Imagine if Ahụdi's husband didn't die at the Split. Imagine if my family wasn't such a disaster.' My voice was sharp and acidic now, slicing into my friend. 'Imagining these things is a waste of time. We're never going to live in a world like that. *I'm* never going to live in a world like that, where these gifts didn't destroy my family, and it is pointless to sit here and consider what that would be like!'

It was very quiet after I stopped speaking, like the forest was holding its breath. Water gurgled softly from the stream, but even that seemed muted.

'You know, you can always talk to us about what happened,' Ụwafụlamiro said gently. Nkadi gave him a sharp look, but he ignored it. 'We've all been worried about you. What happened with Chidị was—'

'Stop!' I put my hands to my head. 'Don't say his name. Don't talk about it. Just . . . just leave it alone. Please. I beg you.'

Ụwafụlamiro fell silent, dropping his eyes apologetically. I put down the food and went to the bank of the stream, crouching down to drink from it. We always found our way back to the water, close to the water. Crocodile children. Deity servants. We needed the river. My sister and my best friend left me alone and I was grateful for it. The water was cold and sharp in my mouth when I drank from it.

'I'm going for a walk,' I called over my shoulder.

'Be careful,' Nkadi replied. 'Don't go too far!'

I could hear the worry in her voice, but I didn't look back as I stood up and walked into the greenery that was draped around us. Pushing through the vines and undergrowth made me feel better, and after a few minutes, once I was out of sight and earshot, I stopped and sat on a large stone. It was slick with moss and I stayed there for a while, hugging my knees and brushing my spirit against the strained twin bond. I wondered what Jayaike was doing, if he was afraid in this moment, if anyone was hurting him. Would I even be able to tell? Would I feel his terror trickle along the old bone, or was he truly alone in whatever hell Ejike had placed him in? I slid off the stone and curled up on the ground, letting the damp grass cool off my skin. My eyes drifted closed and images flashed through my mind – my mother's face with orange flowers blooming at her feet and crawling up her legs, flames obscuring her eyes. The flames died down and a cloud of ash whirled around me. Chidị's body was standing there with a broken eye socket and Chiotu's voice screaming from his throat. I matched her scream and woke up trembling, my body sticky with sweat.

A bird sang something lonely from the branches above me, and I forced myself to get up and walk back to our little encampment. There was a small fire crackling and Ụwafụlamiro was roasting fresh fish over the heat. He looked up and worry entered into his eyes as soon as he saw me.

'Is everything all right, Sọmadịna? Did something happen?' He was about to get up, but I waved him back down as I sat next to him.

'I'm fine,' I said, bumping my shoulder against his. It felt good to be close, to not be alone with the nightmares. 'Where's Nkadi?'

'She went to see if she could forage some supplies as we continue. I don't think she wants us out here when night falls.'

I made a face. 'I know Grandfather said we should stay around people, but at this point I'm wondering if it's safer to be away from towns, you know?'

Ụwafụlamiro nodded. 'All these people are strangers, and we're already strange enough.'

Faint sorrow passed over his face as he said it, and the words pierced me too, but then he shook it all away and gave me a smile. I didn't smile back, because there was something too practiced in the way he'd brushed it aside, so instead I took his pale hand in mine. His skin was freckled and reddened from the sun and his fingernails were blunt squares, stray scales from the fish glistening against the tendons on the back of his hand.

'Is it difficult?' I asked. 'Being friends with Jayaike and me?'

Ụwafụlamiro blinked in surprise. 'Why would it be?'

I didn't let go of his hand. 'We have so much trouble between us and our family, between us and the village, and you're always here, helping us. Listening to us. But you have your own troubles too, don't you? I don't know if we have been listening to you enough. It's not as if Jayaike and I are the only ones who are treated differently because we look different.'

My best friend blushed and dropped his gaze, and my heart fell right along with it. He wasn't arguing with me. Pain wrapped a fist around my chest and squeezed tight.

'Ụwafụlamiro, I'm so sorry. I've been self-centered in this friendship. Please forgive me. Don't hold anger.'

He shook his head, but his white eyelashes were damp. 'What's happening with you is more important,' he said, raising his gaze with that practiced smile.

'Don't do that,' I snapped. 'Don't erase yourself to make me feel like the center.'

'I'm not! It's just that . . . my own things don't seem that big when you compare. So what if people still say cruel things? At least they're not trying to execute me.' He gave me a pointed glare and I flapped my other hand dismissively.

'It doesn't matter. Whatever is happening with you is also important. It's not a competition of whose life is the worst.'

Ụwafụlamiro squeezed my hand and nodded. 'I hear you,' he said softly.

'So then talk,' I ordered. 'What are you feeling?'

'Right now?'

I rolled my eyes. 'No, later, when we're trapped in a magical fold trying to hunt down my brother before our bodies give out.'

'Very funny.' He turned my hand over in his and was silent for a few minutes, his eyes tracing my fingers. 'I like being friends with both of you. I don't feel so strange with you, it's like we all fit together. No one else really understands us, but we understand each other and that's enough.'

I nodded, because I felt the same way.

'But sometimes I feel like I don't really exist, not when I'm around you and Jayaike, but when I'm around everyone else in the village. I was so excited for my gift to emerge, you know, but it didn't make me feel like I belonged any better.'

'You have an amazing gift!' I was trying to cheer him up, but Ụwafụlamiro seemed to shrink in a little more.

'I *disappear,* Sọmadịna. Just like people want me to do, to just go away so they don't have to deal with the way I look or how uncomfortable my skin makes them feel. It doesn't make me feel powerful. It makes me feel like even Ala agrees that I shouldn't exist.'

For a moment, I was struck silent. I felt like a complete fool. It should have been obvious why his gift was even more alienating to him, and I had been so busy thinking about myself and my twin that I had never even bothered to check in on how he was doing. We couldn't control the gifts, we couldn't choose them, and my best friend had been hurting in silence while making sure he showed up for me and Jayaike. There were no words I could say to make amends for the ways I had left Ụwafụlamiro alone. Instead, I pulled him into a tight hug, burying my face in his neck.

'I'm so glad you exist,' I said into his skin. 'The world is a better place with you in it. Our town is a better place with you in it. If you ever disappeared, I would come hunting for you just as much as we're hunting for Jayaike, you hear me? You *belong* here, and I'm never letting you go.'

My emotions were a storm behind my ribs, thickening my voice, and Ụwafụlamiro's hands slid around me as he held me tight, his palm cupping the base of my skull. I let myself relax into the embrace, into the smell of salt and the crackle of fire in the background, warm skin against my cheek. When we finally pulled away, Ụwafụlamiro hesitated with our faces a breath away, and it felt like the whole world stopped moving around us. It was different from when we had been fetching water back home, with people all around us, or even at the bathing pool. *We* felt different, under the late afternoon sky. Ụwafụlamiro's eyes searched mine and I could see the uncertainty there, like he wasn't sure how I felt about him, even after the things I'd said.

My pulse was a hummingbird racing through me as I leaned forward and let my lips brush softly over his. He hissed in a sharp breath and I smiled, feeling like the flint that starts a fire. I kissed him again, a little harder, and then he was kissing me back, strong and sure, his hands cupping my face. It felt warm and safe, like I was curled up inside the hollow of a tree where nothing could get me, at the bank of the river where the crocodiles lived. It felt like home. Chiotu had said that kissing felt like lightning was draped over her skin, sparking in bright flashes, like she had drunk the strongest palm wine, like she was flying, but it didn't feel like that for me. Maybe it was because her body changed and mine didn't. I wondered how it felt for Ụwafụlamiro. I wondered if one day he would want more and I would be too claimed by a god to be able to give it to him.

I pulled away, ending the kiss, and we stared at each other

in a new silence. He opened his mouth to speak, but then we were interrupted by a whistle of air as Nkadi skidded back into the clearing. She was breathing hard, yet a near-silence moved with her as she ran, just as she had been trained. Ụwafụlamiro and I leaped up as soon as we saw her.

'What's wrong?' I asked.

'Pack up. We need to move.'

Ụwafụlamiro immediately took the fish off the fire and began wrapping it in the banana leaves. Nkadi grabbed her bag and twisted her fingers in the direction of the flames. The smell of iron flashed briefly in the air and then the fire was out. She glanced at me impatiently.

'*Move,* Sọmadịna!'

I picked up my spear and slung my bag across me. 'What *happened*?' I shouted.

Nkadi threw a worried look over her shoulder. 'Leopards,' she bit out.

'Leopards?' I didn't understand at first.

'They're feral,' she said. 'We broke into their territory.'

Blood drained from my face and I helped Ụwafụlamiro shove the last of the parcels away. I'd heard of feral leopards and they were nothing like the wild leopards we had deep in the People's Forest. The stories said that when the Split happened and the magic washed over the land, it drove many animals mad – mad enough to dash their own heads against stones to make it stop, mad enough to eat each other and their children, and those that survived remained as the feral ones. Sometimes, the crocodile's bite infects. I'd known we could face wild animals during our travels – any child who grew up by the People's Forest knew that – but I'd never seen a magical feral and I didn't want to.

My sister was readying herself for the fold, reaching her hands out for me and Ụwafụlamiro. Before we could grab hold, a low and multilayered growl filled the clearing. Nkadi cursed under her breath.

'Can't we still fold?' Ụwafụlamiro asked, his eyes darting around the clearing.

'Too dangerous,' Nkadi replied. 'We'd be vulnerable as the fold starts.'

I hefted my spear into position. 'So we fight, then?'

Nkadi sighed and braced herself. 'We fight,' she answered, her voice grim. The undergrowth rustled, and a large, mottled paw stepped out, claws digging into the ground. Ụwafụlamiro pulled his wind whip out, and I heard it crack through the air as he took position next to me. The leopard stalked into the open and I swallowed a shocked sound. It was bigger than the cats we'd seen in Obi's town, and its muscles rippled under a sleek dappled coat. Yellowed fangs curved out of its mouth and it glared at us through slitted eyes, prowling in a loose arc around us.

'Well, there's only one,' Ụwafụlamiro ventured. 'That's not too bad, right?'

A branch cracked behind me and I spun around to see several other leopards slipping into the open, threatening growls spilling out of their throats. Despite their size, they moved with alarming grace as they stalked around us, hackles raised and fangs bared, saliva dripping onto the grass. Terror danced a fine and cold line up my spine as they encircled us, their shoulders sloping under the skin.

'*Nkadi*,' I whispered, and fear shook my voice. 'What do we do?'

My sister pulled out matching daggers. 'They're not attacking yet,' she said.

'Is that normal?' Ụwafụlamiro was glitching in and out of invisibility, his fingers tensing around the handle of his whip.

'It's strange,' Nkadi replied, keeping her voice low. 'It almost seems . . . premeditated. This is not how ferals behave.'

I clutched at my spear and tried to imagine sinking it into one of the cats, but the thought made me faintly nauseous. 'Nkadi, I—I don't know if I can do this.'

She threw me a sharp assessing look, then clenched her jaw. 'One afternoon with a weapon was not enough,' she replied, almost speaking to herself. 'It's not your fault. Just stay behind me.'

The cats were prowling closer now, tracking us with their yellow eyes.

'I don't know if I can do this either,' Ụwafụlamiro confessed. 'It felt different in the training circle.'

'Well, this isn't really what I was preparing you for,' Nkadi bit out. 'Stand back to back, please. Do what you need to do to protect each other. I will handle the leopards.'

I stared at her. 'By yourself?'

Nkadi flicked her wrists, and a deep red flame burst to life on her skin, running down the length of her daggers. She flashed me a wild smile and her eyes glowed like burning coals. 'How many warriors is one dịbịa worth?'

The leopards roared in unison and leaped as if they were one creature. I slammed my back against Ụwafụlamiro's and screamed, jabbing my spear in front of me in a wild arc. I could hear the whistle of his wind whip as it cracked through the air, and Nkadi was a burning blur as she sliced her way through the leopards. The fire from her daggers burned unnaturally, eating away at the flesh of any cat it came into contact with. They snarled with rage each time she made contact, swiping their claws at her and lunging to bite, but she was never there long enough to be caught in their paws or teeth.

I jabbed my spear in the direction of the leopard that was trying to get to me. A howl went up from the other one as Ụwafụlamiro's whip bit into it. Three of them were dead on the ground, red fire gnawing at their skin. Nkadi slid under another one and ran her daggers down its midsection, rolling out of the way as it collapsed to the ground. The remaining leopards roared even louder in what sounded like anguish and redoubled their efforts. I swallowed a short scream as the one in front of me leaped for my throat, claws extended, and before I knew it, my body fell into the motions Nkadi had drilled into me. My shoulder drew back, my arm extended, my body twisted, and the spear released from my hand, piercing the feral through its abdomen. It made a horrific sound and crashed down, one of its limbs knocking me over in a brutal blow that slammed my head against the ground.

Sound echoed around me, ringing through my ears. I tried to get up, but the leopard's paw was too heavy to move, and blood was pooling around us. I could feel the warm liquid against my legs. It made me gag and struggle even harder to free myself, my hands pushing against the dead feral. Ụwafụlamiro cried out suddenly, his voice laced with terror.

'Sọmadịna, *look out*!'

I whipped my head around and time seemed to slow down. Ụwafụlamiro had his whip coiled around a leopard's throat and was fighting to keep it restrained. Nkadi was clutching her side and facing off against another leopard in the shallows of the stream, her daggers sputtering flame as the current carried them away. The last cat prowled in my direction, death boiling in its eyes. I whimpered as I tried even harder to free myself from the dead leopard, but its weight had me pinned. 'Nkadi, help!' I screamed.

My sister glanced my way, then back at the leopard in the stream. She was holding out a trembling hand, and there was a shield of air between her and the cat. *Sọmadịna.* Her voice was clear and urgent in my head. *I can't get to you in time. You have to use your gift.*

'What?' Panic surged up my throat.

You can stop it. Just like the grass in the training circle.

The fear took my voice at the thought of touching that emptiness again. *I can't.*

There's no time. You have to.

I squeezed my eyes shut and tried to reach for the emptiness in my head. I wanted the god to pulse through the ground and leap up in me like she had before, but Ala was silent. All I could hear was the rumbling growl of the approaching cat. My muscles burned as I shoved against the heavy weight lying across me. What had been the point of discovering the emptiness in me and what it could do if I couldn't use any of it when it was needed? I should have listened to Nkadi when she told me to practice on small creatures. It would have been terrible, but at least I wouldn't have failed like I was failing now. My lungs burned and tears stung my eyes. I was never going to find Jayaike. I was a liability who couldn't control her gift when it mattered the most. I was just Ala's tool; I was useless otherwise. It would have been better if they had gone to look for my twin without me.

Sọmadịna! Do it now! Nkadi's voice was harsh and desperate, with a strange growl underneath, but I couldn't do it. I wasn't her. I wasn't good enough. The leopard's breath rolled across my face, rank and hot, and I let my body go limp. Even the Oracle back at Obi's village had told me not to run from the leopard. She must have seen these ferals in our future and known how useless I was, how Jayaike stood a better chance with Nkadi than with me.

I can't, I whispered to my sister. *I'm sorry.*

Nkadi hissed in my head and then the air exploded around me. I flinched as bits of earth and grass hit my face, but then my chest wasn't being crushed anymore and I could breathe. When I opened my eyes, a golden leopard was standing above me, its eyes bright with intelligence. It was smaller than the ferals had been, but more than that, I knew it. I had never seen it before, but I *knew* it.

'Nkadi?' I whispered. The leopard huffed and walked a short distance away from me. I watched in horrified shock as bones cracked and popped, as the pelt slid into skin and then my older sister was standing in front of me again, picking up her cloths and tying them around her. The feral leopards she and Ụwafụlamiro had been fighting lay dead on the ground, one of them half drowned in the stream. Ụwafụlamiro was vomiting next to the remains of our fire, his whip abandoned next to him. I pushed myself up and stared at my sister.

'What just happened?' I asked, keeping my voice level and careful. If I didn't, I would start screaming.

'I killed them,' she said, her nostrils flaring. '*You* certainly weren't going to.'

I blinked, confused. She had been injured in the stream. I had *seen* her. It had looked like her ribs were cracked at the very least, but now she was standing straight and sure. Her hands weren't trembling anymore. *She had turned into a leopard.* Too many realizations were in my head, slamming violently against each other.

'You turned into a leopard,' I said.

She didn't reply. I had *seen* her hands tremble. She'd looked like she was about to collapse.

'Could you have killed them this whole time?' I needed her to say no. She wouldn't have done that to me. 'Were you pretending to be more injured than you were?'

Nkadi shrugged and pulled my spear out of the dead cat with a squelching sound. She handed it to me without a word and I kept staring at her in shock. She was a far better fighter than she had let on. She was a beast doling out death. She was a *leopard.*

'You had all this under control from the beginning, didn't you? From the moment you ran in here acting like our lives were in danger.' Anger was beginning to fill the spaces in me that had been emptied by fear. She was a dịbịa and a leopard and a *liar* and my *sister.* 'Why did you let it go so far?'

Nkadi picked up her pack and wiped some blood off her face. 'You waste your gift, Sọmadịna, when there is so much at stake.'

There was no anger or contempt in her voice, just disappointment.

'You almost let it kill me, just to make a *point*?' My hands clenched into fists, tightening around the bloody spear. 'You pretended to be injured?'

Nkadi didn't look at me. 'Clean your weapon,' she said. 'We fold in a few minutes.'

I didn't recognize the person I was talking to, the calculation she'd shown while I was there, terrified and alone. 'I thought I was going to *die,*' I whispered. 'How could you do that to me?' She had been walking away, but she stopped at that, and I continued, betrayal burning in my chest. 'Is this what it means to be a dịbịa before being my sister? That you run these kinds of tests on me, try to manipulate me to use a gift I told you *I didn't want to use*?'

Still, Nkadi didn't say anything. I didn't care. I had too much to say, knocking at the back of my teeth.

'How long have you been able to turn into a leopard? Does Grandfather know?'

Ụwafụlamiro was watching us with big, sad eyes that were watering from how hard he'd been vomiting.

I shook my head. 'Of course Grandfather knows. We're the ones you lie to. We're the ones who don't deserve the truth. How *long,* Nkadi?'

'Get ready to direct us,' she said. 'We have to fold.'

I exploded. 'What is *wrong* with you?! Why are you acting like a monster!'

Nkadi turned her head slightly, just a slim golden profile dappled in blood.

'At least you're not the only one in the family,' she said.

I didn't know if she meant it to be as cruel as it sounded, but it felt like a blade reaching into my chest and slicing away something important, something that had held us together. I let out a low sob and took a step back, away from her and Ụwafụlamiro. Nkadi's eyes widened.

'Sọmadịna. Wait.'

It didn't matter anymore. Every thought I'd had when that leopard was about to finish me was back in my head, louder than before. I couldn't do it. I couldn't do anything. Everyone lied. My family pushed me away, always. Mama. Papa. Even Nkadi. I didn't belong. My twin was gone. I didn't belong. The town wanted me dead because I didn't belong. Not with my lying leopard sister. Grandfather loved her, not me, and I didn't belong. Not even with the ghost boy I had loved so poorly. I was selfish. I was dangerous. I wasn't worth the truth. I wasn't worth my mother fighting for me. My father.

Ụwafụlamiro stood up, alarm in his face. *'Sọmadịna.'*

It was too late. I turned and I ran. I ran into the green. I ran into the wild. I ran away from the water and the kisses and the lies. I ran and I ignored the voices behind me screaming my name.

CHAPTER SIXTEEN

THEY SHOULD HAVE CAUGHT ME.

I was fast, but I was no leopard. I ran anyway, ripping vines away when they hit my face, vaulting over and ducking under low branches. The bone bond sang to me, soft and whispery, but just enough. Just enough. Leaves crunched under my feet; birds whirled up startled as I tore through their trees. Thorns cut my legs. I ran.

I could hear nothing except my broken heart clattering in my ears, my breath tearing out of my lungs. I had dropped my spear and my pack. Only the bags at my waist remained, leather slapping against me as I ran. I was a coward. When that leopard had faced me, my own life had been at stake and I had given up. If I wouldn't fight for my own life, what would I fight for? I had given up on myself and so I had given up on my twin. I ran. In another life, voices called my name and ran behind me, after me. I didn't know. I didn't hear. It wasn't real.

They should have caught me. If they loved me enough, they would've caught me.

Instead, I followed the bond because I had nowhere to go, and I ran by an oil bean tree, and a man in blue stepped out from behind it and caught me by the throat and all the air left me. I choked and gasped as my feet left the ground, and Ejike smiled a hungry, *hungry* smile.

'There you are,' he said.

Prophecy hit me like a slap. *The hunter has snares that even a small god does not see.* Oh, I was such a fool. *I would strongly suggest that you do not run from the leopard.*

This was all my fault.

I had been so betrayed by finding out what Nkadi could do, I had completely forgotten what the Oracle had told me, and now I was lost. Ejike tightened his fingers as I tried to scream for my sister, and darkness tumbled over me.

CHAPTER SEVENTEEN

WHEN I CAME BACK TO MYSELF, I WAS ALREADY WALKING, AS IF MY body had been doing it without me for a while. The sky was a spread of inky indigo above me and the landscape was dark and unrecognizable. I inhaled a deep breath and immediately knifed over with hacking coughs as foul air filled my lungs.

'Don't do that,' a voice recommended. I flinched as Ejike handed me a square of cloth. He was strolling beside me as if it was nothing. 'You didn't take well to traveling through the spirit world. I had to move your flesh for a while. I'm glad you're back in it.'

I opened my mouth to scream but the air was rank and poisoned, so much so that I grabbed the square instead and held it over my nose and mouth, tears streaming from my eyes.

'It's better like that, isn't it?' he said. 'Shallow breaths now.'

I kept walking, if only because I was sure I would suffocate if I tried to stop or run. 'Where have you taken me?' I choked out through the cloth. My heart shouted my brother's name. The bond wasn't stretched. If I was with Ejike, then Jayaike was close, and that realization was what kept me calm. The earth was cracked beneath our feet and everything felt *wrong*. 'Where is my brother?'

Ejike was walking in confident strides, nothing over his face, just breathing in poison because that's what he was. He belonged here, in this sickening gloom. I could feel it.

'Jayaike is close,' he replied. I *hated* the sound of my brother's name in his mouth. 'We're all very close, small god.'

'I'm going to kill you,' I promised, and he laughed out loud.

'I am sure you'll try,' he replied. 'It's only fair. Every animal fights against the incoming death. No one wants to be eaten.' He looked down at me and grinned. 'I'm going to eat your gift anyway, and there won't be much left of you afterward.'

Nausea roiled in my stomach. 'Have you done that to Jayaike?'

He didn't reply and a scream started building in my throat, but then he winked at me. 'No,' he said, his voice amused. 'Not yet. I wanted to wait for you. It felt right to consume you together. A better chance at reaching the god.'

I hated him. I hated how he told me everything I wanted to know because he didn't think it mattered. He didn't think I could do anything about it, and if the god didn't pulse her way through my body, I wasn't sure I *could* do anything. I closed my eyes for a second and tried to reach for the emptiness inside me, but the poison was too loud and my body was fighting to get enough air.

'Did you like my leopards?' Ejike asked, and my feet stumbled over a crack in the ground.

'You sent them.' I shouldn't have been surprised. He knew we were hunting him. We should have expected him to make a move. 'You wanted them to kill us.'

Ejike let out an exasperated breath. 'I swear you don't listen,' he complained. 'Why would I kill you when I want to *eat* you? I need you alive for that.'

'Then *why*?'

'It was a sudden decision. They had been on another assignment.' He glanced sideways at me. 'Another town. Someone who was foolish enough to give you my name. Their little brother screamed so well, I heard. When they tore out his throat.'

Blackness hummed in my ears. *Obi. Uju.* 'No.'

He crooned, a low, satisfied sound. '*Yes.* I told you what I might do. I always tell you what I'm thinking. But did you warn them? You could've warned them. I might not have bothered to chase them if they ran. But you said nothing, small god. You said nothing and now they are dead.'

I stopped walking. I wanted rage. I wanted grief and power and an emptiness that would pull all the life out of him, but when I reached for it, all I could get was poison, poison, poison. This was my fault. I'd thought he was just threatening

Obi to scare me, but he'd meant what he said and he was right, he was right, *it was my fault they were dead.*

Ejike paused next to me but he kept talking. 'We're near the Split, you know? Gifts have a little trouble working this close to it. Too much fallout. Too much corrupted residue. It's not easy. I'm not saying it's your fault. I'm just saying things could have been different, but sometimes the roads change. Maybe the lesson is for you to accept that you cannot save people. Not Jayaike. Not the siblings that my leopards killed for me.'

'Shut *up,*' I gasped. I was going to *kill him.* Uju had been so young. Obi had been so kind.

'We can't stay here long. Your lungs will shut down. I don't lie to you. Not like your sister, so full of surprises. I wanted her to be honest with you about what she is.' Ejike wasn't as ravenous as he'd been in my dreams before. Now that he had both Jayaike and me, he was calmer. Close to satisfied.

I looked up at him and my hate felt like embers in my eyes. 'That's why you sent the leopards? You couldn't have known that Nkadi would transform.'

Ejike shrugged. 'I have my own diviners. I know how to pull threads one way and then another. And you ran exactly right, exactly broken, exactly betrayed again.' He started walking again. 'We're close to my palace,' he threw over his shoulder. 'The air isn't poisoned inside. Your brother waits. You can try to kill me there if you like.'

'You could be lying,' I snapped. 'About everything. Obi and Uju. Where we are. Where we're going.'

'Lies are for people who are afraid.' He smiled at me, almost kindly. 'There is nothing I fear.'

I didn't want to believe him. I didn't want to think that the leopards had ripped through Obi and their waistbeads, through little Uju, all because they *helped* us. There was so much poison in the air. I stumbled and fell to my knees, coughing so hard my ribs felt like they would break. My vision was beginning to blur. The world swooped as Ejike picked me up, lifting me into his arms. My head lolled against his shoulder.

'Let's go home, Sọmadịna,' he murmured against my hair.

'I never—' I hacked up a clotted cough. 'I never told you my name.'

'Oh, your twin did.' His voice turned sharp with delight as darkness began to creep into my eyes. 'You can't imagine what I had to do to get it out of him.'

I wanted to scream. I wanted to run.

I fell into the darkness instead.

A woman with a round face and eyes full of cataracts shook me awake, her teeth sharpened to points as she gave me a cutting smile.

'What a beautiful child,' she said. Her voice was a broken

calabash, all edges and fragments. Her fogged eyes swept over me, and a chill traced up my spine knowing she could see despite the milk clouding her pupils. 'Ejike is going to eat you all up.' The dim light shone on the keloids marking her face. She had deep laugh lines around her mouth, and her breath smelled like fresh blood.

'Who are you?' I asked. Everything in my head was shouting that she was going to hurt me, she wanted to hurt me, it was going to be so painful. It was a wave pushing off her and hammering into my skin. I crawled backward to try and get away from her, and she allowed it.

'I think you'll have such a pretty scream,' she said. My skin crawled along with me.

Another voice cut in, deferential. 'Mivwodere.'

The sharp woman gave me another smile and then turned her head away from me. 'Ejike is waiting.'

An older woman with long silver braids stepped into view, then leaned over me and smiled gently, showing teeth like white maize. 'Hello, little one.'

I didn't reply. Instead, I looked around, my eyes wide and my nerves trembling. I was indoors and the air was clean. The room I was in was as large as a hall, filled with furniture and woven fabrics. A small group of women stood in a loose circle around me but at a good distance, their eyes lined with charcoal, their lips stained like blood and sunsets. They looked curious and they whispered among themselves, strong and unfamiliar accents changing the shapes of the words.

'Where are her breasts?' someone was asking.

'Maybe she's too young,' another one suggested.

'At that height? Impossible.'

'Look at that skin! So firm.'

'Her body is like a child, but her power!'

'She won't look like that anymore when Ejike is finished with her.'

Laughter broke out but it had an edge to it – it was the kind of laughter you pushed out of your mouth instead of screams or tears. There was something bitter and furious underneath, something helpless and snapping.

'Where am I?' My voice was hoarse, as if I'd been screaming for days. I was seated on a wooden table and my skin was clean and fragrant. I reminded myself of a corpse being bathed for burial.

The woman with silver hair reached out and I flinched, but she didn't react. Instead, she smeared a daub of red on my lower lip with her thumb. 'Welcome,' she said.

All the women had brass rings decreasing in size from their knees down to their ankles, clanging against each other when the women moved. They kept looking at each other and then at me, and I could recognize pity behind their eyes.

'You're in Ejike's palace,' Mivwodere said, and again, the

smell of fresh blood from her mouth washed over me. I tried not to gag as she reached out and lifted my chin, examining my face as if there was an answer to something there.

'We did keep her simple, as you asked, Mivwodere,' said the woman with silver hair. I noticed that even though she spoke boldly, her body drew away from the bloodmouthed woman.

'Yes, I see,' Mivwodere replied, her voice a drawl. 'Ejike will appreciate that.'

'Where is my brother?'

I was molding my fear into anger, building in quick blocks. I had barely completed the question when Mivwodere's tight fist caught me in the mouth. The other women gasped as my head snapped to the side and slick red blood fell over my lower teeth and onto my chin. I went numb with shock – no one had ever struck me before in my life. I reached inside myself to touch my gift because *how dare she,* but the emptiness lurked out of reach. Mivwodere shook out her hand fastidiously.

'I don't like that tone. Avoid it.' She snapped her fingers at the woman with the silver braids. 'Afan! Clean her up.'

The woman hurried forward and dabbed a soft cloth against my mouth, her eyes giving a warning. I already knew I was too desperate and angry to listen – not now, not when I had come this far, not when I was this close. Another woman passed her a cup of water and Afan gave it to me.

'Rinse your mouth,' she whispered. I rinsed quickly and spat into a bowl, glaring at Mivwodere. Oh, she was next on my list after Ejike and I did not care anymore to run from the version of me that had dropped Chidị on the farm. Maybe I was now desperate enough, driven to the edge, but I wanted that version of me. I wanted to be walked by the god again, if that's what it took. Afan took the cup and bowl and quickly retreated, looking down at her feet. I moved my jaw tentatively as Mivwodere cracked her knuckles and smiled at me.

'Ejike told me a lot about you. I'm his right hand, you know. Usually, I kill those who seek to kill him, just because I take it personally.' Her smile morphed into a cold, clouded stare. 'Usually, I would kill you. But Ejike has plans, and they will be carried out.' She snapped her fingers at me. 'Let's go.'

I climbed off the wooden table, pushing all my emotions deep inside me because my bond was short now, shorter than it had been since that terrible moment when my bedroom was empty. I had to choke down the anger. I could take all this if it meant I was close to finding my brother. I could be quiet until the moment was right. In the silence as I followed Mivwodere out of the room, watched by a relieved knot of frightened women, I said a prayer to Ala for the first time since all this started.

Do what you want with me. I give my life over to you. All I ask is when the time is right, let me touch my gift, the great emptiness. Everything was becoming clear to me. *YOUR great emptiness. The mouth of the crocodile.*

When the time is right, allow me to kill the man who took my brother.

I didn't even know if the god was listening. Mivwodere dragged me by my arm down a corridor made from a stone I had never seen before, veined red and gleaming. I shouted and struggled until she stopped and leaned close to my face.

'Don't make things difficult,' she said. 'I would prefer your pretty face to be intact when I return you to Ejike, but I'm a flexible person.' She patted my cheek with her hand and flicked her thumb across my mouth, her smile happening. 'Change my mind.'

'Please,' I begged. 'He's my twin. I just want to know where my brother is, and then I'll go quietly. I swear.'

She gave an exasperated sigh. 'I hoped you wouldn't be so convincing,' she said, drawing back her fist again to hit me, but then she stopped as my words registered. 'Wait, your twin?'

'I've been looking for him, please—'

Mivwodere slapped her palm over my mouth, leaning into my face with fascination and tilting my head sideways to examine me from another angle.

'He really does look just like you,' she murmured. 'Amazing. I knew you were siblings, but I didn't know you were twins. No wonder Ejike wants to eat you both together.' She took her hand off my mouth and wiped it against her cloths absentmindedly. 'How lovely it will be to watch you suffer next to each other.'

'He's here, then.' I ignored everything else she was saying because relief was drowning me. 'He's really here.'

I'd known, and Ejike had said so, and it seemed so from the lack of pain from the bond, but Ejike's dark fog was still blocking my connection to Jayaike so I couldn't have been sure. I wasn't even sure now.

'Where are you keeping him?' I demanded. 'I want to see him.'

Mivwodere raised an eyebrow. 'I'm feeling almost sentimental about your face now, so I won't rearrange it for that question.' She grabbed my arm and pulled me along down the corridor again. 'But do stop tempting me.'

We halted in front of two enormous doors made of ornate iron. Mivwodere snapped her fingers and the doors flung themselves open, then she dragged me in and dumped me unceremoniously on the floor. I landed on soft carpets with a thud, rage and hope and panicky grief writhing in my chest like a bundle of snakes. I looked up at Mivwodere, tears in my eyes. Jayaike was so *close.*

'Please tell me where he is,' I choked out as the tears blurred my voice. She dropped to one knee and took my chin in her hand.

'You're exquisite when you beg,' she murmured.

A tendril of rage curled up from the writhing bundle. 'I will curse you,' I whispered. 'It will follow you all your life.' I sounded like a useless god. If I could have used my gift then, I would have skipped Ejike and killed her first, just for her taunting.

'I sleep in a bed of curses,' she replied. 'They keep me warm.' She kissed me with her fogged eyes open, a harsh and unkind thing, her sharp teeth drawing blood.

'Exquisite,' she repeated, then stood up and called to someone behind me, inside the rich room. 'She's yours, Ejike. Has a mouth like ripe fruit.'

'You're so good to me.'

My skin rippled uncomfortably at that voice, the one that was becoming too familiar. Ejike stepped gently onto the carpet I was sprawled on and crouched down to see me better. He smelled like absolutely nothing at all, so much nothing my senses recoiled from it. His eyes loomed close to my face, the pools of black with the sliver of yellow cornea around them. I wanted to gouge them out.

Ejike put both his hands on either side of my face and leaned in, pressing his nose to my cheek and inhaling deeply. His hunger was back, and it was louder than it had been in the dreams. My skin pebbled in apprehension. I knew I should have been terrified, gibbering with fear, but I was still so angry, so drunk off knowing Jayaike was somewhere around. I was almost delirious. I prayed to the god again. *Ala.*

Ala. Ala. Cover me in scales. Ejike grinned up at Mivwodere. 'You were right,' he said, and his voice had turned guttural. 'She is perfect.'

'I'm never wrong,' Mivwodere answered as she turned to leave. 'Enjoy her.'

'Where is my brother?' I asked Ejike. 'I thought you wanted us together.'

He nodded. 'I do. I just wanted to see you first.'

Mivwodere stopped and turned her head. 'You're not doing it now? Do you need me to take her back to the women?'

Ejike's empty eyes ran over my body, across my naked and flat chest. The women had dressed me in a small wrapper tied at my hips and left my beads at my waist. 'No,' he said. 'She can stay here with me until it's time. I don't want to let her out of my sight anymore.'

Mivwodere nodded and left as I glared after her.

'You want to kill her too, don't you?'

I jerked my head toward Ejike in surprise. He just smiled.

'I don't blame you for it. She's a little brutal in how she does things.' He reached out and stroked a splotch of blood off the corner of my mouth. 'I am sorry that she hit you.'

I recoiled from his hand. 'Don't touch me.'

He leaned in and put his mouth to my ear. Nothingness beat against my cheek.

'Do you want to know what I'm going to do?' he asked. 'How I'm going to eat your power?' He waited close to my face until I nodded, and then he stood up and reached out a hand. 'Come on, then. We have a long night ahead of us.'

I hated myself for nodding, for taking his hand, but I needed to know. I needed to know everything I could so that I could keep all my promises and make up for all my secrets. It was a mercy that Nkadi and Ụwafụlamiro weren't here. I wanted them to be safe. I wanted this to be between this monster and my twin and me.

His palm was cool as he pulled me to my feet. The space was larger than I had realized, with a domed ceiling and hundreds of lamps flickering everywhere, shadows hiccuping in corners. Tall windows looked out into an unknown night.

'This is your palace?' I asked.

'Yes,' Ejike replied. 'We're almost at the edge of the Split, you know. This palace was built soon after the war, out of the residue. It's taken years to make it livable, keep the poison outside.'

'But the poison doesn't affect you.'

Ejike smiled down at me. 'No, it doesn't. But I have humans living with me here – you've met my wives – and I prefer to keep them alive.'

I frowned at his phrasing. 'Aren't *you* human?'

The Oracle had said if he was human then he could be killed. He needed to die, and if he wanted to talk and talk until he gave me enough information to kill him, then so be it. I would chatter away as if he hadn't hunted my brother and me down, as if he hadn't put his foot on my spirit and crushed it by taking Jayaike from me.

'Am I human?' Ejike considered the question. 'I'm not sure at which point I lose enough humanity or gain enough power for that to change.' His tone was conversational as always, as if I was just a normal guest in his house.

'Did you build this palace?' He couldn't have. Ejike looked like he was my father's age; he wasn't old enough to have been here when the Split happened. But he had said the palace was built after the war and that it was *his* palace. When he smiled again, a pit opened up in my stomach. 'You did,' I said slowly. 'You were here for the war.'

'I was here for the war,' he agreed. 'I was one of the dịbịas who created the Split.'

I couldn't help it – I gasped, air emptying out of my chest, leaving only shock behind. Ahụdi had told us the stories. The dịbịas were trying to save us. They were *good.* They weren't like Ejike, not this twisted, poisoned dark thing. 'You're lying,' I said, and he laughed.

'We know each other better than that by now.' He went to a table made of black wood and poured chilled water from a jug into intricate sculpted clay cups, handing me one. I didn't take it.

'I can't drink anything you offer me,' I pointed out. 'Do you think I'm a fool?'

Ejike sighed and sipped from my cup. 'There,' he said, offering it back to me. 'Are you satisfied?'

My eyebrows pulled into a scowl. 'No? You were breathing poisoned air with no problem. Why wouldn't you be able to drink it as well?'

His eyes crinkled at the corners with amusement, and he put the cup back down on the table. 'You're no fool, Sọmadịna.' He tipped his head to one side indulgently. 'Ask me your questions. I know you have them.'

I did. Zerenjọ had said Ejike's description didn't fit any dịbịa he knew, and my grandfather had been at the Split when it was made. He wouldn't forget a single detail, not a dịbịa like him. Ahụdi said every memory from that time haunted the survivors. None of them could forget, even if they tried. 'You didn't die in the Split,' I said. 'Why didn't you just go home? Why stay here? Why become *this*?' I let my disgust at everything he was show in my voice, but it didn't seem to bother Ejike.

He sank gracefully into a chair, his blue cloth draping around him. I remained standing.

'I almost died,' he said. 'I fell into the Split. I felt it tear my flesh and break my bones as my body was thrown from rock to rock. I felt my breath bubble with blood. I *should* have died.' The black holes that were his eyes were unfocused, slipping into the past. 'I did not want to die, Sọmadịna. There was another dịbịa close to me, close to death. Their legs had been torn away, their skin split from chest to hips, showing their organs. With their eyes, they begged me for mercy.'

I shuddered as I listened. I could almost see the blood, the viscera, hear the screams. This was not what I had pictured when Ahụdi had told my siblings and me these stories, but she wasn't a dịbịa. She hadn't been at the exact location, she hadn't seen the Split form. Every story she told us about it was secondhand.

'I wanted to go home to my wife,' Ejike was saying. 'At any cost. To my young son, my firstborn. So I made my choice. I reached over and I carved and cracked the other dịbịa open a little more, just so I could reach their heart. I cut the symbols I needed into that slick muscle and then I burned their organs with my gift.' His eyes wandered over to me. 'It is a sacrifice, do you see? And in exchange for giving them release from this life, I took on their gifts and it saved my life.'

There was a name for people like him. *'Ritualist,'* I whispered. Those who committed human sacrifice for their own gain – stealing what belonged to deities alone. 'You're a ritualist.'

Ejike sipped at his cup. 'That's what it's called, yes. I'm a survivor of the Split. Do you know how rare that is, Sọmadịna?'

I actually did. Ahụdi had told us how few dịbịas returned, how many died. Zerenjọ was a survivor. This monster before me was something else entirely. 'You should have died there,' I said. 'It would have been better.'

'Than what?' He raised an eyebrow in question. 'Than returning to be killed by my brothers? Than becoming an abomination?'

I flinched at the word.

'I chose life, small god. I put all the dịbịas who were dying out of their suffering.'

'You *stole* from them!'

He waved a dismissive hand. 'I took payment for the kindness I showed them. Besides, you have no idea what it feels like, to hold so many gifts. You asked if I was human before. I don't know. No human has ever held as many gifts as I do or been changed the way that the Split changed me.'

I swallowed back my bile. 'But you didn't go home?'

A shadow crossed Ejike's face, but it passed quickly. 'My healing was tangled with the Split. I need to stay close.'

'But you came to my home.' *You took my brother.* 'You came to the forest when I was running.'

'Quick trips,' he replied. 'Through the spirit world. It took me decades to learn how to do that.'

'You ran out of victims.' He narrowed his eyes at me, but I knew I was right. 'How long did it take before there were no other survivors from the Split for you to feed on? Is that how you kept yourself from getting old?'

Ejike gestured to himself and laughed. 'This? This isn't even my body. I stepped out of it a long time ago and stepped into someone else.'

I hadn't known that was possible. He laughed again at my surprise and his voice sounded like a ghost, like laughter I'd heard from a different mouth.

'Power can give you many things, Ṣọmadịna. I almost wish I could keep you and your brother.' He swirled the water in his cup and looked down into it. 'That's what I did with some of the survivors, you know. Kept them in the palace for a long, long time. I couldn't let them heal, but I couldn't let them die, so I kept them as they were. They screamed until I cut out their voice boxes. Then they screamed with only their eyes.' His voice was heavy. 'They had been my comrades, but I was trapped here. If I had known my survival would have meant that, I never would have touched the first dịbịa or taken their gift. I would have let myself die. But once I started, I could not stop.' He shrugged. 'I was changed. I want what I want, like a never-ending blaze of hunger is burning me up. I have built a palace, a life, companions. This is who I am now.'

I stared at him. 'Does your wife live?'

He *flinched.*

'Is this who she would have wanted you to be?' I pushed, and something dark entered Ejike's face.

'Enough,' he said. 'You don't want to press your hand against that wound of mine, Sọmadịna. It will take you somewhere you won't like.'

I felt halfway mad. 'According to you, I'm about to be carved open and used for a ritual, made into a sacrifice. I think I can ask you anything I want.' A thought bloomed in my head – a memory from one of my dreams where he'd told me that he had eaten a god's power before. It hadn't made sense then, but knowing he was a ritualist changed everything. 'You ate a god's power through a ritual, didn't you? How did you do it?'

Ejike was no longer casual. He drew up from his chair and malevolence seeped off him like dripping rot. 'The same way I will do it on you and your brother,' he answered. 'Small gods. I met someone like you before, partially possessed. I made the deity rise within them and then I marked and burned their heart anyway and *I ate their god.*'

I laughed in his face, ignoring the rage in his eyes as I did so. 'What kind of weak deity allowed someone like you to eat them? Do you know what a deity even is?' There was no way he could do that to me, not with Ala. She was the most powerful, the earth everywhere under our feet, the underworld and the source of life.

Ejike sneered at me. 'I am a *dịbịa.* I have spoken with countless gods. You know nothing, little one.'

'My grandfather is a dịbịa. My sister is a dịbịa. *You* are a vulture.'

He was in front of me faster than I could see him move, and his nothingness slammed against my face, scraping on my skin. His voice shook and I wondered if this was what his rage sounded like. 'You don't know who I am. But I know who you are, Sọmadịna, daughter of Olejeme, the son of Ahụdi. Sọmadịna, sister to Nkadi and Jayaike. *I know who you are.*'

Terror gripped my chest as he recited half my lineage and my siblings. 'How?'

Ejike's smile was cruel. 'I tore it out of your brother's head. And your crocodile god did nothing to stop me. Once I had his name, that was all I needed. I told him you gave that to me, by the way. He wept and wept.'

Grief filled my eyes with water, a flood of exhaustion and dreams and sheer loud want for my twin. I had betrayed him in so many ways. Ejike wiped a tear as it spilled down my cheek.

'Don't cry, small god.' His voice was soft now, gentle as a silent snake. I looked up at him and the darkness in his eyes threatened to swallow me up. I might have been lost, I might have given up again like I had with the feral leopards, because I was just a child, I was so tired, and there was more evil in this world than I had ever thought possible. But then, Ejike asked me a question that reshaped everything, that tore strength from my legs and stabbed hope through my chest. He leaned close and slid the question into my ear like a barbed fishing hook.

'Would you like to see your brother?' he asked.

CHAPTER EIGHTEEN

I SAID YES. *PLEASE, YES, LET ME SEE HIM.*

What else could I say? I had come all this way, flawed as I was, broken as I was, because I loved Jayaike and I wanted to bring him home with me. I had no idea if that was possible anymore, not with the emptiness sunk so deep in me that I couldn't reach it, not with the deity ignoring my prayers, a crocodile sleeping in the water with its eyes closed. I sank into a chair, feeling dizzy, as Ejike rang a bell and summoned one of his servants.

'Bring me the other one,' he said.

All I could hear was my heart, beating and beating like a maddened drum. I reached out through the twin bond, along that old bone, hoping Jayaike would finally be there, but it vanished into Ejike's darkness. I didn't ask him to lift it – I knew he wouldn't. He enjoyed cutting me off from my brother, blocking that road of spirit we shared. I wouldn't beg him for that. It would lift once he died.

The great iron doors swung open without any noise. I was almost too afraid to look up. Ejike put a hand on my shoulder and it felt too heavy, too wrong.

'You don't want to miss this moment, Sọmadịna,' he said gently. 'Raise your head.'

I raised my head.

My twin walked into the room.

I felt my heart shatter and re-form in a split second. Pain filled my whole chest, grief and shock and a relief so sharp it sliced me up.

'Jayaike,' I said, and my voice was a croak, muted and scratched up. My brother looked at me, and there he was, his beloved face, my other soul, finally, *finally*. His face cracked open with emotion, his eyebrows pulling down, confused.

'Sọmadịna?' My name stuttered on his tongue. 'Are you . . . are you real?'

Ejike bent to whisper to me. 'I didn't tell him you were here. Isn't this a nice surprise?'

Jayaike had lost some weight but not too much. He was wearing a wrapper in Ejike's blue, and I wanted to rip it off my brother and burn it. His skin was slightly grimy and his dark gold hair was tangled, but he didn't seem injured, not until I saw his eyes. They were haunted, skittering from left to right as he tried to understand what he was looking at.

'Of course I'm real,' I said.

Jayaike faced Ejike instead of me. 'Please don't do this to me again,' he said. 'I can't take any more of this.'

I snapped my gaze to Ejike, shaken by my brother's broken uncertainty. '*What is he talking about?*'

Ejike shrugged. 'Your brother and I have spent a lot of time together. I was hospitable at first, but he was . . . uncooperative. I became less hospitable.'

Jayaike wouldn't look at me. I ignored the dead man next to me who didn't know he was dead yet, and I walked closer to my brother. 'I'm real,' I told him, as I put my hand on his arm, my loam skin against his clay. 'See?'

My twin's eyes shot up to me the moment we touched, and a low hum vibrated from the point of contact, traveling up our arms. I could tell the moment he realized I was real. Whatever had been dead in his eyes sprang immediately to life, blazing with sharp awareness. The emptiness deep inside me inhaled and I almost laughed as all the time apart dissolved into nothing. We were together again, looking into each other's faces just like we had done every night for our whole lives. Our flesh recognized each other – how could it not, when we were formed at the same time from the same material? The vulture should have never let us get this close. With my back to Ejike, I gave my brother a sharp smile.

'Jayaike,' I said.

One corner of his mouth pulled up. 'Sọmadịna,' he answered. 'What took you so long?'

I stared at him. 'Are you making a *joke* right now?'

Jayaike smiled fully, and it was like the sun had just thrown itself into my eyes. 'Maybe,' he said. 'Was it funny?'

I made a face at him. 'No, not particularly.'

I didn't take my hand off his arm the whole time. Ejike would be paying attention to our voices, our words, because that's all he could witness. He couldn't feel the thrum that was pulsing under our skin now that we were reunited, or the emptiness letting itself float up from what secret dark places it had been buried inside me. I felt it settle in my chest, close enough for me to reach. *Thank you, Ala,* I whispered silently. If she was allowing my gift to rise up, then I would have enough of my power to fight Ejike. I wouldn't need her to possess me, and if the god never rose in me, then Ejike wouldn't be able to eat a deity's power. Still, my gift was too destructive to let someone like Ejike use – he would kill everything he could reach. We couldn't let him steal anything, not anymore.

Jayaike placed his hand on top of mine and squeezed. His palm felt unnaturally hot, like something was building up in him. I was sure he had gifts I didn't know about yet – weapons we could use against Ejike now that we were together again. My twin and I didn't need the bond to communicate when we stood this close. We had been one person. We *knew* each other.

I raised my eyebrows at him in a silent question. *Are you ready?*

Jayaike gave me an imperceptible nod, and then he darted to one side, sank to one knee, and *pushed* out a hand toward Ejike, sending a wave of force that caught Ejike on the side of his body and knocked him down to the floor. I ran over and grabbed one of the chairs, smashing it over Ejike's head. He raised an arm to defend himself and the chair broke apart, the wood snapping into pieces. I reached for the emptiness inside me, but before I could contact it, Ejike snarled in anger and surged up to his feet. He held out his palm to me and my body flew back, slamming against the wall. I was pinned there with my arms and legs extended to the sides as a wild hum filled the air. Jayaike moved toward Ejike and got slammed to the wall right next to me, his body in the same spread position.

'Don't irritate me,' Ejike growled. 'I didn't want to use my magic on you like this.'

I bared my teeth at him, furious. I wanted to roar at him, but no sounds came past my throat. Ejike smiled but his eyes were cold.

'I told you how many gifts I have, Sọmadịna. Did you think it would be that easy? Did you think I have survived these decades, eaten this much power, to be bested by two *children*?'

He lowered his hands, but Jayaike and I remained pinned to the wall.

'To be fair,' he continued, 'I wasn't expecting both of you to access your gifts so quickly. I'm glad to see it, though. It makes my work easier.' Ejike shrugged off his robes so all he had on was a pair of blue trousers. His chest was covered in scars, designs that I couldn't look too long at without getting dizzy.

'Go inside yourselves,' he urged. 'Call for Ala, reach for her, think that she's going to save you. I *want* her here.' He opened a carved wooden box and started taking out iron tools, sharp wicked little things. Nausea boiled in my stomach. Ejike held up a blade and let the lamplight catch the edge. 'And when she is filling you up, we will see who moves faster for the kill.' He glanced over at us and flicked his fingers. The silence in my throat lifted and I coughed out loud, Jayaike coughing next to me.

'You can't kill a god,' my twin said, his voice hoarse.

Ejike rolled his eyes. 'I don't intend to kill Ala. I just want to eat some of her power through you. It might be enough to finally free me from this forsaken place.'

'What then?' I spat out. 'Will you go *home*? To your *wife*? As if she'd want you like this. As if she's even *alive*.'

Jayaike made a small sound next to me, something stricken and hurt. I struggled to turn my head to him.

'What is it?' I asked. 'Is he hurting you?'

'I'm not doing anything to him,' Ejike said. He was sharpening one of his tools, but he wouldn't look over at us. 'Jayaike and I have had many conversations in our time together. I always told him the truth, even when it was difficult for both of us.'

'Shut *up*!' I yelled at him, hating how distraught my twin looked. 'You are not a victim here. Which part of this is *hard* for you?'

'His wife,' Jayaike whispered. 'His wife is alive.'

'I don't *care*! He was a dịbịa and now he's become a *ritualist* – there's no coming back from that. I hope it hurts knowing that he lost her, that she thinks he's dead.' I was snarling, bitter and hateful. 'I hope she never finds out what he turned into, for her sake, and I'm *glad* that losing her has caused him suffering. He is a *monster*! He doesn't *deserve* a family!'

I broke off, reeling from my own words. All of a sudden, I could see Chidị's father shouting at me with hate in his eyes. I could see the people of my town watching me with suspicion, even though they had all known me since I was a baby. I could see Mama's face the night my twin and I got our gifts, her face in our doorway, her mouth forming the word *abomination,* the last time she walked away from me and wouldn't even look at me. Papa leaving me with tears in his eyes. I gasped in shocked pain, and next to me, Jayaike was weeping softly.

'It's Ahụdi,' he whispered. 'His wife is Ahụdi.'

Ejike's hands stilled for a moment, then returned to their work. I looked between him and my brother, frowning. 'What are you talking about?' I said. 'What do you mean, his wife is Ahụdi? Our *grandmother*?'

Jayaike raised his wet eyes to meet mine. 'Sọmadịna,' he said. 'It's true. It's true.'

'But—' It was impossible. Ahụdi's husband had died in the Split. His name was Kesandụ. He was gentle and good. I remembered the stories. She'd told us the stories and his name was *Kesandụ* and he made her smile and he was gentle and good and he was our *grandfather.* He was with me in spirit. Ahụdi had said so. Nkadi had said so. My stomach sank like a stone drowning in a stream, falling past where the light could hit, burying itself in the silt. I looked over at Ejike, who was still laying out the tools of his blasphemy on the black wood table.

'Kesandụ?'

His shoulders tightened. 'Don't.' His voice was coiled and tight. 'Don't use that name.'

I couldn't believe it. I opened my mouth again and all that rolled out was laughter, loud and spilling laughter, racking my ribs and echoing through the room. Both Jayaike and Ejike turned to look at me in surprise. I kept laughing until tears fell down my face and I ran out of air, then I gasped and gasped and looked at my grandfather, living inside a stolen body on stolen time.

'You're going to sacrifice your own *grandchildren*?' Another laugh spilled out of me. 'You knew this whole time and it didn't even matter, did it? Anything for power, even us. What would Ahụdi say?' She had been more right than she knew about the company his spirit kept me in, the terror of my dreams.

Ejike's face darkened, and he pointed one of his knives in my direction. 'Don't you dare say her name to me like that,' he bit out.

'Why? Because you still love her? She loves *us,* you vulture, you thief! She loves us more than you can ever understand, as corrupted as you are now. But you'll still kill us anyway, won't you?'

Ejike took a moment to compose himself, and when he looked at us again, he was gathered, resolute. 'Yes,' he replied easily. 'And it will be the most powerful ritual I have ever done, precisely because you are my blood, the children of my child.'

Jayaike drew in a sharp breath. *'Papa,'* he said. 'You would do this to your own child? Your only son?'

Ejike picked a thin and curved blade off the table and walked toward us.

'If Olejeme was here, if he held the power I needed, I would slit him open from chest to hips like I'm going to do with you. I would crack open his breastbone to reach his heart. I would carve the symbols I need into it and then I would burn his organs in offering to the power I would eat from him. I would leave him alive while I did it, small gods, just as I will do with you.' His eyes were the blackest thing I had ever seen in my life. 'You cannot appeal to me with blood, with family,' he sneered. 'I am beyond that. I have lost everything already. And then I found you, what gifts. When you stop existing, my life will not know any loss, do you understand? You did not exist before. All I have here is gain and gifts and a god's power to unlock me from this place.'

Jayaike tilted his head a fraction. 'Why do you think Ala's power will free you?'

Ejike stopped a breath away from us and looked us over. 'Because although she shows herself to your little town as the crocodile, she is the earth. She is everywhere and everything, all the islands, the Split and beyond. Once I take part of her in, I will be able to move everywhere she is.'

'Who was the god you took part of before?' I asked, and Ejike's head swiveled to me, his teeth baring in a pleased, sharp smile. His eyes turned cloudy.

'I'm so glad you asked.' Outside the tall windows, lightning cracked across the sky and thunder sounded. 'He was a storm deity, for what it was worth. Not as useful as this is about to be.'

I exchanged a look with Jayaike, and he appeared just as shaken as I was. We needed to get out of here.

Ejike reached out with the curved blade and made a small incision on my brother's chest. Jayaike screamed, and I could feel heat radiating off him like surging fire as a thin line of blood trickled down his body.

'No!' I shouted. 'Leave him alone!'

Ejike smiled at me. 'Your turn will come soon enough,

Sọmadịna. And then your sister – I can feel her on my land, approaching the palace. I'll make sure we welcome her and your pale friend.'

Nkadi and Ụwafụlamiro. They had found their way even without me. Ejike cut my brother again, deepening the cut, and more blood spilled out. Jayaike sobbed and moaned while I fought uselessly against the chains of Ejike's power. I couldn't move, and he was going to slice my brother up in front of me. Forcing my breath under control, I closed my eyes and reached inside myself, calling up the emptiness.

It came willingly and I dove into it like I was a child again, swimming in the spring, losing myself. I thought of the grass dying in the Sacred Forest as Zerenjọ made me show him over and over. Maybe I should have listened to Nkadi. Maybe I should have practiced more. Jayaike was so close to me, but with a marrow-deep certainty, I knew that he wouldn't be hurt by my gift. If it could not kill me, then it could not kill him, for the god had touched both of us. Still, I poured all my energy into focusing the emptiness toward Ejike. I wasn't sure what would happen when it brushed against his own nothingness, the blank space where I assumed his conscience had once been, or maybe his soul. I wanted life to be stopped within him. I wanted to see him crumple to the ground, but instead I kept hearing Jayaike scream and scream, so I opened my eyes.

Ejike took his blade off my brother's skin, his hands covered in blood, and looked over at me with interest.

'That's a fascinating gift you have,' he said, sounding almost thoughtful.

I didn't understand. I could *feel* the emptiness spreading through the room, the way it felt like it sucked out the air. The lamps all started dying, one by one, their flames flickering into darkness, until we were illuminated only by the moonlight through the windows. The iron doors opened, and we all looked in that direction just in time to see a servant walk in with a concerned frown.

'Is everything all right?' they began to ask, but then the emptiness hit them, and I watched in horror as their eyes widened and their voice cut out. A strangled cry was forced out from their throat as their flesh shriveled, the skin puckering and darkening, everything pulling to their bones until they were swaying in front of us like a desiccated skeleton, before finally toppling to the ground, dead. I choked back sour vomit and tried to let go of the emptiness before it spread more, but it felt bigger than me, pulsing. Like the god was already in the room.

'No, no, no,' I whispered. 'Not like this.'

It wasn't supposed to hurt anyone else. It was only supposed to hurt Ejike, and he was just standing there staring at his dead servant, delighted. When he looked back at me, his eyes were shining.

'You are a wonder,' he said reverently.

Jayaike gasped for breath next to me. There was a deep cut

over his breastbone and blood soaked the front of his wrapper. He felt like a sun, so hot that it was singeing my skin.

'Sọmadịna,' he whispered. I started crying.

'I'm so sorry,' I said. 'I don't know why it's not working.'

Ejike laughed and returned to the table to swap out his tools. 'I'm sorry to disappoint you, granddaughter.' It sounded mocking in his mouth. 'The only thing that could stop me is if your god herself showed up in your skin. Pray harder, Sọmadịna. We both need her here.'

I had thought my gift would be enough. Why would Ala have let it rise up in me if it couldn't do anything against Ejike? I'd asked her to take me, to use me, and instead she had left me with a gift that was toothless against this man carving up my brother. She had left us here to *die,* just like the Oracle had warned me she might.

'Sọmadịna,' my twin said, and I made myself look at him. His eyes were so soft, tears tracking underneath, and he kept his voice quiet, just for the two of us. 'I already told her never again,' he said to me. 'Because you belong to yourself. It's your body.'

I frowned. 'You prayed to Ala for me?'

'Of course. I saw what it did to you.'

I clenched my fists, my arms still stuck to the wall. 'It wasn't your place to choose,' I hissed, trying to keep my voice down. 'If she possessed me now, we could *kill* him.'

Jayaike shook his head stubbornly. The heat coming off

him was almost unbearable. 'I won't let you turn yourself into a vessel when you don't actually want it,' he insisted. 'You don't understand.' He stretched out his fingers toward me. 'We're two halves of the same weapon, Sọmadịna.'

I stared at his fingertips as they wiggled just out of reach of mine. The hair on my arms crisped up from his heat. Jayaike was staring at me so intently it felt like he was trying to pierce through my skull.

'Do you see it yet?' he asked urgently, then he dropped his voice even more until it was nothing but a sibilant slide through the boiling air between us. *'He should have never let us so close to each other.'*

It was as if I had been underwater, hearing sounds muffled from above, and now I had thrust my head through the surface, and the light was bright and sharp, the sounds clear. Jayaike was almost trembling with heat and life, while I was death and the void. This is what it had always been, since that night when we looked into a chasm in our room and saw different things – this is what the dịbịas taught us when we were all children. The aspects of Ala. The underworld and the source of life. It had been so clear, if only I hadn't been so terrified the whole time, I might have seen it sooner.

Ejike didn't know the god who had given us to our mother, but I did. Or at least, I was starting to. Ala hadn't answered my prayer for possession because my brother asked her not to and she respected his request. While I may not have forgiven her for what she did to me on the farm, she had returned us to each other. She had given me these gifts and made me what I was. I could resent her for that, for not being normal, but I remembered something Ahụdi had said to me one moonlit night when we lay out on mats in our compound, looking up at the stars. I had been talking to her about Mama and Nkadi and the babies that had died before my sister lived.

'Gods are not *fair,*' my grandmother had said. 'Do not expect it from them. They are not human, Sọmadịna, they are unknowable. But we work with them and we serve them, and we petition and bargain, and we share these physical and spiritual worlds as best we can. They are here for us too. Yes, your other siblings died. But Nkadi is alive, Sọmadịna. Nkadi is *alive.*'

Maybe I would never understand the deity who had claimed me. But I was not powerless, and as Jayaike had shown, she could listen to our requests. She had given us these gifts, but I had been using mine alone, which was where the mistake was. I stared into my brother's eyes and the Oracle's words came back to me. *Your eyes are too narrow and you need more of them. Every cutlass needs a handle.*

I *wasn't* alone.

I had never been alone, not even in Mama's womb. I had been a spinning blade with no handle the whole time my twin was gone, but I wasn't born alone and even if Ejike won, I wouldn't have died alone. He wasn't going to win, though, because Jayaike was right – Ejike had made a mistake too.

He had pinned us next to each other.

'I see it,' I told my brother. 'Jayaike, *I see it.*'

Ejike was annoyed as he went through his tools – he seemed to be missing something. I didn't think he would let it distract him for much longer, so we didn't have a lot of time. I stretched my hand out as far as I could, straining each fine muscle and ligament, trying to touch Jayaike's fingertips. My head hurt and the emptiness was still spilling through the dark room. Our fingers were just a whisper apart. We panted out breaths as we kept pushing, and then Jayaike let out a cry as the wound on his chest tore a little bit further.

Ejike whipped his head around, thunder echoing outside the windows, and his eyes blew open in alarm when he saw what we were doing. He was an intelligent man. He had been doing magic for a long, long time. He could feel the fire of life burning off Jayaike and the rumbling emptiness pouring off me, and everything he thought was impossible was becoming alarmingly possible in the space between our skin.

'No!' he shouted, and he raised his hand, but it was too late.

Jayaike screamed as his wound stretched, and then his fingertips touched mine, and the whole room fell into the river. Ejike's spell tore off and I grabbed my twin's hand as the water rushed over our heads. There was no storm, no lightning or thunder, just bubbles and clear pale green water above, below, and around us. I stared at Jayaike and he looked down at his chest to see the wound seal itself up. A crocodile's tail swept by us and we both spun in the water to watch its large body swim through the swirling currents. It was enormous, the largest crocodile I had ever seen, with a body the size of the ancient trees in the forest, limbs like hundred-year-old branches, and slitted eyes that watched us above a jaw full of massive, edged teeth. My twin and I clung to each other as we stared in awe. The water churned and air burned in our lungs. Everything was green and scales and that slitted eye that dug into my spirit, deep, deep, deep until I was turned inside out and spat out, and then I was back in Ejike's palace, crouched on the floor, still with Jayaike's hand tight in mine.

We stood up together and looked around. All the furniture in the room had been blasted away and now lay broken in corners and against the walls. Ejike's tools were scattered everywhere, abandoned blades and lost iron. He was on his hands and knees, his trousers torn, and there was no lightning outside the windows. We watched as he stumbled to his feet, his body swaying, and fixed a furious stare at us.

'What have you *done*?' he cried out. He tried to take a step toward us, but Jayaike raised a hand and Ejike could no longer move.

Sọmadịna. It was my twin's voice, but without words, and

with a sob, I realized that the darkness Ejike had used to interfere with our twin bond was gone. We were fully connected again, and Jayaike was gleaming with relief over the old bone.

You're back! I said, and he smiled.

We're back, he replied. *I think we broke the palace.*

Something was definitely wrong. The palace walls were creaking ominously, and in the distance, we could hear shouts and the sound of running feet. 'They're coming,' I said out loud, and Ejike growled at me.

'Release me now!' he ordered.

Jayaike laughed and my heart jumped. It had been so long since I'd heard that sound. 'No,' my twin said. 'We're taking you to the Split to finish this.' I wasn't sure exactly what my twin meant to do, but he was clear and strong and alive, and I was happy to let him take the lead.

Mivwodere rushed into the room, barely pausing to glance at the body of the desiccated servant on the floor. She was already drawing a sword and was followed by a contingent of servants, some armed.

'What have you done?' she shouted, then stopped in her tracks when she saw Ejike immobilized, Jayaike and I standing free and alive before him. 'Ejike,' she said slowly, lifting her sword as she shifted into an offensive stance. 'Why are they still alive? What happened to the magic?'

Ejike looked alarmed, an expression I never thought I'd see on his face. 'What happened to the *magic*?' he echoed, then he made a terrible sound, like a gutted animal. 'My gifts, why can't I reach my gifts?'

I could feel my emptiness inside him, like a wall around his magic, threaded through with Jayaike's fire. I smiled at him without replying, then the ground tilted and rumbled loudly under our feet. We all stumbled and many of the servants fell to the floor. My twin and I exchanged glances. The earth groaned again and this time the walls cracked, dust blooming out from them. The smell of iron assaulted my nostrils and a high-pitched whine pierced the air. I clapped my hands to my ears.

'Let him go or I will run you through,' Mivwodere shouted. Her eyes were frantic. She was afraid – she had no idea what she was dealing with. Jayaike flicked a hand, and Mivwodere was thrown against the wall. She dropped to the ground, silent, and I watched in fascinated horror as my twin walked past her to the iron doors, Ejike's body stiffly following behind. The servants scrambled out of the way and Jayaike looked back at me.

'Come on, Sọmadịna,' he said. 'We have work to do.'

CHAPTER NINETEEN

THE PALACE WAS IN COMPLETE CHAOS AS WE WALKED THROUGH IT. The floor kept rocking under our feet, and the walls shivered around us. Everyone who saw us fell back as if Ala's power was radiating from my twin and me, and maybe it was. They certainly recognized Ejike as defeated, his body jerking after us unwillingly. I didn't know how Jayaike was doing that, but I could feel that he had a deft hold on our intertwined gifts. It was a relief. I never wanted power like this, except to get him back and kill Ejike, and frankly, I trusted my twin far more than I trusted myself.

When we walked through the main doors into the palace compound, I stopped short in shock. The air was no longer poisoned. People were running around and screaming as the ground cracked open and closed back up with no recognizable pattern. A girl with muscular shoulders and an iron collar with a broken chain dangling from it slit a servant's throat. I stepped back from the spray of blood as Jayaike looked around.

'Sọmadịna!' I spun around and nearly fell as the ground hiccuped again. My eyes lit up when I saw who had called my name.

'Ụwafụlamiro!'

He was running across the compound toward me, then he was there, alive and well, sweeping me up in his arms. 'We found you!' he gasped. 'You're alive!'

I laughed aloud and hugged him fiercely. 'I'm so glad you're safe!'

I looked over his shoulder and I wasn't disappointed. Nkadi strolled behind him, blood splattered over her arms. I already knew it wasn't hers. She let out a fractured cry when she saw Jayaike and ran to him, throwing her arms around him.

'She found you.' Nkadi's voice shook. 'I knew she'd find you.'

'Big sister.' Jayaike smiled and hugged her back. 'You're right on time.'

Ụwafụlamiro put me down and pulled my brother into his embrace, dragging him away from Nkadi. 'You're alive, you're alive.' Our best friend was crying, his eyes already red. Nkadi grabbed me and pressed me to her.

'Thank Ala you're safe,' she murmured against my hair. 'Grandfather would have killed me.'

I smothered a laugh. 'We did it,' I told her. 'We got the man who took Jayaike.'

She looked over my shoulder at where Ejike was standing, his eyes burning with a visceral hatred. 'How?' she asked in awe.

'Jayaike has his flesh under control,' I told her. 'I don't really know how he's doing it.'

My twin and Ụwafụlamiro were crying and laughing together, but then the ground dipped again and we all fought to balance ourselves.

'What did you do?' Nkadi asked, and I almost laughed at how many times people kept asking us that question.

'We combined our gifts,' I said. It was the best way I could think of to explain what had happened. There were no words for the water and the scales and the endless green.

'We were walking through the poison and then the air contracted and expanded,' Ụwafụlamiro said. 'It felt like something had exploded somewhere, and all the foul air just . . . tunneled away.'

Jayaike's eyes sharpened. 'In what direction?'

In the end, there was really only one place it could have gone to. I wasn't surprised when Ụwafụlamiro pointed north, in the direction of the Split.

The land outside the palace grounds was even sicker than where we'd arrived. The air was no longer sour, now that the poisonous magic had been pulled away, but the soil was still wounded and dying. We heard the Split before we saw it. It sounded like countless voices weeping and wailing on the wind, and I felt it in my chest, like my heart was rupturing over and over again. Ejike kept wincing, as if the weeping was cutting into his skin.

'Why does it sound like that?' Ụwafụlamiro asked.

'Torn land,' Jayaike replied, giving Ejike a stern glare. 'Torn people.'

Nkadi followed his look and frowned at Ejike. 'Who is he, really?' she asked. 'There's something very wrong with him.'

Jayaike and I exchanged worried silent words. *We have to tell her,* I said.

He didn't disagree. *I just don't want to tell Ahụdi when we get home.*

I couldn't imagine how painful that was going to be for all of us. *Let's just get through this first.*

'He used to be a dịbịa,' I said to Nkadi. 'He's a ritualist now.'

Pure disgust crossed her face. 'He's a *what*?'

Jayaike grimaced. 'He used to be Ahụdi's husband.'

Nkadi stopped walking. 'You're lying,' she said flatly. Beside her, Ụwafụlamiro's eyes were huge and round.

'That can't be true,' he said. 'Sọmadịna?'

My mouth twisted. I hated saying it because it didn't mean

anything other than old blood. 'Look,' I said, addressing my words to Nkadi because she was the one who needed them. 'He's not our grandfather, not anymore. Not since he did human sacrifices and stepped into a new body and changed his name. He's Ejike now, and he's going to die.' I looked at my twin. 'He's going to die, right?'

Jayaike's gaze had drifted toward the Split and its cries. 'Probably,' he said. 'We have to see what the Split needs.'

Nkadi's mouth was hanging open. 'He stepped into a new *body*?' She turned to Ejike as we kept walking. 'How? How did you do that?'

'Nkadi!' I pushed her gently. 'Not the time.'

Ejike cackled. 'Oh, I like this one,' he said. 'I could teach you many things, Nkadi. Things your dịbịa grandfather will never teach you, because they don't want us to have real power. Help me get away from these two, and all I know is yours, I swear it.'

Nkadi frowned and I nearly rolled my eyes. He was so transparent in his desperation, but also, he knew nothing about my sister and her dedication to who she was.

'He did a ritual on someone possessed by a deity,' I told her. 'He ate their power so he could have a piece of the god.'

Blood left Nkadi's face even as rage entered her eyes. 'That's unholy,' she said. 'That's punishable by death. That's a perversion of everything a dịbịa is supposed to be.'

Ejike snarled, realizing that his freedom didn't lie with her. 'You're all fools, you dịbịas,' he said.

'Enough,' Jayaike said. 'We're here.'

I looked in front of us and every story Ahụdi had ever told us coalesced into a terrible true thing right before our eyes. The Split was a gouge into reality itself, a gorge so huge that it was impossible to even *think* about the other side of it. It looked like the earth had simply ended there, dropping off into a dry, jagged nothingness, a fractured horizon as far as we could see. All the poisonous magic that had left the air was now hovering in a black cloud above the Split, with lightning streaking through it. The ground was boiled a hard ugly red-black and it was hot against the soles of our feet as we approached the edge.

'Take my hand,' my twin ordered, and I obeyed. Immediately, it was as if another world was laid on top of this one. I could see the fire of Jayaike's gift shot through with the emptiness of mine, and it was all floating over the gorge, herding that unclean magic into the cloud, containing it.

I looked from the gorge to Ejike and back. 'It's all one thing,' I said. 'We contained him and it contained the poison.'

Jayaike nodded. 'Look there,' he said, pointing down.

Pale reddened swirls were pushing up from the chasm itself, throbbing in pain as they connected to the black cloud.

'That's coming from the land,' I said. Nkadi was looking over the edge, her gaze filled with awe.

'It's all just a big wound,' Jayaike said. 'What the dịbịas had to do. Just like Ahụdi told us.'

'What do we do, though? And what about Ejike?' I felt less bloodthirsty now that Jayaike was safe, now that I was reconnected to him and balanced with his life instead of spiraling into the dark of my own emptiness and rage.

Jayaike's mouth curved into a soft smile. 'We heal the land,' he said. 'That's what we're here for. That's why everything that has been allowed was allowed.' He nudged my shoulder with his. 'Ahụdi told us. Gods are unknowable.'

I sighed. 'So we're tools after all.'

Nkadi shook her head. 'We're servants, Sọmadịna. That's how it works, the give and take. We help where we can. Imagine what this poison has been doing to anyone who lived too close to it. Jayaike is right; it's a wound.'

'Fine.' I knew they were right. I could feel how much the earth was hurting. 'I'm sorry,' I whispered to it. 'I'm sorry we did this to you to save ourselves.' Ejike gave me a strange look, but said nothing.

Everything Ahụdi had told us about the costs of war seemed very real now. I had known her stories were true, of course, but there was a gap between the history of the Starvation War and the gorge lying in front of us now, so wide we couldn't see any land on the horizon. I'd never thought about the people we fought in that war, but now I found myself wondering what lay on the other side of the Split. Was their land sick there too?

Did they have an earth deity who was in pain from what our dịbịas had done?

'What will you do with the poison?' Ụwafụlamiro asked. 'You have to put it somewhere, right? You two can't be here to hold it caged forever.'

Jayaike frowned. *Maybe my fire can burn it off,* he said to me through the bone bond. I knew he didn't want Ejike hearing us.

No, I said slowly. *I think I know what to do.*

Ever since that terrible void had opened up in our bedroom, I had wondered why it was in me, what was wrong with me. Why had Jayaike seen life, while I was tied to death? Why did the grass die around my feet and the wind give up in my presence as I walked through the Sacred Forest with my true grandfather? All these questions had haunted me, and I'd felt cursed by Ala. I'd even resented my brother for not having the same gifts, for seeing life, as if the deity had spared him. But I remembered his eyes when Ejike brought him to me, and I knew now that he hadn't been spared. I also knew he had survived something I might not have. I had lain on the ground beneath a feral leopard and almost let it kill me, surrendering to the emptiness inside me instead of using it.

This was how I could use it. I held a place other people couldn't go to.

I was a terror built for this.

I spoke without words to both Jayaike and Nkadi. *The magic has to go somewhere,* I explained. *I have a void in me that can eat it all.*

Nkadi recoiled. *No,* she shot back. *It's too dangerous.*

Jayaike looked at me, his brow furrowed slightly. *Are you sure?*

I would have laughed, but I thought it would worry them, make them think I was losing my mind. *I'm sure,* I replied. *Let it go, Jayaike.*

Ụwafụlamiro shifted uncomfortably. 'What are you doing?' he asked, suspicious.

I didn't answer. Jayaike pulled back his fire from the roiling black mass of magic, and it came for me with a scream, flooding my spirit, lifting my feet off the ground, and bowing my spine.

'Sọmadịna!'

Nkadi held Ụwafụlamiro back as he tried to rush to my side. Ejike's eyes rolled up in his head and he dropped to his knees.

Sọmadịna, my twin said. *Do you have it?*

I took a deep breath and let the magic channel into me, burning like hot iron inside my skin.

Yes, I answered. *I have it.*

I could taste the poison trying to overwhelm me, but it was pointless. It was dark, but I was the emptiness and the emptiness was me. The crocodile yawned its jaws open inside my spirit and I dropped all the magic down, into the god's mouth, where everything begins and ends.

Just like that, it was gone. Ejike screamed and fell to the ground. His rituals had tied him inextricably to the Split; he had become the poison, fed the poison, and it had grown with his power. He would not survive this healing.

Next to me, Jayaike exhaled slowly, spreading out his hands. The night around us *broke* as time folded forward and the sun gasped at the horizon. Grass grew under our feet, and the land wrenched as trees sprang up, sending chunks of soil flying in every direction. I could hear Nkadi and Ụwafụlamiro shouting, but their voices were drowned out by a deafening thunder coming from the chasm.

Water rushed up from the bottom of the Split, deep greens and blues churning with foam, more water than I could ever imagine, like a thousand wide rivers. Everything was trembling and it was dawn and my eyes burned from the light, my nostrils scorched with the smell of salt from the waves slamming into each other beneath us. Was *this* what my twin was capable of? This much change, dragging the sun forth? My knees were weak with awe. The new waves kept rising up until what was an empty chasm was now a body of water, clear sand in front of us leading to gentle ripples washing up against the land.

Jayaike opened his eyes to look at me, and I started crying.

I forgot about Ejike and Nkadi and Ụwafụlamiro and everything behind us. It was just my twin and me, standing in soft grass with an improbable beach in front of us. We grabbed each other into a fierce hug and held on for a long time, our spirits too overflowing to say anything.

'We did it,' he finally whispered.

I nodded, still too shaken for words. Nkadi and Ụwafụlamiro tackled us with hugs, and for a while it was nothing but a babble of wonder and words and tears and laughter. Finally, we all pulled ourselves together. Jayaike walked over to Ejike and turned him over to his side from where he had fallen. We all recoiled when we saw his face.

Ejike was now an old man, and I could sense that's all he was. Just a man, and an anomaly of one at that, with no gifts. No power, no magic, no nothing. His breath was rattling through his chest.

'I think he's dying,' Nkadi said. I didn't know how I felt about that.

'People are coming.' Ụwafụlamiro gestured back toward the palace, and true enough, a crowd of noise was approaching to see the healed Split.

Ejike coughed and blood speckled his lips. 'Free,' he gasped out, his voice thin and weak. 'At least . . . I am . . . free.'

We all looked at each other in silence for a moment as the wind blew over the new water. Nkadi knelt by Ejike's side.

'You all go,' she said. 'I'll stay with him until he passes.'

'You don't owe him anything,' I said, because I felt I had to. 'He's not our real grandfather, not like Zerenjọ.'

My sister smiled sadly. 'I know, Sọmadịna,' she replied. 'I'm a dịbịa here, not a granddaughter.'

It twisted my chest to hear her say that, to watch her hold the dying man's hand, to think that Ahụdi's first love was going to die like this, next to a miracle of a new story and the smell of salt.

Jayaike took my elbow. 'He's not alone.'

I nodded and let my twin lead me away. As we walked through the grass, I looked back at the water, still marveling at its existence. There was grief in my chest for Ejike that I didn't want to look at. Behind us, Nkadi's head was bowed over him.

'I suppose they can't call it the Split anymore,' I said. 'It needs a new name.'

Jayaike had a small, satisfied smile on his face.

'The Split Sea,' he said. 'I wonder what's on the other side.'

EPILOGUE

OUR LAST FOLD ON THE WAY BACK HOME RETURNED US TO THE packed red earth of Nkadi's training circle inside the Sacred Forest. A smile stretched across my face when I saw the man standing at the edge of the circle, his eyes crinkled with joy and relief.

'Grandfather,' I said, and Nkadi spun around, a soft breath escaping her mouth.

He held out his arms and she ran to him so fast that she was simply a blur colliding with his chest. Zerenjọ held her tight and murmured into her head as Nkadi sobbed, her body collapsing in the only place I realized she felt safe.

Zerenjọ fed us a feast of roasted goat meat, blackened plantains packed with red oil and pepper, pounded yam with okro and periwinkles, and even gourds of young palm wine back at his house. We washed it down with cool spring water and told him all the stories we had in us, everything that had happened. Our grandfather's eyes were sharp and keen as he listened, and I felt a small wonder at being the storyteller this once, instead of the audience under the moon. I had told Jayaike everything that happened after he was taken, and we had wept over it together. Still, I wasn't prepared when Zerenjọ looked at us and asked the question I least wanted to hear.

'Do you want to go home?' he said.

Jayaike squeezed my hand. On our way back, he and I had taken a walk away from the others and I'd told him of our parents' betrayal, the terrible things Mama had said. I thought I could get through it as if it was just another story, but Jayaike had shared and breached her body with me. The grief had cut me in half and I had broken down, crying so hard in my brother's arms that I thought my throat would bleed from it. Jayaike had wept as well, his face pressed against my hair.

'I'm sorry I wasn't there,' he said, his words thick with sorrow. 'I'm sorry she turned her back on us, Sọmadịna.'

'If you want to go home, I understand,' I told him. I'd practiced the words many times. 'But I can't go with you, Jayaike. I can't do it.'

His face was grim. 'They should see me,' he replied. 'They should look at what they threw away.' I had sniffled and his eyes softened as he held me tighter. 'But only when you're ready, Sọmadịna. We'll be home with Ahụdi soon.'

He'd told me his theory that the deity had allowed all this

– Chidị's death, Ejike kidnapping him, Zerenjọ not being allowed to come with us, maybe even Mama's reactions – all so we could heal the Split. It didn't make me any more inclined to forgive any of the things that had been done to us. I might have been a god's tool, but I was a *person.* I was someone's child, or at least, I used to be.

Now Zerenjọ was asking us what we wanted to do, and though I knew Jayaike wanted to confront the people our parents had become after he was taken, to look them in their eyes and let them know they had been seen, I still wasn't sure I wanted to do that. I had already seen more than enough from them.

'Maybe we can see Ahụdi and Ọlụchi first,' I suggested.

'They're visiting your parents,' Zerenjọ said. I bit my cheek, feeling trapped.

'Look, Sọmadịna.' Nkadi leaned toward me. 'You can stay here as long as you want and you know that. But looking away doesn't make things disappear. They will always be there, just waiting.'

I looked down. 'I know.'

She placed her hand on my arm. 'We are with you. We are your family. A razor cannot sever the forearm from the elbow. You will *never* be alone, you hear?'

I was surprised by the force in her voice, but I nodded. I knew she was right. I still had her and Grandfather and Ahụdi and Ọlụchi. I still had Ụwafụlamiro. I still had my twin. The wounds from our parents didn't have to be healed by our parents.

'I know it hurts,' Nkadi said. 'I feel it too.'

Jayaike was silent and I knew he would only go if I was ready to face them, not one moment before. Ụwafụlamiro leaned his shoulder against mine in solidarity. I loved my best friend, but too much had happened and we had decided together to allow our friendship to remain unchanged for now. I had no home. I didn't want to think about kisses that felt like warmth and comfort. I wanted to heal with my twin and understand how the two of us fit into the world after everything Ejike had done to us. We still didn't understand if or how healing the Split would affect all the other islands, including our own. Our grandfather had told us not to worry about that, that it was dịbịa business now and we could shift the burden over to them. I wasn't sure how true that was, or if Ala was really done with us or not. All the answers I wanted were buried, and only time would uncover them.

Zerenjọ waited patiently for my answer, his face calm and steady, his love certain and unshakable. The Sacred Forest glowed around us, its faint music whistling out. I knew this was a place for dịbịas, but could it ever be a place for children owned by a god? I couldn't hide out here forever.

I couldn't say the words, but I nodded and it was Jayaike who met our grandfather's eyes and spoke.

'We're ready to see our parents,' he said.

The journey back to our village was gentle. We soaked up the Sacred Forest and its odd beauties, took care with the shortcut lines, and before too long, we were back by the tallest palm tree, looking toward the town.

'I can't believe I'm really standing here.' Jayaike's voice was low and wondering. 'There were moments when I wasn't sure this would ever happen.' His voice spoke of shadows and muffled screams. When it sounded like this, I was always glad that Ejike was dead, that I had kept that promise.

I took Jayaike's hand and laced my fingers into his. I didn't have words to use in that moment, but it didn't matter. We were there together.

A girl walking past with a water pot took one look at us and dropped her pot in shock. It broke into shards, and we watched her run off into town. We all looked at each other, then burst into laughter.

'No need to hire a town crier,' Ụwafụlamiro said. 'Everyone will know we're back in the next few minutes.'

I wasn't entirely sure about seeing the rest of my family again, but if Mama or the rest of the town couldn't see our worth, then the problem was with them, not with us. Jayaike and I had never been abominations. We had done and survived unimaginable things. Our world was so much bigger than our town, the river full of crocodiles, and these forests we'd grown up in. There was an entire sea out there to prove it.

I turned to Zerenjọ. 'You don't need to come with us, Grandfather.'

He raised an eyebrow and Nkadi looked at me with surprise. 'It's helpful to have him there, Sọmadịna,' she said. I knew she was thinking about the trial and that she was worried about me, but Zerenjọ understood.

He looked into my eyes and his face creased into a smile.

'Small god,' he said, and tapped his staff on the ground. 'Let's go home, Nkadi.'

My sister hesitated, and I put my hand on her arm. 'Jayaike and I can handle this,' I said. 'Trust us, Nkadi.'

Our golden leopard sighed and I felt her muscles relax. 'Well, you created the Split Sea. I suppose you can do anything.'

Ụwafụlamiro grinned at her. 'I'll take care of them,' he said.

Nkadi inclined her head. 'I know you will.'

We all embraced and then she left with our grandfather. Jayaike held my hand and Ụwafụlamiro slung an arm across my shoulders. We watched them until they vanished around a bend, then the three of us exhaled together and turned back to the town. It felt a little like we had let one world go with Nkadi and Zerenjọ and were preparing to face another.

This time, I was ready.

When the armed men came to meet us, Jayaike greeted them politely.

'Is there a problem?' he asked.

Their leader hefted the handle of his ax over his shoulder and replied just as politely. 'Of course not. The elders merely wished to provide you with an escort back into town.' He inclined his head with a little irony. 'Welcome home.'

They formed a circle around us, and I took my cue from my brother, remaining courteous and calm. People came out of their houses to watch us, whispering loudly and staring with barely concealed fascination and fear. Soon enough, I realized that the men were herding us toward the main square, not to our home. I stopped walking.

'We are not going to the square,' I said flatly.

The man with the ax frowned. 'The elders wish to welcome you back.'

I was starting to get irritated. 'The last time I was here,' I said coldly, 'the elders wanted to put me to death.'

The man lowered his ax from his shoulder.

'I'm under orders,' he said, but he didn't look like he minded carrying them out.

I moved aside and my brother stepped forward, brushing his hand over the ax handle. It sprouted leaves and buds, and the metal head fell off with a heavy thud. The man cursed out loud and dropped the blossoming handle on the ground.

'We're not subject to those orders,' my brother replied. 'We just want to go home.' The crowd around us was thickening.

'Are those the twins?'

'It's the girl that killed Chidị!'

'That blacksmith has been looking for her, o!'

'Open road, her father is here.'

I spun around as the people jostled and created a path that led straight to Papa. He was searching anxiously, and then his eyes fell on me. He didn't move. The moment between us stretched out like rubber. I gazed at the details of his face, so familiar and yet, somehow, a stranger's now.

Forgive me, Papa said.

Tears sprang to my eyes. I could hear Ahụdi's voice in the crowd. My father looked at my twin and his eyes went even softer. *Jayaike,* he whispered. *You found him.*

I nodded, short of words, afraid to move. When the person behind Papa took a step out and forward, my heart stopped.

'Mama.'

I didn't recognize my own voice. I barely recognized her face. New lines had mapped themselves over her skin since I had been gone. As she looked at me, I watched her face crack open with grief and she reached out her arms, taking another step toward me. I took a step back and her heart visibly broke in her eyes. She lowered her arms.

‘Sọmadịna,’ she said, then she looked at my twin and a sob wrenched itself out of her mouth. *‘Jayaike.’*

My brother came up and took my hand in his. ‘Mama,’ he said, his voice cautious. I could feel his tension radiating through our bond.

Our mother pressed her hands to her chest and spoke in a rush. ‘I shouldn’t have said those things, done those things. I was—I was stubborn and I turned away from a god and then I ran from the consequences. I have been—’ Her voice broke and Papa patted her back. ‘I have failed you so badly.’

I stared at her. She was just a human, a terrified creature, just a small flicker of light who hadn’t known how to look at the terror she had given birth to. And yet, I wasn’t ready to forgive her just because she now felt bad about what she had done. I didn’t even feel ready to forgive Papa for how he had kept loving her at her worst, how he had kept choosing her. Jayaike rested his chin on my shoulder and I knew he understood.

Our mother’s mouth was wet and loose. ‘I will do better, you hear? I swear it, Sọmadịna, Jayaike. I will do better. I will heal what I have broken.’

Everyone was looking at us. Ụwafụlamiro’s parents had shown up and were holding him so tightly it was surprising he could still breathe. I stayed silent and then Ahụdi pushed through the crowd. ‘Leave this conversation for inside your house,’ she scolded. ‘The children just got back.’

She pulled Jayaike and me into her arms, and suddenly I was

a child again, safe and loved and listening to stories about magic and sacrifices made out of love. I shook with exhaustion and relief, letting myself sink into her embrace. Jayaike was crying softly next to me, babbling in a low stream of words. 'We saw the Split, Ahụdi. Just like you told us. It was just like you told us.'

Our grandmother kissed his temple roughly. 'I missed you both so much,' she said. 'Have you eaten? Ọlụchi is cooking.'

I started crying then, my face pressed and hidden against her chest. Ahụdi made soft, comforting sounds in my ear. 'It's going to be all right,' she whispered. 'Everything is going to be all right.'

She leaned back slightly to tip my head up so she could see into my face. I sniffled and looked into her eyes, and it was like watching the sea fill up again, with love and compassion and endless acceptance. My brother was safe and pressed to my side. Ahụdi smiled down at me.

'Welcome home, Sọmadịna.'

I looked at her and I thought about who she had been, a woman who watched her love go off to save their people, a mother who sat under moonlight and made sure we never forgot who or where we came from. I thought of a man who betrayed his beliefs and corrupted his spirit trying to get home to her, who had died in the grass next to a newborn sea with his son's firstborn holding his hand. I reached up just like I used to when I was a child, and I touched the soft skin of Ahụdi's face.

'Grandmother,' I said. 'I have a story to tell you.'

ACKNOWLEDGMENTS

Funny story – I actually wrote the first two chapters of this book as an entry for the New Visions Award hosted by Lee & Low Books back in 2012. I was a baby writer applying for as many opportunities as I could and I didn't expect anything to come of it, so I was quite shocked when I was listed as a finalist and asked to submit the rest of the manuscript in two weeks. This was a problem because I hadn't actually *written* the manuscript – cue panicked screams. I spent the next several days desperately cobbling it together to make the deadline, creating a clunky and incredibly rough draft that, spoiler alert, did not win the award. It was the first novel I ever wrote.

Over a decade later, I want to thank my editor Michelle Frey for turning that clumsy first attempt into what it is now: a book I believe both of us are quite proud of, my third novel for young adults, and a fantastical foray into Igbo culture, drawing on both postwar and precolonial aspects of the place I come from. My grandfather was killed in the Biafran Genocide when Old Ụmụahịa was bombed, and twenty years later, I was born there. As someone who is very publicly queer and trans in flesh terms, it's not safe for me to return to that land I miss so much. I find myself in a halfway exile, writing this story of a strange spirit-touched child rejected by the community she was born into. Sọmadịna learns how to ground herself despite this – in the family she does have, in the deity she belongs to, in the power she learns how to use. I am grateful for all the deviant African spirits, queer and trans folk, those in flesh and not, those on the continent and in diaspora, who hold the line with me because we belong to our cultures and our cultures belong to us.

Thank you to everyone at Knopf who worked on this book and helped bring it to our young readers. It's rather magical for me to watch it finally be made after twelve years! Thank you to Paul Davey for the utterly gorgeous cover art – Sọmadịna's defiant stare is my favorite thing. As always, enormous gratitude to Jacqueline Ko, Kristi Murray, and the entire Wylie Agency. Nine years since I signed and nine books out at this count.

As I write this, the world is burning at the hands of the greedy and the cruel. It is an old, old story made painfully new by the way it is live streamed through our phones now. My work continues as it always has – in service of liberation. I believe that re-indigenization is key to this, and that is where this story comes in, centering our Indigenous realities, our deities and dịbịas, threading it all with the magic that makes everything possible.

To my beloved readers, thank you so much for holding my work and entering my worlds! I hope we all step into our power. I hope we all get free.

ABOUT THE AUTHOR

AKWAEKE EMEZI is the author of many books for both teens and adults. Their YA titles include *Pet,* a finalist for the National Book Award for Young People's Literature, a Walter Honor Book, a Stonewall Honor Book and a longlistee for the Carnegie Medal and *Bitter,* a YALSA Best Fiction for Young Adults Pick. Their adult titles include *The Death of Vivek Oji,* a *New York Times* bestseller and a finalist for the Dylan Thomas Prize; *Freshwater,* which was longlisted for both the Wellcome Book Prize and the Women's Prize for Fiction, named a *New York Times* Notable Book and shortlisted for the PEN/Hemingway Award; and bestselling *You Made a Fool of Death with Your Beauty,* which is being developed by Michael B. Jordan's Outlier Society. Selected as a '5 Under 35' honoree by the National Book Foundation, they are based in liminal spaces.